HAUNTED

By H.G Ahedi

For dad

A special thank you!

Uttam & Poonam

Shwetha D'Souza

Paul Trinies

Dr. Mithun Rajeshekar, PhD

Anitra Wilson

The OPAL girls

&

Treasured friends

Contents

1

The Secrets She Keeps

January 10, 2015

Egypt

The massive, golden sun rose over the edge of the barren world, and its lights fell on a lonely camel caravan. Dr. Marian Watson watched as it disappeared behind the dunes. She wondered if she should call for help, but her colleagues were marching in the opposite direction.

She left the jeep behind and sipped the last few drops of water from her bottle. Rolling hills of sand surrounded her, and the wind whipped the dust around her face. The wreckage could wait. She strolled, admiring the sunrise, for once in her life wishing to stand still and admire the wonders of nature. As a dedicated archaeologist for the last twenty years, she felt she deserved it. Egypt had lost its lustre. She remembered being excited about discovering old artifacts and solving ancient mysteries. Now it was just another job.

"Marian! C'mon!" called Walter Weldon.

She increased her pace. Walter was her boss, a good man, a philanthropist, and a multibillionaire obsessed with the Nefret. The cursed ship, the doomed ship.

Marian looked at her bruised feet, no thanks to Zachary. She hadn't planned on walking. He'd underestimated the distance, hadn't checked the fuel, and now they were stranded. She thought she shouldn't be so judgemental; it was just half a mile, and help was on its way.

Breathing hard, trying to hold on to her hat with her right hand, Marian climbed up the next hill. When she got to the top, she spotted Zachary Hilton in the lead. He marched ahead like a soldier, straight, tall, and fast. The dryness in the air and the howling wind didn't bother him. Her eyes drifted ahead, and her heart stopped in her chest. She blinked twice to make sure what she was seeing was real. Zachary was right. It existed—the mysterious tourist ship that had disappeared forty years ago.

The Nefret sat tilted at eighty degrees, partially buried under sand. It was around thirty feet long and ten feet high, and its anchor was half-submerged in the earth. The desert had swallowed the vessel's stern. Marian forgot all her aches and almost ran towards it, breathing hard. The ship's hull was black, and the wood bore dozens of fractures. The middle and lower decks appeared intact, but the upper deck had perished. A big crab crawled out through a crack, slithering over a statue of a woman at the helm of the vessel and disappearing into another hole.

"Let's go inside," Walter said, pointing toward a large opening in the lower deck.

The ship could crumble at any moment, Marian thought, but it was worth the risk.

Inside it was dark and cool, and the air was foul. Sand formed a thick layer on the floor. Many panels stood in silence, almost hidden under years of dirt. Marian stepped forward, and the wood groaned under her feet. She noted something on the wooden deck and cleared the gravel with her shoe. The deck was smeared with small, angular stains. She kneeled and cleared the dust, revealing more oddly shaped black marks. Marian recalled the massacre. Suddenly, she felt an icy touch on her neck. She gasped and turned; no one was there. Breathless, she stared into the void. The wind howled.

What if the locals were right? What if this ship is cursed?

Marian didn't believe in the supernatural, but the history of the Nefret bothered her. The locals thought a green demon haunted this ship, and it had slaughtered all those passengers forty years ago.

Dismissing her thoughts, Marian tried to focus and headed upstairs. On the upper deck, she found Walter staring at a wall. It was covered with the black splatter, and the roof was smeared with countless clusters of irregular black dots. She considered offering comfort, but maybe it was best to leave him alone.

On soft feet, she headed for the bridge. Perhaps she could access the Captain's logs and find out more. Questions ran through her mind.

How did those people die? What actually happened?

Something clattered, and Marian spun. A cabin door hung open. She approached it but soon halted. In a corner lay a hand, a skinless human hand. The desert became silent. The wind died out.

Marian took a deep breath and stepped inside the cabin. The bright light from her flashlight cut through the darkness. Pictures on the walls had degraded, and the wallpaper had disappeared. There was a crack in the roof, and sand dripped in an unsteady trickle. Nothing remarkable. As Marian turned to leave, her foot came into contact with something solid.

"Oh."

A pair of black eyes shone in the dim light. She picked up the head of what looked like a Jackal made of hard-baked clay. She felt it with her fingers. The Jackal was the guardian of the dead and a well-known symbol of Anubis, the Egyptian God of the dead, especially popular in the First Dynasty (c. 3100–c. 2890 BC).

Marian wondered where the Jackal had come from. It did not belong on a ship that was only, at most, fifty years old. Pots full of Jackal heads were available as souvenirs in markets of Cairo and other parts of Egypt, but this one seemed authentic, its markings deep, its bottom rough and pointed. Near the door lay several pieces of clay. She gathered them and put them together to create a small jar, placing the Jackal's head on it. It fitted perfectly. To Marian, a jar topped with a Jackal's head could mean only one thing. A warning. A sign of danger.

A tingling sensation crept through Marian's hands, and when she looked down, she found that her fingertips had turned green. Her head spun. Screams echoed in her ears. Visions of fire danced in front of her eyes, and something unseen passed through her body. The jar fell from her hands, and she ran out of the cabin screaming.

The fresh air calmed her down. The dizziness eased, and embarrassment sunk in. Marian wiped her hands on her coat, trying to get rid of the green tinge. She couldn't deny it, she sensed it, there was something here. Something horrible, something unknown. In all her years of experience, she'd never felt this way. She rushed toward the bridge but paused at the sight of an open door. She peered inside. Walter sat on a broken bed, pearls resting in his palm, glittering in the dim light.

They were here.

He looked away, as if aware of her presence. She left him in peace.

The door of the bridge opened with a loud cracking noise. Like the ship, the bridge was old, rusted, and dusty. It was a constricted place with a couple of consoles and a big chair in the middle. Zachary stood in the middle, unblinking. She followed his gaze and saw a tilted head lolling in the Captain's chair. She covered her mouth, her heart drumming in her chest as she stepped closer. A brown fleshless skeleton sat in the Captain's place; a large hole carved roughly out of its left temple. Its jaw was open, and its hollow eye sockets gawked unseeingly. A small scorpion clambered out of its right eye socket, crawled downwards, and disappeared into the rib-cage.

Marian shut her eyes. She knew they ought to leave and turned to tell Zachary so, but her words fell silent before they left her mouth. Zachary stared straight into the skeleton's eyes, as if he were willing it to come back to life. Marian looked between Zachary and the skeleton. Did Zachary know who it had been?

2

Early Demise

June 2, 2015

City Morgue, New York

D r. William Sterling sat in silence in his dimly lit office on the third floor of the City Morgue. In his mid-thirties, William was a medium-built man with broad shoulders, and he stood at five feet, eleven inches. He had a square face, dense coffee-colored hair, dark brown eyes, and a well-kept French beard.

The old air conditioner groaned, trying to fight the New York summer heat. William's office was small, crammed with six cabinets, a desk, and two chairs. Files and papers were scattered across the floor waiting to be sorted, but William was too busy to worry about housekeeping. Having worked as a medical examiner for over ten years, he'd learned to follow his instinct, and right now, his intuition told him to keep looking. Everyone thought these three men had committed suicide. He didn't believe it. The autopsies were scheduled for tomorrow morning, and he wanted to be prepared.

William focused on the first victim. Don Wagner, a 49-year-old wealthy industrialist, died sometime between ten thirty p.m. and midnight on May 30, 2015. Twelve hours before his death, he'd made breakfast plans with his daughter, Rachael. When he didn't show up, Rachael stopped by his penthouse, finding it trashed and her father lying in a pool of blood with a gun in his left hand. She called the police. The patrol officers found no sign of a break in, and interviews with the neighbors, the doorman and the daughter revealed no clues. The CSU unit dusted the entire apartment but only found fingerprints matching Mr. Wagner and his daughter. Just one shot was fired. The rest of the bullets were still in the gun's barrel. The cops collected the cartridge, and the medical examiner extracted the bullet from Wagner's brain. Ballistic reports showed a match. It was Wagner who'd pulled the trigger. But why?

Perhaps Mr. Wagner had fought with his killer and the killer prevailed. But security cameras confirmed that no one had entered or left the apartment. A thorough search of the penthouse showed it wasn't a burglary. William combed through the crime scene pictures. After he shot himself, Mr. Wagner fell on the glass table which smashed into pieces. Blood soaked into the carpet and spread away from the head. William stared at the stocky, bald man in his blue Italian suit. His eyes were open, his chubby face had turned whitish, and blood stained his mouth. One hand was above his head, the other near his torso. Mr. Wagner did not have a history of depression, alcoholism, mental disorder or any financial issues. He'd had an accident two weeks before his death but had suffered no significant injury, and everyone said he was a happy-go-lucky, compassionate, and a kind man. He had no reason to kill himself.

William turned his attention to the next file. Clark Garrison died around ten hours after Mr. Wagner, between nine and eleven a.m. Mr. Garrison was a 45-year-old Caucasian with two kids and a wife, Amanda. After spending a weekend at her mother's, Amanda returned home and found her husband dead on the kitchen floor. Crime scene photos showed that Garrison had been an athletic, average-looking man with dense, brown hair and a well-trimmed beard. His eyes were wide open, staring upwards with a horrified look on his face. William looked closely at his skin. The victim had scratched himself on his arms, legs and stomach, leaving deep tears.

Garrison's fingerprints were found on the butcher knife, and there was no evidence of forced entry. The neighbors saw no one enter or leave the house. He was healthy, but unlike Wagner, Garrison had financial issues. He worked for a filtration company, and the neighbors told the police tales of quarrels between him and his wife, usually over money. Amanda did not deny the fights but said that things were improving. Her husband wouldn't have committed suicide, she said; he wasn't the type.

William turned to the last file. Nigel Hawk, a wealthy, divorced businessman, died approximately eight hours after Mr. Garrison on May 31, 2015. At seven p.m., Hawk shot himself on the balcony of his penthouse, tripped over, and fell eight floors before landing on the driveway. The doorman witnessed the fall and called the police who rushed to the scene, broke into the penthouse, and found no one. No broken locks, no struggle, and no murderer. The gun was found coated in Hawk's own fingerprints. Four hours of interviews, which included his two ex-wives and two daughters, led to nothing. Hawk had everything to live for: a thriving business, diplomatic immunity, expensive vacations. Hawk's history with his ex-wives was volatile, but with no evidence of foul play, cops ruled his death as another suicide. William examined the pictures. Hawk looked stern, like a school headmaster. He had a military cut, a trimmed mustache, and a skull that was smashed in from the fall.

William had fought for these cases. The other medical examiner had ruled the deaths out as suicides, but William wasn't so sure. He convinced the victims' families and his boss that they could've been murders. He wanted to do the autopsies and visit the crime scenes. Finally, his boss and the families agreed.

Detective Tom Nash from the NYPD was William's friend. They had worked together on many occasions. But because the evidence showed that these three cases were suicides, he refused to get involved. To make matters worse, Tom was adjusting to a new situation. After an exchange program passed by the police commissioner, Tom was forced to let go of his old partner, John White. He wasn't a happy man. Adjusting to a new partner was tough on him mainly because he lost his best friend and didn't trust his new partner. From William's prospective Joan Chase was a fine detective, but trust between cops is earned not given. Since, Tom had been wound up and moody. William knew it would be difficult to convince him of anything without evidence.

A knock sounded against the door; a figure leaned on the doorframe. Even in the dim light, William could make out Dr. Juliet Wave.

"Juliet, what are you still doing here?" he asked, turning on the lights.

"So, that's the secret of success? Sit in the dark."

William chuckled. "No. It's not. What about the kids?"

"They're with Albert. I was working late, and since you were so eager to get tests done, I started with Mr. Wagner."

"That's great," said William.

"Don't get so excited. I only had time for one test," Juliet said, handing him a file.

William scanned the report quickly. "Low serotonin?"

"Yes. Because of their behavior, I thought I'd measure their levels. Metabolized in the liver, serotonin is derived from the amino acid tryptophan. It's produced by the nervous system, mainly found in the brain and gastrointestinal tract. As you know, it helps convey nerve impulses and constrict blood vessels, and it manages sleep and mood. The test shows inhibited serotonin generation."

"Could it be drugs?"

"I'm unsure. If it affects one neurotransmitter, it might also affect others, like dopamine. By the time you've done your autopsies, I'll have finished the toxicology reports. We should have more answers soon."

"Thanks, but I don't think it's enough to get the NYPD interested."

"Well, it's a start. I had limited time today. Goodnight."

"Goodnight." William watched her leave as the clock beside him flashed eleven p.m. He should head home soon, but he was unlikely to sleep. He rubbed his hands over his face. Low serotonin. What could it mean?

William picked up his phone and dialed. No answer. Tom was ignoring his calls. So, he called his new partner.

"Yes?"

Williams' heart skipped a beat. Her voice sounded hurried and puffed.

"Who's this?" Joan asked.

"Err ... It's Dr. Sterling."

"Doc, do you what time it is?"

"Doesn't sound like I've disturbed you," William replied slapping his head with his left hand. He didn't need to say that.

"Who is it?" asked a male voice.

"Oh! I'm so sorry," said William.

"It's fine. Why did you call?"

"I don't think these are suicides. I think these were clever murders."

"You don't give up do you?"

"No, I don't. We found low levels of serotonin, which means that the suicides could have been caused by a drug."

"Do you have anything else?"

"Not yet. I'll have more evidence tomorrow. I'm calling because I want to see the crime scenes."

There was a momentary silence.

"Is that really necessary?"

"Yes."

"Fine," said Joan. "Meet me at the 234 Freeway Apartments tomorrow at nine thirty a.m., and don't be late."

Cab, New York

It was past midnight, and William was sprawled in the back seat of a cab. He watched the streets out the window. New York never slept. Bright street-lights hid the stars and cut through the darkness. William laid his head on the seat and tried to relax, but his mind wouldn't settle. Joan. Her voice kept echoing in his head. He'd met her in person a couple of times, and she'd occupied his thoughts since. Somehow Roumoult Cranston, his best friend knew he liked her and kept pushing William to ask her out. But he wasn't certain. The situation was compli-cated; he wasn't over his ex and wanted to avoid developing feelings. Fear dominated his heart when it came to Joan. What if he messed up again? The past two years with Rylee had been strenuous, he wasn't sure if he wanted to go through it again.

Sitting up straight, he pulled his phone out of his pocket and called Roumoult, who was due to return from his Europe business trip tomorrow.

"What took you so long?" William asked when Roumoult finally answered the call.

"Good evening to you too," he replied sarcastically. "I was going through security. My flight out of London leaves in thirty minutes. Why aren't you in bed? Its midnight in New York!"

"I know I'm right!"

"Oh, dear Lord," said Roumoult. "You got permission to do the autopsies, didn't you?"

"I am telling you, these are murders," William spluttered. "I have reasonable cause, and we should do the autopsies."

"You don't have a reasonable cause, you are obsessed."

"Roumoult, just listen," William said before telling him everything he'd found. He heard Roumoult yawn. "Am I boring you?"

"I'm exhausted."

"Fine. I'll see you tomorrow morning."

"No. I plan to sleep all day. I'll call you."

"Okay."

"Goodnight."

"Bye," William said half-heartedly. He recalled the day he had met Roumoult. Everyone else in high school thought of him as cold hearted, rich, spoiled brat. William found him reserved, observant, and extremely curious. Over the years he discovered he had the same qualities. He peered outside the window. He missed his friends. He missed life before the only thing that mattered was work.

3

Gone

June 3, 2015

Wellington Heights Apartments

William woke at five a.m. Four hours sleep wasn't enough. He suffered from insomnia since his breakup. Roumoult had told him repeatedly that he should seek help, but work was his medicine. Today, he didn't feel tired or groggy.

He got up and walked around his two-bedroom apartment in his pajamas. He'd taken over the property, bought by his sister, after his brother-in-law was transferred. It was lucky timing; William had just been kicked out of the navy for punching a senior officer. His father was an Admiral in the Navy and wanted him to apologize and return to duty. When he refused, his father threw him out of the house. That was when William had come to New York and started his medical career. It had now been ten years.

After a jog, a shower, and breakfast, William reached work at seven a.m. He stayed in his office for a while checking his email, and then he decided to check in with Dr. Wave before starting the autopsies.

He took the elevator to the basement, switched on the lights, and marched along the corridor toward pathology. He passed the storage room, the freezer, the pathology lab, the locker room and the room set aside for boxes and coffins. He reached the end of the corridor and was about to swipe his card when he heard a crash.

"Hello?" William called out, feeling his pulse rise.

Then came voices. The low tones of two men.

William retraced his steps. The changing room was unoccupied. He peered through the glass door of the storage room and noticed something metallic on the floor near the freezer. Twisting the doorknob, he entered the room. The desk was untouched, and his eyes rolled over towards the sizeable ugly gray freezer.

Suddenly, a figure appeared and raced towards him. Before he could react, something struck him on the head. William cried out, and the room twirled before his eyes as darkness fell.

John F. Kennedy International Airport

"Finally," muttered Roumoult as the plane touched down on American soil. Glad to leave the last three-weeks of meetings and conferences behind, he couldn't wait to get home and sleep in his own bed. The pilot announced that passengers could disembark in a few minutes and urged them to remain seated. Once the seatbelt sign was switched off, Roumoult got to his feet and stretched.

He ran his hand through his thick, wavy brown hair. He had striking features, bright green eyes and an oval face with a prominent jawline. He was smartly dressed in a blue, small-checked designer t-shirt and black trousers.

As he waited in the queue, he subconsciously rubbed his hand over his jaw. He needed to shave. Moving through customs and luggage retrieval took half an hour. At last, Roumoult stood outside the airport, his coat draped over his shoulder and his bags dragging beside him. He didn't call his secretary immediately, instead taking a moment to soak in the warmth of the sun.

Roumoult looked forward to catching up with his friends. He felt that he'd complicated his life by agreeing to help his father in his business. He wished he could only focus on his Law Firm and solving mysteries. Being the only son, he'd hardly had a choice.

His phone buzzed with four waiting messages.

The first was from his father: "Let me know when you reach NY. Happy Journey."

The second was from William. "Hey. Welcome back."

Roumoult started to call Alice, his secretary, when a loud horn distracted him. His sparkling, gray Audi RS 7 glided swiftly along the road before coming to a stop in front of him. A stranger stepped out of it.

"Mr. Cranston?"

"Yes."

"Jim Meadows, your new driver."

"I don't have a driver," said Roumoult. "My father does, and he was going to pick me up."

The young man looked uncomfortable. "I was told I am your driver," he repeated.

"Who hired you?"

"Fred Cranston," Jim replied.

Dad would never change, he thought. His attempt to have some control over Roumoult's life was increasingly annoying. First, he sneakily tried to set up Roumoult with women, which never worked. And now this, a driver he didn't need. He was too tired to argue. "Just take me home."

Roumoult watched Jim like a hawk as they left the airport. When he was satisfied that he wouldn't wreck his car, he turned his attention back to his phone. "You have a voicemail," the third message read.

He played it: "Hi, Mr. Cranston. It's Jonathan here. Sorry to disturb you, but I need help. Dr. Sterling is gone. He came to work this morning, and no one has seen him since! Could you please come to the Morgue? I think he's in trouble."

Roumoult sulked. "Tell me when he is not in trouble."

"Sir?" asked Jim.

"It's not you. Change of plans. Let's go to the City Morgue."

Jim nodded and changed lanes.

William had done it again. Being hooked on a case was like being on opium for him. Once he began working, he forgot to eat, destroyed his health, and ignored his family and friends. He wouldn't see him or hear from him for days. It was also his way of dealing with pain. The last time he'd vanished, it turned out he'd checked into a motel for forty-eight hours to work on a case without telling anyone. Lapses like this weren't unusual. Jonathan had called an hour ago. Maybe he'd reappeared.

Roumoult dialed. "Jonathan?"

"Mr. Cranston. Oh, thank God. At least I got through to you!"

"How are you?"

"I'm good. Good, but I'm worried about William," Jonathan said.

"So, he hasn't shown up?"

"No."

"Did he leave any messages?"

"No. Are you coming?"

"Yes. Call me if you find him."

Next, Roumoult called Angelus, a dear friend and a private detective who worked with his Law Firm. His conversation with Angelus was short and disappointing. William hadn't contacted him. Roumoult felt his anxiety rising.

"Jim, can we get there faster?"

"I'll try."

The car picked up pace.

The Audi parked on the roadside opposite to the old building. Roumoult asked Jim to stay in the car. Across the street, a Range Rover pulled up and Angelus stepped out. Roumoult crossed the road and shook his hand.

"Welcome back," Angelus said.

"It's good to be back," Roumoult replied.

"He's done it again."

"Disappeared?" said Roumoult. "It seems so."

"Are you sure he isn't hauled up in some motel?"

"I don't know. That's why I am here."

Angelus just shook his head. Muscular, taller than Roumoult, and with a large, square face, Angelus' military background shone through his every move. He was the picture of calmness, strolling casually toward the Morgue.

As he climbed up the stairs, Roumoult caught sight of Jonathan standing next to a lady. He recognized Detective Joan Chase instantly. She was a curvy woman with high cheekbones and a sharp nose. She brushed her silky, brunette hair away from her face and folded her arms as he approached.

"Mr. Cranston and Angelus. Meet Detective Chase," Jonathan said awkwardly.

Roumoult and Angelus shook hands with her.

Jonathan was a shaggily dressed man with a weather-beaten face. He shifted his weight from left to right and rubbed his palms together.

"Don't worry, we will find him," Angelus said.

"We'd better! I called the motel he checked into last time; he's not there."

Roumoult turned to Joan.

"Dr. Sterling wanted to see the crime scenes and called me last night," she said. "I was supposed to meet him, but when he didn't show up, I called the Morgue, and Jonathan told me he'd disappeared."

Roumoult remained quiet.

"Did he call you last night?" Joan asked.

"Yes, but I didn't think he was in any danger," Roumoult responded. "Let's just work together to find him. Where's Tom?"

"I don't know," said Joan. "I called him several times, no answer. I left a message."

Roumoult led the way to William's office. "What time did William come into work?" he asked Jonathan.

"Around seven a.m."

Without another word, Roumoult called Angelus, who had set off in search of the security guard. "Did you find the guard?"

"Yep, I'm in his office now."

"Okay, look through the camera footage from seven to eight thirty a.m."

"I'll call you as soon as I find anything."

The office offered no clues, nothing out of place. Roumoult, Joan, and Jonathan took the elevator to the basement. The numbers on the screen climbed down as the elevator descended. Roumoult closed his eyes, a throbbing pain piercing his temples. The elevator shuddered to a halt, and he walked out before the doors had finished opening.

"We should begin in the storage room," Jonathan suggested. "I saw blood there."

Roumoult eyed him and quickened his pace.

"I'll get Juliet. She was the last person he called."

Roumoult nodded, trying to remain calm.

"Who's Juliet?" Joan enquired.

"A pathologist who works here."

In the storage room, files littered the floor. A water filter had been tossed and surgical instruments were scattered on the floor. Roumoult kneeled to examine a red splatter of blood.

"I'm calling the CSU unit," Joan announced as Jonathan and Juliet entered the storage room.

"Hello, Dr. Wave. How are you?" Roumoult asked.

"I'm well, thank you," said Juliet. "Have you found him?"

Roumoult shook his head. "What can you tell me?"

"He called me in the morning, but I was busy with the children and thought I'd see him when I got to work. By the time I arrived at the lab, Jonathan told me he was gone."

Roumoult paced back and forth. "Did you look everywhere?"

"Yes! His office, the pathology lab, the cafeteria, the reception. And I asked everyone. No one saw anything."

"What about the freezer?" Roumoult asked, pointing towards the big door.

Jonathan's face fell, "I-I didn't check in there."

Roumoult reached the door and pulled it open. An enormous cloud of mist hit him and then evaporated. He stepped inside, and the others followed. The freezer was at least ten feet wide and fifteen feet deep and had eight aisles of samples.

Footsteps boomed as they searched for William. Roumoult walked up and down the narrow corridors, examining the various samples suspended in liquid. He paused in front of a human head. Its hollow eyes stared at him. He felt a knot in his stomach and looked away. When he reached the other end, Joan was waiting. "No sign of him?" Roumoult asked hopefully.

"No."

They exited the freezer, shutting the door behind them. "Where is Dr. Wave?" Roumoult asked after a moment.

Joan and Jonathan looked at each other.

"I thought she was behind you," said Joan.

From inside the freezer, they heard a loud rattling sound, followed by a crash.

"Jonathan, stay here," Joan ordered. She armed herself with a gun and walked into the freezer. Roumoult followed her.

"Dr. Wave! Dr. Wave!" Joan yelled.

Fog surrounded them, and Roumoult's legs shook in the cold. They followed the rattling sound to the third aisle. Joan put her gun away and folded her arms. Juliet was rifling through shelves muttering something to herself.

"Juliet, what are you doing?" Roumoult asked.

"Someone took them! They were right there!" she cried, moving away from the shelves "Oh God, what am I going to do?"

"What's she talking about?" Joan asked Roumoult.

"Beats me."

"It can't be. I left them right there!" Juliet wailed.

"What? What's gone?"

"The tissue samples, the blood samples, everything! It's all gone!"

Roumoult swallowed thickly. "Do you mean samples from William's cases?"

Juliet's silence was answer enough.

Everyone left the freezer and Roumoult closed the door.

"Someone's stealing evidence," Juliet said.

"It doesn't matter. You have the bodies. You can..." he paused. "You have the bodies, right?"

"Well, we had them yesterday!" Juliet exclaimed.

Roumoult dropped his head into his hands.

"This is nuts. I'll check, wait here," Jonathan said.

Roumoult paced. No one spoke. Worries about William's wellbeing were building, and they weren't helped by Jonathan's breathless return. "Someone took the bodies! They're gone!"

"How can that be? Are you sure?" Joan asked.

"Yes. I checked! They're not where I left them."

"What does this mean?" Jonathan asked.

"It means William could have entered the basement when they were stealing evidence," Roumoult said darkly. Everyone looked at him, then the silence was broken by Roumoult's phone ringing.

"Can you come to the security office?" Angelus said eagerly.

"Okay."

The group marched to the ground floor and stepped into the small office.

"Everyone, Ben Hast, the security guard," Angelus said.

Ben was a big man in his fifties. He had broad shoulders, large blue eyes, and a bald head. They exchanged short pleasantries.

"Did you find out what happened to him?" Angelus asked.

"I think William got in the way when someone was stealing evidence," said Roumoult.

"I see," Angelus said. "Perhaps the surveillance videos can shed some light."

Roumoult peered at the monitor. The footage showed William entering the premises. Then the camera on the third floor showed him entering his office. The group watched as William stepped out of the office and made for the stairs. Ben produced another piece of footage, which displayed the basement corridor. They watched as William walked straight towards the pathology lab. Then the screen went blank.

"What happened?" Roumoult asked.

Ben frowned. "Someone sabotaged the basement and the parking lot cameras. I fixed them half an hour ago."

"How did they get in the building?" Joan asked.

"Through the back door," Ben replied. "It's a spring lock. They probably used a skeleton key."

He played another video clip. At six fifty a.m., a white van drove into the parking lot. Two men in masks climbed out of the vehicle, rushed to the back door, and broke in. Then the screen went blank.

"It's not enough to identify the crooks," Joan said.

Roumoult wasn't worried about them. He wanted to find William. "It is possible he's still in the building. They could have dumped him somewhere."

"I looked everywhere," Jonathan said.

Roumoult bit his lip. "Let's say they wanted to hide him as long as possible. How would they do that?"

"The cameras in the basement and parking lot were out for two hours. They could have hidden him anywhere," Angelus pointed out.

Roumoult turned to Ben. "Can you show us what happened in the past three hours?"

The guard nodded, and Roumoult waited for him to access the system. A short ring echoed through the office. It was Joan's phone.

"The CSU unit is here," she said after taking the call. "I'll take them to the basement and arrange a search party."

"Thank you," Roumoult replied. He turned his focus back to the screen, eyes narrowed at the shapes flitting across it.

"Who's that?" Roumoult asked after a few minutes, pointing out a black van that had entered the parking lot at seven thirty a.m.

"The cemetery guys," Ben answered apathetically.

"Cemetery guys?" Angelus asked.

"They pick up the coffins of homeless and unidentified people and take them to the graveyard," said Jonathan.

"Did they take any coffins today?" Roumoult asked.

"Hold on." Ben skipped through the security video.

Roumoult wiped the sweat off his brow and watched as the men loaded three coffins in the van and drove away. Ben paused the video. "They took three coffins today."

"Do you have a record of the coffins?"

Again, Ben shuffled through the footage. After a few minutes, he said, "We don't know their names, so we give each coffin an ID. Today, we sent coffins with IDs 10010, 10012, and 10013 to the First Calvary Cemetery."

"Okay. One possibility: William could be in one of those coffins."

"I don't like that possibility," Angelus stated.

"What else happened?" Roumoult asked.

They watched as several staff members entered and left the building, but nothing unusual stood out.

"Okay," said Roumoult after a long silence, "two possibilities. One: he's in a coffin. Two: he's in the cold storage."

"What makes you say that?" Angelus asked.

"The thugs only disabled the basement cameras, meaning they didn't need to go to the other floors. William could only have bumped into them in the basement. He has to be there. Jonathan, did you check the coffin room or cold storage?"

"No, I checked for bodies but not for ... William."

Hurried footsteps approached. Joan stepped back into the guard's office.

"Okay. The CSU units are processing the crime scene, and five cops are searching the entire building. We'll find him." She paused, sensing their despair. "What's happened?"

"Jonathan, please check the cold storage. We will check the coffin room," said Roumoult authoritatively.

Joan swallowed. "Why the coffin room?"

As they returned to the basement, Angelus brought Joan up to speed. They walked past the CSU unit. Following Ben, Roumoult almost ran to the end of the corridor. The guard opened the door and switched on the lights.

Roumoult surveyed the gray and dreary room. He looked at the six coffins. "They don't check them before they take the coffins?"

"No. They sign the register and take the sealed coffins with IDs." Ben pointed towards a register on the table next to the door.

Roumoult and Angelus leapt into action. Angelus opened the first coffin. Empty. Roumoult opened the second. Nothing. He was about to prize open the next one when he spotted a casket at the far end of the room with something written on it. He stormed towards it, then he stopped to stare at the numbers *10013*.

"Oh, good God," he muttered. Angelus moved to stand next to him. Roumoult bowed his head. He moved to one side as Angelus dug a claw hammer under the coffin's lid, forcing it open. Inside, a chubby old man dressed in shags lay peacefully with his hands crossed over his belly.

Angelus ran his hand through his hair. "They took the wrong coffin."

Footsteps echoed, and Jonathan appeared. "He's not in cold storage."

Roumoult shut his eyes.

City Morgue

Roumoult pushed the door open and ran out of the building. He could hear Joan calling his name, but he didn't stop. William was locked in a coffin, sent off to a graveyard for cremation. Roumoult felt bile rise in his throat.

Noticing his haste, Jim unlocked the car door and moved to the backseat. Roumoult climbed into driver's seat and took the wheel. Joan threw herself into the passenger seat. Roumoult turned the key.

"Hey, Mr. Cranston!" Jonathan called out. "I'll call the cemetery and make sure they don't cremate anyone."

"Good idea!" yelled Joan.

People on the sidewalk stopped to stare.

Roumoult pushed the accelerator. Tires whirled and screeched as the car raced. He touched the small screen, and the GPS came to life.

"First Calvary Cemetery," Roumoult said clearly.

The route appeared on the screen: *The First Calvary Cemetery is approximately six miles from our current position. Total time to destination: twenty minutes. For the best route, please take a left at the next intersection.*

Roumoult tried to ignore the urge to speed, pushing the brakes and bringing the Audi to a halt before the intersection. The Range Rover was right behind him. He thought about the last twenty-four hours. His eyes were gritty, and all he wanted was a shower and some sleep. William's disappearance changed everything. The lights turned green, he pushed the pedal, and the car shot forward. Joan grabbed her seat.

"Sorry."

She didn't say anything. A moment later, her phone began to ring. She spoke low and fast.

"What happened?" Roumoult asked when she'd hung up.

"That was Jonathan. No one's answering the phone."

Roumoult gripped the steering wheel firmly to keep his hands from shaking. Traffic forced him to slow down. He banged the horn.

The First Calvary Cemetery

As soon as he drove through the gates of the cemetery, Roumoult felt calmer. He'd made it. The beautiful, green driveway led to a three-story structure. Various plants and flowers grew in round spaces in the middle of the thick, green meadow. Roumoult parked in the driveway and stepped out. He noticed an old man sitting in a chair on the deck reading a newspaper.

Joan said to Roumoult, "Let me do the talking."

He nodded.

"Hello, sir. We're from the NYPD. We're looking for three coffins that arrived from the City Morgue about four hours ago. Do you know where they are?"

Instead of responding, the man stared at her.

"What's your name?" Joan asked firmly.

"George Cores," said the man. "I'm the caretaker and the gardener."

"Okay. I need you to focus. We need to find three coffins that arrived from the City Morgue this morning. Do you know where they are?"

"They must be in the storage room."

"Good. Who's in charge?"

"Father Kristen."

"Good. Now take us to the storage room and please call the Father."

"But..."

"Just do it," Joan interjected.

The group hastily followed the caretaker. Roumoult felt Mr. Cores' agitation and confusion tangle with his own. He noted a medium-sized chapel to his left and followed the group down the long corridor. They came to a stop in front of the big wooden door. Cores inserted the key and opened the door.

Roumoult's heart sank. Coffins of different shapes and sizes lay silently on tables. The room's few lights emitted a yellowish glow, casting over the caskets. Sweat dripped down Roumoult's neck, and his palms were wet, but he had no choice. They started looking.

"Could be one of these," announced Joan.

Roumoult felt hopeful.

"Wait a minute," Angelus said. He counted. "There are four coffins here."

"I thought there were three!" Joan said.

"You can't open them!" shouted Cores.

Roumoult raised his hands. "Quiet everyone. Why are there four coffins?"

"I don't know...Wait a minute," Angelus said slowly. "Remember what we saw in the Morgue. Maybe we don't have to open any of them. The coffin at the Morgue had an identification number."

"So?" Joan asked.

"So logically, William should be in the one without an ID," Angelus concluded. "Doesn't that make sense? The culprits must've hit him over the head, put him in the coffin with no ID, and sealed it."

"Then the cemetery guys took the first three sealed coffins without checking for IDs," Joan added.

Roumoult set about searching. A few minutes later, they met near the door.

"They all have IDs," Joan said, voice rising. "He's not here. We were wrong."

They heard loud footsteps, and a tall man with short, curly hair and piercing gray eyes appeared at the door. "What's going on here?" the Father demanded.

Roumoult noted the panic on everyone's faces. He took the lead and explained the situation. The Father's face softened.

"Please help us," Joan said.

The Father nodded.

"Have you cremated anyone this morning?" Roumoult asked anxiously.

"No. The morning funeral took more time than I'd expected."

"Thank God," Roumoult muttered, leaning against the wall. He rubbed his face with his hands.

"Why do you have four coffins from the Morgue?" Angelus asked.

"Bodies of three unfortunate souls were sent to us day before yesterday. We were too busy, so we rescheduled their cremations."

"And City Morgue sent three more bodies for cremation today,"

"Yes,"

"There are four coffins here. Where are the other two coffins?" Joan asked.

"There was no space here. We put them in the second storage room."

Father Kristen led the group further along the corridor before opening a large door. Roumoult felt his anxiousness drop in the fresh air.

"When we have a lot of funerals, we put a few caskets in this extra cold storage unit," the Father explained. The group followed him across a small meadow to an ancient-looking structure.

Angelus walked up to Roumoult. "Are you okay?"

"I'll be fine when I find him."

Soon they came to stand in front of the structure. Father Kristen took out a big bunch of keys.

"Could you please hurry?" Joan pleaded.

"I'm trying—" The father replied, but he broke off mid-sentence.

A loud thud distracted everyone.

Father Kristen found the keys and unlocked the door.

Roumoult entered the structure. A chilly draft hit him. The lights turned on, and he found himself in another large room filled with coffins. "All right, let's just find that casket."

They spread out and searched fanatically.

"Here!" shouted Joan.

Roumoult rushed to her and saw a familiar-looking coffin. He banged the top. "William?"

There was no reply, but he heard a soft bump.

"William," he repeated, pressing his ear against the top.

"Roumoult..." came a soft whimper.

He looked at Angelus, who pushed him aside and unlocked the coffin with a claw hammer. They shoved the top away, and there was William, his face covered in blood. His lips moved as if he was trying to say something.

"Get him out!" Angelus said.

Roumoult and Angelus helped William sit on the lawn. The Father draped a blanket over him.

"I'll get some water," Angelus said.

Roumoult sat at William's side. "William?" He noticed a wound on his forehead and dried blood on his face. He looked exhausted. "Look at me. Are you okay?"

"What took you so long?" William grumbled.

Roumoult closed his eyes and then lay back on the grass. Finally, he could relax.

In an hour, an ambulance arrived, Detective Tom Nash was not far behind it. Tom's light brown hair glittered in the sunlight. He was a bit shorter than Joan, with baby blue eyes and a heart-shaped face. Roumoult thought Tom's personality was a bit unsuited for a homicide detective. He was too gentle, too good-humored.

Roumoult thanked them for their help. A paramedic approached him and said that someone had to stay overnight with William. Roumoult wanted to say no, but he couldn't. William needed him. The medic returned to the ambulance.

"Well, stealing evidence indicates the possibility of a homicide," Tom told Joan.

"We'll have to reopen the case," Joan agreed.

"So now this is a homicide investigation?" asked Roumoult.

"Yeah. Dr. Sterling got what he wanted," said Joan.

Roumoult rolled his eyes. "Good luck."

Upper East Side New York

Tom regretted that he hadn't acted sooner. He could have prevented the theft of the bodies and saved William from a near death experience. It didn't matter anymore; it was done. Another case reopened by William.

He had strong instincts.

Tom smiled involuntarily when he remembered the first time, he had seen William. He was an underpaid assistant and Tom was a lieutenant trying to solve a murder of a young girl. All hopes of solving the case had faded, but the young fellow toiling alone in the Morgue at midnight, wasn't going to give up. Two weeks passed without a word, and then the phone rang. William had traced the unidentified DNA on the murder weapon to two other unsolved murders. He contacted his friends in the forensic department and pinned down a suspect at the local bakery in the area. Tom took over and within twenty-four hours made an arrest.

Then began a friendship that lasted for a decade. Through him he was introduced to Roumoult. He was smart, uncanny, visionary, resourceful and twisted the law and his family's power to get what he wanted. No one knew what he would do next. It was handy to have a powerful man on his side but there was one thing about their friendship Tom despised. If Roumoult got involved in a case, he would take over, use any means necessary to solve it, leaving him and his friends behind and often inviting danger.

Tom spent the rest of the morning going through the case files. The best place him to begin was the victims' families. They drove to Upper East Side to question Hawk's first wife.

He sat in Mrs. Longburn's large, well-decorated living room. She was a nice-looking woman with short hair, brown eyes, and a full figure. Next to her sat Kera, Hawk's eldest daughter.

Tom informed Mrs. Longburn about the theft of Mr. Hawk's remains.

"Why?" asked Mrs. Longburn.

"We don't know."

"Why would someone steal my father's body?" Kera sobbed.

"We're trying to answer that question," Joan told her gently before turning back to Mrs. Longburn. "What can you tell us about your ex-husband?"

Mrs. Longburn appeared uncertain. "Nothing much. We parted ways ten years ago. He was stubborn, hot-tempered, and career-minded. He was secretive and kept things from me. I didn't like that."

"Had you seen him recently?"

"No."

"Kera, did you see your father before he died?" Joan asked.

"I saw him about a month ago for dinner and ice cream," she replied morbidly.

"I'm sorry for your loss," Tom said.

"Oh, stop it." Mrs. Longburn rolled her eyes at her daughter. "He didn't love you. He loved no one!"

"Shut up, Mom!" Kera screamed.

Tom gulped but pressed on. "Mrs. Longburn, we understand that this is a difficult time, but we need your help. Where were you on the night your husband died?"

"I already told the police. I was at a charity ball. Hundreds of people must have seen me."

"And you, Ms. Longburn?" Joan asked Kera.

"I was at my best friend's birthday party until midnight."

"And your dad called you three days before his death?" Tom asked, referring to his notebook.

"Yeah. We talked about usual stuff. He said he fell the other day and hurt his knee. He was taking painkillers."

"What about the gun?" Joan asked.

"He had a gun registered in his name. He usually kept it in the study desk," Mrs. Longburn huffed. "I didn't approve of it, but no one listens to me."

Once they were outside the building, Joan turned on Tom. "That wasn't useful."

Tom sulked. The trouble with his new partner was that she was too impulsive. She wanted answers quickly. To him patience was the key. "Let's keep going." He said longing for the good old days with his old partner. There were no surprises, no second guesses. With Joan, it was too complicated. He never knew what she would do next.

St. George Hospital

William tried to settle in the bright hospital room. It was simple yet elegant, painted white with red trimmings. He lay on a big, comfortable bed, looking out the window at the city view. The room was furnished with a couch, a tallboy, and two comfortable chairs.

William didn't feel good. The thick bandage above his left eye bothered him, and the four stitches near his hairline were itching. He tried to sit back and watch TV, but he felt restless. Every time he closed his eyes, he imagined he was back in the casket. He wanted to go home, but the doctors told him they were waiting for his test results. Guilt and despair hung over him. He wished he could erase his memories and start over.

Roumoult entered the room, talking with his father on the phone. William was glad for his company. He tried to focus on the TV. After a while, he noticed Roumoult was silent and looked over to find him reading a Playboy.

"Where did you get that?"

"I borrowed it," said Roumoult.

"From whom?"

"A patient next door. He was in a coma."

"So, you stole it?"

"Lighten up, I'll return it. It's not like he needs it." Roumoult returned to the magazine.

Sometimes William had a tough time understanding Roumoult. Just this morning, he'd turned everything upside down to save him. Next thing, he was rifling through a stranger's room, taking whatever, he wanted.

Lower Manhattan

Their first interview wasn't very revealing, so Tom hoped Mr. Hawk's second wife could give greater insight into his death. Mrs. Angus owned a small apartment on the second floor on Hudson Street. Her living room was neat and well-decorated. She was a young and lean woman with silky, brown hair and large, gray eyes. Lacey, Hawk's stepdaughter, looked very much like her mother. Tom thought it was best to jump right in.

"What can you tell us about your ex-husband?" he asked.

"I don't see the relevance," said Mrs. Angus. "First the medical examiner and now the NYPD. What's going on?"

"We're just following a line of inquiry," Joan reassured her.

"He killed himself, and there's nothing more to it. I'm tired of this. Please ask the City Morgue to return his remains so I can arrange a funeral."

Tom and Joan exchanged an uncomfortable glance. Tom explained the situation.

"Oh my God! This is disturbing! Why? Why would someone steal his body?"

"That's what we're trying to find out."

"What about the funeral?"

"It will have to wait," Tom said.

"You will find him, right? Intact?"

"We will try," Tom said earnestly.

"And you'll notify me immediately?"

"Yes," said Tom. "Can you tell us anything that might help us locate him?"

"I honestly don't know," Mrs. Angus said. "People change, and things fall apart. It's hard to love a man and lose him. Nigel used to share everything with me, but he just stopped. He changed. You know when you have the feeling that someone's hiding something from you. Last year, whenever I asked him about his business trips, he would change the subject or get angry. He made excuses like 'I don't mix business with personal life.' Things got worse, and his relationship with Lacey fell apart. So, I left him."

"Did you speak with him before he died?"

Mrs. Angus shook her head. "No. He spoke to Lacey."

Tom turned to the daughter.

"He called me two days before," Lacey said. "He mentioned a fall, but the injury was minor. I didn't think he was in trouble."

"Was he agitated, stressed, or worried?" Joan asked.

"Not that I noticed," answered Lacey.

Tom asked Mrs. Angus about the gun. She knew nothing. He asked if there were any issues with their financial agreement after the divorce. She told him that Nigel never neglected Lacey's needs; he always took care of her.

Lower Manhattan

Tom was getting tired of all the driving. He parked the car and cast an eye over the exclusive building. He hoped talking to Mr. Wagner's daughter might shed some light.

Rachael Wagner received them gracefully and made them comfortable in her penthouse apartment. She was a sophisticated woman in her late thirties. Her makeup was precise, and her hair perfectly tied up in a neat bun. But her dry lips and swollen eyes told another story. As soon as they told her that her father had disappeared, Rachael broke down and wept. Joan tried to console her, and Tom got her a glass of water. They waited for her to calm down.

"This is unacceptable! Why? Who would steal his body?"

"We don't know, but we will find him," Joan assured her.

"I don't understand! This is ridiculous! Why weren't the bodies kept in a secure place? Does this mean anyone can steal a dead person?"

"It is an unusual situation," Tom said.

"Please tell me you will find him. He was all I had!"

"We'll try our best," Tom said solemnly.

"Did anything happen before his death?" Joan asked.

Rachael tried to compose herself. She drew in several deep breaths. "Yes, he had an accident."

"How did it happen?" asked Tom.

"Every Friday, Dad went to a poker game at his friend's house. When he was driving back home, he saw something on the road, an animal. He reduced his speed. Suddenly, the animal moved and ran toward the car. He lost control and crashed into a tree. He passed out, but when he woke up, he called me and an ambulance." She paused and twisted the tissue in her hands.

"Did something else happen?" Tom pressed.

"I-I really don't think it's relevant."

"It might be."

"Well, after he called me, I asked him to stay in the car. I grabbed a friend and got there in forty minutes. The ambulance arrived, but I couldn't find my father. It was horrible. We looked everywhere! Finally, we found him hiding behind some rocks, but he wasn't himself. He pushed the paramedics away. When I reached for him, he screamed like a madman. He picked up rocks and threw them at us. The paramedics seized him, sedated him, and took him to the hospital. The ER doctor did some tests, but everything was negative. They thought he was hallucinating but didn't know why. The next morning, he was himself again, charming and caring. I was so relieved that he'd recovered. Then... I asked him about the accident, and he looked confused and said he remembered nothing."

"He denied it?" Joan said.

"Yes!" Rachael exclaimed. "He said he didn't remember throwing stones, or screaming at people, or even coming to the hospital."

"You think he changed his story. Why?" Tom asked.

"I don't know, but I know he lied. I just know it!"

"Did anything else happen after the accident?"

"No," Rachael dabbed at her eyes. "He acted like it never happened."

The Bronx

The wobbly chair caused Tom to shift uncomfortably. Amanda Garrison watched him with narrowed eyes. She was a middle-aged woman, skinny and dressed casually in all black. She did not welcome the inquiry. Joan told her what had happened to Mr. Garrison's body. Tom braced himself for a response, but there wasn't one. Amanda's expression remained cold and unchanging.

"Are you sure?" she asked curtly.

"Yes," Joan replied. "We're sorry. We're trying to locate his body."

"Hmm." Amanda looked away. "What can I do for you?"

"Could you tell us anything more about your husband's death?" Tom asked.

"No. Not really. I told the police everything I know. I came home, and he'd stabbed himself. That's all."

"How was your relationship with your husband?" asked Joan.

"Just like any other marriage. We fought a lot. We have two daughters, a mortgage, and no one to support us. I can't find a job. I wanted to move to the country; he wanted to stay. But things were improving. Clark got some extra work, and we had some more money."

"Did he have any medical problems?" Joan asked.

"High blood pressure and migraines."

"Migraines?" Tom repeated after Amanda.

"Yes. Over the last few weeks, he had frequent migraines. The doctor diagnosed him with myopia and told him to wear glasses. Although he had to take pain killers for a while, he felt better after that."

Tom asked about the butcher's knife. Amanda said they'd had it for years and that her husband had used it often.

St. George Hospital

William opened his eyes, his headache returned. The light was dim, and the curtains drawn. He sat up slowly and found a visitor at his bedside.

"Hey. You're awake." Joan said softly.

"Hi." William could feel his heart hammering. He watched Joan flick through Roumoult's magazine. "Where's Roumoult?"

"He went home to freshen up. I volunteered to stay until he got back."

Just then, Roumoult entered the room. "Hey, how are you?"

"Fine."

44

"Thanks for staying," Roumoult said to Joan.

"No problem."

"It's addictive, isn't it?" Roumoult commented pointing the magazine.

"Oh, yeah!" They laughed, and Roumoult started to tell her about his trip.

William fumed. Roumoult hadn't told him anything about the trip.

Joan smiled and blushed as they chatted. William seethed, glaring at Roumoult.

"So, you reopened the case?" Roumoult asked.

"We did," Joan said. She told them about their interviews with the victims' families. "Let's just see what we find." She rose and left, the room falling silent in her absence.

"How are you?" Roumoult asked William again after a while.

"Get that thing out of here!" William spat, pointing at the magazine.

Roumoult looked confused, "What's the matter with you?"

"Just do it."

"Maybe you hit our head somewhere and it didn't show up on the MRI."

"Roumoult!"

"Ok, Grandpa," Roumoult muttered. He rolled up the magazine. "Wait a minute, you're jealous!"

William felt heat rise in his cheeks. "Just drop it."

"Fine," said Roumoult, a smirk playing across his lips.

4

Mystical Creatures

June 4, 2015

St. George Hospital

Tom didn't like the Emergency Room, but evidence called. Dr. Myer was the resident who had treated Mr. Wagner after his accident. Tom wanted leads. He'd spent all day waiting for the toxicology reports on the medicines collected from the crime scenes. He speculated that the killer substituted the pills, leading to the murders. One look at the toxicology report slashed his theory. It showed that the victims' medicines were genuine.

Tom wracked his brains. All the victims' family members had been interviewed except one. Clark Garrison had a sister in London. Tom had tried to call her, but there was no answer. He'd left a message, hoping for the best.

A woman in scrubs walked into the waiting room.

"Dr. Emma Meyers?" Tom asked.

"Yes," she replied, crossing her arms.

"Detectives Tom Nash and Joan Chase."

"Can I see a badge?"

They showed her their badges.

"Are these real?"

Tom smiled. "Dr. Meyers, we want to talk to you about Mr. Wagner."

Dr. Meyers' face softened. "Is it true he killed himself?"

"Maybe," said Tom. "Anything you can tell us about the accident?"

"Why do you ask?"

"We're trying to tie up a few loose ends."

"Sorry, I can't help you."

"Why not?" Joan demanded.

"I'm busy," Dr. Meyers said simply. "Have a nice day." She turned to leave.

"Hey, hold on!" Joan called out.

Dr. Meyers paused.

"We just want to know—"

"Correct me if I am wrong: I don't have to talk to you, do I?" Dr. Meyers tapped her foot impatiently.

"No," Joan conceded, "but if you are withholding—"

"I know the law. It's a suicide, and you have nothing."

Tom stepped forward. "What's your problem? Helping the police is a—"

"The police?" Dr. Meyer spat. "Damn the police! The first bloody cop who spoke with Mr. Wagner scared the old man to death."

"What?" Tom asked. "Did you report the incident?"

"No. It was an accident, not a hit-and-run. But this cop shows up and talks to the old guy for five minutes, just five minutes! After that, Don Wagner changed his story. And now he's dead. Dead! I've never lost a patient before. I should have gone with my instinct and kept him under observation."

"Hold on, what did he say? What did he tell you?" Tom asked.

"It doesn't matter. He's dead."

"Look," said Joan, trying a new angle. "You cared for him. He was your patient. Don't you want to know why he died?"

"What about that cop?"

"We'll track him down and question him. You have our word," Tom said.

Dr. Meyers nodded slowly. "Fine. Let's take a seat." She pointed to a small table with four chairs.

Joan and Tom sat side by side facing Dr. Meyers.

"Two weeks ago, Mr. Wagner showed up in our ER," she began. "He was hysterical, and when the paramedics couldn't control him, they sedated him. The injury to his shoulder was minor. I went to see him at about three a.m. He was awake, strapped to the bed, and he looked frightened. I tried to console him, but he said he couldn't involve anyone else. He kept saying that he and his daughter were in danger. 'He will kill her! He will kill her!' he said. It took me some time to gain his trust, and he told me the whole story. After the accident and talking to his daughter, he heard it. The howl of a wolf."

Tom sat back.

"He tried to find out where it was coming from," Dr. Meyers continued. "That's when he saw a large creature moving through the woods. It scared him just about to death. He left the car and took cover behind some rocks. It howled again and again, each time drawing nearer. He prayed for his life. He was alone, helpless. Suddenly, there was silence. He thought it had decided to leave him alone. Then he heard a rattling noise, followed by a hoarse roar. He turned and saw a figure, a wolf-like shape, moving through the woods, dragging something."

Tom was dumbfounded. "Let me get this straight," he said. "Mr. Wagner saw a werewolf in the woods, and it was dragging something."

"He said it looked like a body bag."

"Did he witness a murder?" Tom asked.

"I don't know."

"You should have told the police," Joan said.

"Everyone thought he was under the influence of a drug."

"Did you test him?"

"Yes. His tests were normal. He was hallucinating due to an unknown cause. The next day, he denied the whole thing. There was nothing I could do."

Before heading back to the car, Tom and Joan asked hospital management to track down surveillance tapes of the mysterious cop's visit to Mr. Wagner.

"A fourth murder?" Joan said.

"Maybe Wagner witnessed a murder. Maybe that's what got him killed," said Tom.

"But what about Garrison and Hawk?"

Tom shook his head. "I have no idea, but we have to find out if Wagner was telling the truth."

East Village, New York

Roumoult drove wordlessly. Jazz music played over the radio. The windows blocked out the chaos of the city, and the air conditioner fought against the raging heat. Long queues of cars lined every street. Roumoult looked at William; he still looked exhausted and sick. The doctors had released him from the hospital, and William refused to stay at the Cranston house. He insisted on going home.

"So, what's your plan?" Roumoult drummed his fingers against the steering wheel.

"I'm going back to work tomorrow," William replied.

"What? Take a few days off!"

"No, I need talk to Juliet and Jonathan. The autopsies and tests must be done by now."

Roumoult felt as if a rock had fallen on him. In all the commotion, he'd forgotten. "William," he said, "the bodies have disappeared."

"What?"

"The thugs were stealing evidence when you showed up. That's why they attacked you." He glanced at William, who sat with his mouth open.

"Oh, hell! This is unbelievable! Why didn't you tell me?"

"Oh, I am sorry, I was busy saving you!"

"What should I do?"

"Wait for Tom to find them," Roumoult told him. William grumbled.

Roumoult stopped the Audi at the next intersection. They were near Madison Square Park, still about thirty minutes from William's apartment on 8th Street.

"I need to ask you something," William said. "Why did you ask Joan to stay?"

"I didn't. She volunteered."

"Why?"

"You already know the answer. She likes you."

"No."

"You like her. Admit it, you're jealous when she so much as looks at other men."

"I'm not," William said defensively, settling back in his seat. "I don't think it's a good idea to date cops."

"And dating Rylee was a good idea?" Roumoult asked.

William rolled his eyes. "There you go again. You hate her, don't you?"

"Yes, I do. Shall I tell you why I hate her chronologically or alphabetically?"

William fell silent. Roumoult realized being brash wouldn't help. He was sensitive. The lights turned green, and he eased his foot onto the accelerator.

"I'm sorry. I didn't mean..."

"You did."

"Fine, I apologize."

"That's not an apology."

William folded his arms, and Roumoult realized the conversation was over.

"So, you are not going to help me?" asked William breaking the silence.

"I already did."

"I mean to find those bodies."

"Nope,"

"Aren't you curious? This is not your garden-variety case. Three people killed themselves and they have no suspects or a murder weapon. As if he killed them and vanished into thin air. Then as I am about to do the autopsy someone attacks me, and the bodies disappear."

"Sounds like your type of case,"

"Oh, don't jerk me around. You are doing this on purpose."

"No, I am not. You know what happens if I get involved."

"Yes. I know. You get answers. Tom is too slow."

"William, you need to trust Tom. He will find the bodies and solve this case."

"I trust him, but I have a bad feeling about this case. It's unusual."

They spent the rest of the trip in silence, and when Roumoult was sure that William had everything he needed, he left.

Roumoult spent the rest of the day at work. He couldn't focus. His body felt heavy with fatigue. William's words kept echoing in his mind. Of course, he was interested but wasn't sure if Tom would welcome his input. He wanted to help William, and perhaps he could do it without trespassing over Tom's territory. He called Tom and asked for an update. Tom proudly told him about the werewolf, a possible fourth victim, and their plan to search for the body in the woods. The werewolf intrigued Roumoult. He volunteered to join the search and picked up William on the way. Tom was a bit hesitant, but Roumoult assured him he was just doing it to indulge William.

"You changed your mind." William said sitting in the passenger's seat.

"No. I was getting bored. And it has been a while since we chased Werewolves. I thought it would be a fun night out."

"Just admit it. You are curious about the case and scared of annoying Tom"

Roumoult glared at him and remained silent.

"Did you tell Fred?" William asked as the Audi sped after Tom's car on the highway.

"No, I don't want to tell him I'm going out hunting for bodies at night in the middle of the woods with a high probability of a werewolf sighting."

William laughed.

"But I didn't lie to him," Roumoult continued. "I told him I was taking you and a few friends to dinner." He pointed at the boxes of Chinese takeaway perched on the dash.

To the best of their knowledge, Rachael Wagner had found her father on Interstate-95 about twenty miles from Manhattan, beyond Eastchester. Roumoult tailed Tom's light-gray Ford for two hours. Jet lag made his eyes sting. The horns, bright lights, and fumes bothered him.

When they neared their destination, Roumoult felt as if he'd left New York far behind. Gone was the concrete jungle. Tall trees leaned over the road, which was lined with houses and small apartment buildings. The thick vegetation blocked the moonlight. They drove for another ten minutes, and soon the cars slowed down. Roumoult parked behind Tom, unbuckled his seatbelt, and stepped out of the car. "Damn, it's hot," he said, pulling off his coat.

"Welcome back to NYC." Tom laughed.

They joined a group of ten cops and four police dogs, standing to eat in the cool night air. Roumoult enjoyed the Chinese food and a doughnut but skipped the coffee.

"Are you ready?" Tom asked.

"Yeah, thanks for accepting my offer."

"Huh, you are weird. A normal person would have taken his friend to a bar to cheer him up."

"Yeah. A normal person."

Using the highway as a midpoint, the group of twelve people searched a one-mile radius in all directions. The cops identified the spot where Wagner had hidden, and the CSI unit was busy collecting evidence. Paired with William, Roumoult walked through the bushes. The surrounding area was vast, home to a number of houses, large trees, and three golf clubs.

"It's been over two weeks," William said. "The trail could have gone cold."

"It's possible."

But they searched on.

They were in the North-West grid. Roumoult glanced at the officer with them. Officer Jake Hurtado was a medium-built Hispanic man. He had a small forehead, brown eyes, broad lips, and a bulging chin. He wore an NYPD uniform and carried a radio and a gun. A police dog, Roddy, walked by his side.

Roumoult's flashlight cut through the darkness and although it was helpful grass and muddy potholes covered the ground and were difficult to spot. Within minutes his Italian shoes were soaked and ruined. He shook his head. Bugs and mosquitoes bothered them continuously. During the first hour, Roumoult could feel excitement flooding his veins. The dogs barked, and the cops chattered at a distance. There were no footprints; there was no trail. For the next two hours, the police searched every inch of terrain they could reach. Mosquitoes bit every patch of bare skin. Roumoult picked up the radio. "Hey guys, have you found anything?"

"No, and it's hot as hell!" Tom complained.

At two a.m., everyone met back at the cars.

"Well?" Roumoult asked.

"Nothing." Joan replied.

"If there was a body, the dogs would have picked up the scent," Officer Jake said.

"So, Wagner was hallucinating," said William, stating the obvious.

Everyone nodded.

"But what caused the hallucination?"

"And why was Wagner killed?" Tom asked. After a moment of silence, he brightened. "On a positive note, I'm glad there's no werewolf or a fourth victim."

Roumoult scowled at him. He could have stayed at home and relax in front of the TV for the same result. He could have avoided four hours in the heat, sinking his feet into dirty potholes for nothing.

5

Curious Burns

June 5, 2015

Cranston Law Firm, East Village

Roumoult woke up late feeling tired and frustrated. To make matters worse, he got stuck in Friday morning's traffic and was late for his appointments. His father kept sending him reminders pestering him to attend a party tonight. Roumoult ignored the messages. He drove into the underground parking of his Firm and thanked God that he'd made it.

The Cranston Law Firm chiefly dealt with corporate law and was one of the most well-known firms in New York. It was a two-story building that Roumoult had bought ten years ago. Fred had been pestering him to use the money he'd inherited from his grandfather, but he hadn't been happy with Roumoult's choice. His unhappiness was natural because the old, crumbling, abandoned building had a haunted outlook, and no one wanted to buy it. But it wasn't just that. The building had a history. Two men and women had been found dead in the last decade. The neighbours had reported hearing screams and voices from the abandoned building. Out of fear, no one entered it for years. Then it was put on an auction. Roumoult found the advertisement in the papers. He didn't know why, he liked it and bought it. He renovated the old building into a modernised one, and fortunately for him, the ghosts of the past never returned, and the place had earned its fair share of success.

Roumoult left his car and walked up the stairs. The walls of the building were white with smooth, red carpets. The ground floor housed a security office and a reception area next to the main door. The receptionist greeted him. He rushed past her. Most of the first floor was the Law Firm, but there were two big rooms allocated to Jack and Angelus. A narrow corridor connected the Firm to Jack's lab and the Detective Agency. Roumoult turned left, pushed open a heavy glass door, and entered. He walked through a big hall lined with several cubicles, a spacious tearoom, and a waiting room. He marched into his office.

Roumoult's office was rectangular shaped with two wide windows facing each other. He removed his coat and hung it in the small closet, got himself a water bottle from the fridge, and sat down to get to work.

Time passed quickly, and it was late afternoon when Alice Kennecott, Roumoult's secretary, entered the office. She regarded him with her electric-blue eyes. In another life, she could have been a model, underweight, blonde with striking features and a perfect set of almond eyes. She dressed soberly, usually in white or light brown. Roumoult thought she could have done better.

"How are we going?" she asked casually. She must have thought he was doing well.

"Good," Roumoult replied. "You can go home."

"I'll leave soon," Alice promised. "I thought I should let you know you have a new client."

Roumoult checked his calendar. "Not that I can see,"

"He showed up this morning demanding to meet you. I suggested he could talk with Nelson or Angelus and tried to persuade him to come tomorrow, but he insisted on waiting."

"He waited all day?"

"All day," said Alice. "Without a single complain,"

"Interesting," he muttered.

"It must be very important,"

"Tell me about him,"

"He's reserved, scared and suspicious. He has his doubts about being here and keeps nibbling on his fingertips. Probably about fifty, dressed informally, probably unemployed and cannot afford you."

"How do you know he is unemployed?"

"Because he was discussing his next interview with an agent on the phone."

"Fine. I'll see him."

"Okay. Are you coming tonight?"

"You mean to the party Dad's been heckling me about?"

Alice chuckled. "Are you afraid he'll try to set you up again?"

"I know he will. I am happy he's dating Evelyn; I hope he would leave me alone. I don't know why he does that."

"He's a father." Alice shrugged. "He wants you to have some fun."

Roumoult laughed and shook his head. "See you tonight."

Roumoult regarded the man in front of him. Patrick Burns was a short, middle-aged man with an egg-shaped head. He had dark-gray eyes and kept his white beard closely trimmed. Patrick looked feeble and sick, and he took some time to settle into the client chair.

"Thank you for seeing me, Mr. Cranston," Patrick wheezed.

"You're welcome."

"I am sorry to drop in like this. Your secretary said your schedule is full for months. I couldn't wait. I need help now."

"Okay. How can I help?"

"Oh, I never thought life would put me in such a situation. I-I never thought... oh well. I want to sue my employers and get my compensation."

"Who's your employer?"

"Have you heard of the APTOS?"

"Yes." Roumoult folded his hands. "Owned by the Weldon family, it's one of the biggest and oldest companies in the country."

"I used to work at APTOS Pharmaceuticals as a quality control officer, at a branch on Long Island."

"Tell me about the job," Roumoult said.

"It required me to develop, implement, and improve operation procedures for product quality control. I also refined our manufacturing process, which raised the company's revenue by 25 percent. My job was my life. I lost my wife and kids in an accident. That job saved me."

"What happened?"

Patrick's face became grim. "They fired me."

"There must be a reason," Roumoult said, frowning.

"I was just doing my job."

"Tell me what happened."

"At APTOS, we manufacture multivitamins, pills, and powders. Multivitamins are classified as dietary supplements and regulated by the Federal Drug Administration. As per regulations, we examine ingredients of medicine both before and after production. We get our raw ingredients from a supplier called Apex Suppliers. The raw materials come in packages of thirty by thirty centimeters and contain six glass bottles. My job was to check the potency of the raw materials. On the twenty-ninth of April, I came to work as usual, opened a box, and discovered an unusual powder."

"Drugs?"

"I don't know what it was," said Patrick. "The bottles in this box were full of a green powder that smelled funny, and its texture was odd. It was something different. I discussed the situation with a colleague and planned some tests, but the head of the unit, Dr. Wheeler, intervened. I showed him what I'd found, and he took over. He asked us not to pursue it further. We couldn't argue. He's the boss."

Roumoult nodded understandingly.

"I waited for a couple of days. When I heard nothing, I talked with Dr. Wheeler. He laughed and said it was just a mix-up and that the batch was corrupted. He told me to forget about it." Patrick reached for the glass of water and took a sip.

"But you didn't."

"Oh, I did. I did, I let it go," said Patrick, placing the glass back on the table. "These things happen. I forgot about it until something else happened. A week later. I was on the evening shift, and I finished at about eleven thirty p.m. I stepped into the changing room. My locker was near a window that faces the gates and guard office. As I was changing, I saw an unmarked white van and two men dressed in black loading boxes into the vehicle. I was shocked, and I couldn't see the guards. I hurried downstairs and rushed out of the building. They saw me and fled. I shouted at the top of my lungs and ran after the van, but it was too fast for me. Then Dr. Wheeler and the guards appeared. I reported the incident, and Dr. Wheeler assured me he would report it to higher authorities, but he didn't. Within forty-eight hours, I was fired without an explanation or any compensation. They warned me to stay away from the company and mind my own business. I don't understand. What did I do wrong? I was just doing my job." Patrick blinked back tears. "I don't know what to do. I hope you can help me. I don't know if I can pay you, but I will give you every penny I have. I'm thinking of asking the media for help..."

Roumoult raised his hand for silence. "Don't worry, I'll do everything I can, but don't talk to the media."

Patrick blinked several times.

"Tell no one," Roumoult continued. "No radio, no TV, no newspapers. And sit tight. Do you understand?"

"But why?"

"Because it will only make your situation worse," Roumoult told him. "We have only your word against a renowned company. Until we have hard evidence, it's best to wait."

"Okay. What will you do?"

"Get evidence."

"How?"

"Don't worry about that."

Patrick rose, looking dejected. He reached out and shook Roumoult's hand.

After his client left, Roumoult called Angelus. When there was no answer, he left a message.

The next hour passed quickly. Roumoult's phone rang for the third time, and he shut his eyes. It was Fred, urging him to get to the party. Roumoult got up and opened the closet. He was just pulling on his coat when Angelus stepped into the office and sat heavily on the chair.

"Hey," he said, pouring himself a glass of water.

"Hi," Roumoult said. "Where have you been?"

"Remember the case about the missing businessman?"

"Uh-huh. Do I want to know?"

"We found him," Angelus answered. "In the attic, dead."

"Well, at least he wasn't unfaithful."

Angelus gave him a cold stare. "The wife assumed he ran away with the secretary. She hired us to find him. The secretary and managers guessed he was avoiding the stockholders because he blew up a few deals. As it happens, five days ago, he went up into the attic, had a stroke, and died."

"It's a good thing we don't have an attic in the Cranston house."

"Can you be serious for once?"

"No."

"I thought maybe it was murder, but the medical examiner said he died of natural causes. It's funny the wife didn't notice. She said she never goes up there," Angelus said. He poured himself another glass of water.

"Looks like you need a drink."

Angelus paused and eyed Roumoult. "How can you be so ignorant?"

Roumoult opened the fridge, grabbed a beer, and handed it over to him, "Tell me she didn't forget to give you a cheque?"

Angelus sipped his drink. "Oh, she paid us. She wanted things sorted out quickly."

"It doesn't matter as long as she paid you."

"Roumoult, I don't get you. One day you drive through the city like a madman to save William, the next you have no sympathy for a poor guy who died alone in an attic."

"That was William."

Angelus shook his head. "You have a case for me?"

Roumoult told him about the incident at APTOS.

"Wow, APTOS?"

"Yeah."

"What do you need?"

"Everything. A background check on Patrick Burns. Dig out everything you can about the company and his ex-boss, Dr. Wheeler. Put a surveillance team on APTOS."

Angelus lifted his eyebrows. "You think the white van will return?"

"I know it will."

Angelus finished his beer.

"Put Joe on the surveillance job."

"He just finished a case," said Angelus. "How about David?"

"Nope, get Joe."

"He's going to hate you."

"Let him."

"Just admit it, you like his sense of humor."

"And his instincts," Roumoult agreed, getting ready to leave.

"Are you going the party?" Angelus asked.

"I have no choice." Roumoult closed his office door.

Angelus waited for him near the main door. "What is this party about?"

"It's dad's friend's daughter's birthday party. I have never met her in my life. He has invited most of my lawyers and of course Alice."

"Great. Is Jack going with Alice?"

Roumoult sulked. "No. Did you know that she invited him?"

"Alice never goes out with anyone at work," Angelus remarked.

"But she invited Jack. That means something. And have you seen the way he looks at her?"

"Oh, I know he's smitten. You should've ordered him to go."

Roumoult eyed Angelus, "I can't do that."

They said nothing more as they headed for the parking lot. Roumoult wondered if he should intervene. He'd tried to push William towards Joan, and it hadn't worked. Who was he to step in anyway? He couldn't even sort out his own life.

6

Interpretations

June 6, 2015

The Cerulean Hotel

Roumoult stood silently. The birthday party was for Cathy Marlin, daughter of one of the richest guys in New York, who was a friend of his father's. The Cerulean Hotel was located on top of a skyscraper, and its ballroom was a piece of art decorated in various shades of blue and violet. A sapphire skyline in the middle of the ceiling opened to an extraordinary view of the heavens. Men in tuxedos and women in magnificent dresses danced in the middle of the ballroom to a soft Mozart symphony.

He stood next to his father, who had the attention of the entire group. Fred spoke with enthusiasm and charisma, charming everyone, especially the ladies. His sky-blue eyes sparkled with joy and his soft soothing voice enchanted everyone. Paul Carter joined them. Paul was about Fred's age, but his white hair made him look older. Paul loved his ships and spoke excitedly about one of his newest projects.

After the bulk of the birthday celebrations had passed, Roumoult had dinner and wanted to leave, but Fred insisted on introducing him to another friend: Mark Weldon.

"I don't think you two have met," said Fred.

"No," Roumoult said, extending his hand. "It's a pleasure."

"The pleasure is mine," Mark replied.

Roumoult felt like he was talking to Mr. Universe. Mark Weldon was a tall, ruggedly handsome man with a straight nose and dense, copper-colored hair. Roumoult tried to hide his shock. He might sue the APTOS and here he was shaking hands with the CEO. He was glad when Paul intervened and began talking about his ship again. Roumoult excused himself, and in his hurry to leave, he bumped into someone.

A pair of bright eyes caught his attention.

"I'm so sorry," said the lady. She reached into her purse for a handkerchief. It was then that Roumoult realized that she'd spilled her drink on his coat.

"Oh, that's okay," he said vaguely.

"I'm so sorry," the woman repeated, dapping at the fabric of his coat.

Roumoult didn't care. She wore a V-neck maroon dress. In front of him stood one of the most beautiful women he had ever seen. Her jet-black, curly hair flowed to her chest, and her clear complexion and full lips grabbed his attention. She stopped trying to dry his coat and stared deep into his eyes.

"Ah, Emma. There you are," Fred said, introducing her to Roumoult.

They spoke for a while before Emma said, "Mr. Cranston, thank you for inviting me. It's a lovely party. I have to head home."

"Stay!" said Fred. Emma shook her head. Roumoult noticed that she was gripping her purse tightly and looked nervous. "Thank you," she said. "I-I should go."

"Okay. How about a lift?" Fred asked.

"No. I couldn't ask you to do that."

"Roumoult can drop you home."

Roumoult was astounded. Fred had done it again.

"I don't want to trouble anyone," Emma insisted.

"No, it's no trouble," Fred said merrily, turning to Roumoult. "Is it?"

Despite his frustration, Roumoult managed a bleak smile. "I'd be happy to drop you home."

APTOS Pharmaceuticals, Long Island

Joe Kavanagh sat on the edge of the hill. Ian Stanford, his partner stood near him. Joe was an athletic and experienced private detective with a broad nose and a square face, which was highlighted by an impressive goatee. He ran his hands through his short, coffee-brown hair, and handed over the binoculars to Ian.

Joe enjoyed working with Angelus, because he always gave him the best cases. He had more reservations when it came to Roumoult's cases. They were spooky, unpredictable, and oftentimes turned deadly. He preferred straightforward domestic issues, like husbands dying in attics.

Ian was half Joe's age, an average built man with excellent tracking and surveillance skills. He was hungry for action. Curiosity was his compass, and he was always looking for the next challenge.

They'd reached their destination at one a.m., but it was very unusual. APTOS Pharmaceuticals stood on over two acres of land. Masked by tall trees, the building wasn't visible from the highway. It was a massive, daunting complex. Joe spotted the electronic fence perched on top of a ten-foot-high wall. For a second, he thought it was a prison. Thick vegetation surrounded the gray, two-story structure. Joe noted large rocks sitting at the bottom of the hill. Only one road linked the highway to the gates. He spotted two cars parked along the north wall and saw a small office staffed by two guards near the gates. He glanced at Ian, who looked worried.

"What have we gotten into this time?" Joe remarked.

NYPD Precinct

The sunlight streamed through the windows. Tom found himself struggling to get leads. His morning was unproductive and reflected on his phone conversation with irritation.

"Tom," Joan called. "I checked the video surveillance tapes from St. George Hospital."

"And?"

"I think I know who visited Wagner."

Tom moved closer and surveyed the scrawny man in NYPD uniform. "Do we have an ID?"

"Not yet. Did you speak to Ms. Garrison?"

Tom didn't know where to begin. He shrugged half-heartedly.

"What happened?"

"People are so ignorant! For the last twenty-four hours, I've been trying to get in touch with her. Now they tell me she left London for New York the minute she found out about Clark Garrison's death."

"Oh?"

"Yeah. I called Mrs. Garrison. She said that Ms. Garrison told her she was coming. When I asked her why she didn't mention it to us, she said she thought Ms. Garrison changed her mind."

"Did she actually land in New York?"

"Yes. I called the airport. Jenny Garrison landed in New York on the twenty-fourth of May at eleven thirty p. m."

"And she didn't contact Mrs. Garrison?"

"Nope."

"Then where did she go?"

"Beats me. Now we have three dead men and a missing woman."

Cranston House

The Cranston house had two levels, and a well-kept lawn and flowerbeds surrounded it from all sides. An eight-foot-high red-brick wall marked the boundaries of the house. Tall trees stood surrounded the residence. Light poles stood on both sides of iron gates that opened onto a short driveway.

Roumoult still struggled with jet lag, but it was better than yesterday. He thought about Emma and their conversation. He got dressed, came downstairs.

The living room was decorated with exquisite Persian carpets. A fireplace with an oak mantelpiece stood to the right. Above the mantelpiece sat family portraits. Three comfortable couches formed a semi-circle around the fire and the flat-screen TV. He walked into the dining room and found his father reading the newspaper.

"Good morning dad,"

"Good morning. How did you sleep?"

"Just fine."

Charles Austin entered the dining room with Roumoult's breakfast and set it down on the oak table.

"Thanks."

Charles was a tall, slim man of Fred's age. His hair was a mixture of gray and brown, and it always combed back against his head. Charles was very neat and conscientious, keeping the Cranston house in excellent condition. He was Roumoult's godfather and the brother Fred never had.

Roumoult focused on his breakfast.

"What did you think of the party?" Fred asked.

"It was fine."

Fred chuckled. "What did you think of Emma?"

Roumoult smirked. "Dad, if you don't stop, we'll get into a huge argument."

"I can't stop. I'm dedicated to the cause."

"Dad, these set-ups are too much."

"Are they?" Fred replied.

"I know you like to keep tabs on me. I've accepted that, but this is over the top. I'm glad you're dating; I don't need to do the same."

"Just tell me."

"Dad, why are you doing this?" Roumoult complained. He reached for the coffeepot.

"Because you are my son."

Roumoult took his time filling his cup. "I've been that all my life. What's changed?"

"You didn't answer my question. You like her, don't you?"

"No. I don't." Roumoult insisted. He turned his focus to his breakfast.

"You couldn't keep your eyes off her!"

Roumoult's shoulders slumped. "Dad!" he groaned.

"Come on. Tell me,"

"We had fun talking last night. But I felt... she was holding back. There is something going on in her life."

"Oh, I hope its not bad."

"Dad, I think she's trouble."

Fred smiled mischievously. "So are you."

Cranston Firm, Angelus' Detective Agency

Angelus' office was around thirty square feet. It housed a mid-size desk, a row of cabinets, and two large windows. Light green carpet covered the floor, and the walls were white with no pictures or boards. A neat pile of files sat on his desk with a computer, a few pens, and a notepad.

Angelus was accustomed to Roumoult's methods of handling cases. While other lawyers would sit in their offices, make calls, go to court, and wait for the information to come to them, Roumoult was renowned for hiring private detectives to dig out the truth. If no one was available, he became impatient and did the work himself. Angelus read Patrick Burns' file and concluded that the man was honest, hardworking, and dedicated to his job. His slate was clean. Checking the company was next on his list. It had been a couple of hours, and he wondered if Jack had found anything on APTOS Pharmaceuticals.

He left his office and peered into the vacant waiting room. It was an area housing a water filter, a small kitchenette, and a few chairs. His colleagues were working hard in their cubicles. He left the Agency and strolled down the corridor, stopping to knock on the lab door. As expected, there was no reply. He entered the dark room and switched on the lights. Jack Calvin sat on a chair, leaned forward, glaring at the computer screen. Large headphones covered his ears. Jack was a geek and a hacker. He loved computers and spent his time developing algorithms and programs. The lab was full of his stuff. Three boxes sat in a corner. Two big desks were buried under monitors, computers, laptops, keyboards, and other electronic devices Angelus didn't recognize.

Angelus waited for his attention. When Jack didn't move, he smacked him across the back of the head.

"Hey!" Jack cried out and removed the headphones.

"Good morning," Angelus said. He treated Jack like his younger brother. They had a lot in common. Both were orphans with a history of drug abuse and bad company. Joining the military had saved Angelus; computers had saved Jack.

"Can't you just say good morning like a normal person?" Jack said, getting to his feet.

"I tried and failed."

Jack hardly reached Angelus' shoulders. His blond hair was rumpled, his face was tiny with blue eyes.

"Why are you harassing me?"

"Did you get anything on APTOS?"

"You're not my boss."

"Tiny, why do you do this every time?"

"Don't call me tiny!" Jack yelled, standing on his toes in an attempt to match Angelus' height.

"It's Roumoult's case. I want an update."

"I'm working on it."

Angelus let out a huff of disappointment.

Cranston Law Firm

Despite it being a Saturday, Roumoult was overwhelmed with work, but that didn't keep people out of his office. Angelus informed him that Jack was making progress. Alice was still in the party mood, coming in to tell Roumoult that she'd seen him talking to Mark Weldon and his ex.

"I spoke to Weldon, not to his ex," Roumoult said dryly.

"Ah, the nice lady Fred introduced you to."

"Emma?"

"Yep."

That explained why Emma had been so nervous. He thought.

"They dated for four years. Oh my god, people say they looked so hot together. They got engaged, and something happened. I don't know what. Anyway, their engagement broke off six months ago and Emma moved to New York. She's single now."

"Great! Thanks for the boring intel. Now can I get back to work?"

Soon after Alice left, the door swung open again. Roumoult's anger bubbled, but it melted in seconds when he saw William leaning against the doorframe. He looked better and rested. "Hey, you look well."

"Thanks," William replied, walking in and making himself comfortable in the client's chair.

"You went to the hospital?" Roumoult said noticing that William's bandages were smaller.

"Yep. Got rid of the stitches. I'm glad it's over."

"Oh, okay." Roumoult croaked.

They sat in silence for a moment.

"I'm doing great," William said.

"Okay."

Silence again. Roumoult waited for it.

"What the hell am I saying? It's not okay! It sucks!" William shouted.

"Oh, really? I hadn't noticed." Roumoult remarked.

He had expected William to freak out. In fact, he was surprised it had taken him so long. He listened to him complain.

"I can't sleep or eat, and I'm having nightmares. I tried to work today, but I couldn't focus!"

"Have you considered speaking to someone?"

"I'm talking to you, aren't I?"

"No. You should talk to a professional."

"Don't even go there!"

"William, admit it," Roumoult said, looking at him intently. "The breakup and your near-death experience have affected your emotional well-being."

"You are wrong! I'm fine!"

"No, you're not! You fixate on a case because you expect it to solve your problems. You use work to ignore your pain. If that doesn't work, you busy yourself falling for all the wrong women. It is a pattern."

"Hold it. You're lecturing me about dating wrong women. Let's list the wrong women you've dated," William fumed.

"I know the list by heart, and I know exactly why I dated them," Roumoult said coolly.

"Let's see," William continued, ignoring him. "A heartless model, an escort, a car racer, and the latest one was an international thief!"

"What can I say? I like variety."

"Why can't you go out with someone normal? Like Emma."

Roumoult was stunned. "Where did that come from?"

"You like her."

Roumoult was saved by Alice stepping into the room.

William turned to face her, "You have worst timing ever!"

Interrogation Room, NYPD Precinct

Tom considered his day a success. They'd found the name of the cop who'd met Wagner in the DNV database. They picked up Andrew Maxwell and brought him to the Precinct. They still hadn't heard about Ms. Garrison, but at least they had a suspect.

The interrogation room was a lusterless space furnished with a metallic table and four chairs. It was painted pale-blue, and a wide mirror served as part of its largest wall. A wooden door was the only entrance, and opposite it were two small, barred windows with dusty glass.

"Why am I here? I've done nothing," Maxwell said. He was a young, skinny man with black, bulging eyes that peered at the detectives from behind a pair of thin-framed glasses.

Joan placed a photo on the table. "Is that you?"

"Yes."

"Do you know Mr. Don Wagner?" Joan asked, placing Wagner's photo on the table.

Maxwell picked up the photo. "Yes. He was my last prank."

Tom's jaw dropped. "What?"

"Let me explain. I work as a clerk in a crappy office downtown. My job is boring, and I don't earn much. A year ago, I found employment with an organization that helps to set up pranks, parties, and surprises."

"Seriously?" Tom asked.

"You can call and ask Sam Craig, my employer."

"Okay. Let's say we believe you. How does it work?" Tom asked.

"We have a website. People register and make an appointment. They meet with Sam. If he thinks the job is good for me, he calls."

"In this case, who contacted Sam?"

"Ms. Wagner."

"Ms. Wagner?" Tom stifled a laugh. "Okay. What was the prank?"

"Mr. Wagner had an accident. He had this ridiculous story about a creature he just wouldn't stop telling. The daughter thought it was a stupid story and that it made him look bad. She worried he'd lose his reputation, especially with trustees and stakeholders."

"Then what?" Tom asked.

"I played my role, just like she asked. I dressed as a cop and walked into his room. First, I struck up a casual conversation to make sure he was the right guy. I asked about the accident. Then I said to him, 'Mr. Wagner, you know what will happen if you keep telling your story. It will come for you.'"

Tom's face hardened.

"That doesn't sound like a prank," Joan said.

"It sounds like a threat," Tom added.

"I agree. I didn't like it either, but I was desperate. I needed the money."

"How much did you earn?" Joan asked.

"Fifteen hundred dollars," Maxwell replied.

"Wow," said Tom, shaking his head.

"We just do what the client wants. No questions," Maxwell explained. "Trust me, most of the pranks are juvenile, but sometimes you get a really horrible one. Two months ago, I dressed up as a zombie and followed a woman to scare the hell out of her. Why? Someone thought she was a bitch. For that prank, the client paid two thousand dollars."

"Do you have any idea what you've done?" Tom asked.

Maxwell lowered his eyes. "I'm sorry. I was just doing a job. No one had ever died before."

Tom felt frustrated. He stepped out of the room and clawed at his face, knowing that this lead was a dead end. Joan caught his eye. They both knew that if Maxwell's story checked out, they'd have to let him go and lose a primary suspect.

The Little Palace

Roumoult enjoyed his chicken salad, while William ate beef pie with salad.

"So, did you call your mom?" Roumoult asked.

William's relationship with his family was volatile, and Roumoult knew it affected him, but like everything else outside of work, William ignored it.

"No, and don't start."

Roumoult nodded. He knew he'd failed before, but he had to try, for William's sake.

"Why are you so eager for me to get in touch with my family?"

Roumoult sipped his coffee. "You might regret it later."

William face turned sour, and he chewed his pie.

A shadow moved over them. "Hey there," said a familiar voice.

Roumoult looked up and frowned at Angelus, who was followed by Jack.

"How did you two find us?" William snapped.

"Alice," Roumoult replied before Angelus could answer. "Couldn't this wait?"

"No," Angelus said. "Alice told me you have a busy afternoon." He and Jack sat down.

"Let me guess, this is about APTOS?" William asked.

Angelus looked at Roumoult.

"He tells me about his cases, and I tell him about mine," Roumoult said.

"Boss, APTOS was created way before you or I were born," said Jack.

"I figured."

"The Weldon family started it in 1876," Jack began enthusiastically. "It's a massive enterprise involved in shipping, electronics, manufacturing... You name it, they either own it, or they have shares or partnerships in it. These are powerful dudes, and their power grows with every generation. Each Weldon is better off than the previous one."

"They can't all be perfect," Roumoult interrupted.

"Boss." Jack leaned forward. "None of them have ever gotten arrested for a crime. Never got drunk or caught with drugs. No accidents or parking tickets. No scandals or extramarital affairs."

"So basically, they're boring," said William.

Everyone burst into laughter.

"They're model citizens. They donate," Jack continued. "They work with charitable organizations. A year ago, they traveled to Africa and Syria to help people in need. They work closely with the Natural Museum of History. Th—"

"Okay, I get it. What about APTOS?"

"Same story. From what I can gather, records of all employees, including Dr. Wheeler, are clean. APTOS produces and sells high-quality products with excellent customer service. Overall, the company's reputation is impeccable," Jack said.

"At this point, all we have is your client's word," said Angelus.

"Where does that leave you?" William asked.

"Without evidence, we have no case. Mr. Burn's word is not enough. The Weldon's are powerful. The judge wouldn't even consider the case. If we want to win, we need more," Roumoult explained.

Everyone fell silent.

"Angelus continue watching APTOS. If the company is as good as it seems, we'll have our answer in the next few days."

St. George Hospital

As soon as Emma stepped into the hospital, Dr. Luke Lox greeted her. It surprised her, as she didn't realize her boss paid her any attention. She was a new resident, and most of the renowned surgeons ignored her. Dr. Lox was an old man who looked under-nourished. His apron was two sizes too big and slipped from his shoulders. Emma didn't think he ever slept, because he always looked drowsy. They exchanged pleasantries, and Emma walked into the changing room to begin her night shift. The cops hadn't contacted her, and there was nothing in Wagner's bloodwork that would benefit the case. It still bothered her, why did he hallucinate?

Behind the reception was an opaque partition, separating it from the doctors' offices and changing rooms, the storage room, the waiting room, and the nurse's station. But this only occupied a quarter of the ground floor. The rest was the Emergency Department, a spacious hall crowded by curtains.

Emma entered the ER through the heavy, blue door and swiped her card on the panel. The ER was in full swing, with nurses running around and instruments beeping. The air was dank, smelling of blood and antiseptic. Emma greeted the head nurse, Jennifer Cross. Jennifer was a caring and optimistic lady. She reminded Emma of her grandmother—a large woman with short, curly hair, a small neck, and a cheerful face. She missed her grandmother. She was supportive and caring, unlike her mother whose focus was fame and reputation. Her breakup with Mark had caused a big rift between them and fed up with her mom and her family she had moved to New York. The shadows of the past followed her everywhere. The other night she had seen Mark, and it brought back painful memories. She tried to remember why she was here. To finish her residency and to do something good. She looked around for Tim Larson, a senior doctor, her mentor, and her only friend in this city. She found him bandaging a teenage boy's leg.

"Hello, Emma," he said.

"Hello," she said. She felt a knot in her stomach. For the last few months, Tim had been looking sickly, dark bags forming under his gray eyes. He attempted a smile, and the creases in his skin became clearer. He'd become so thin, Emma worried he would faint. She wished he'd talk to her.

After several hours, Emma tore herself away from the ER, heading for the cafeteria on the fourth floor. Even at this hour, it was busy. She enjoyed her coffee overlooking the city lights. As she rose to leave, she was stopped by the sight of a familiar face. Dr. Larson was arguing with two men. Emma squinted, but the dim light made it impossible to see their faces. The conversation finished abruptly, and the men left. Dr. Larson stood motionlessly, looking miserable, as if his world had shattered. Emma thought about asking him what had happened, but by the time she'd decided to approach, he'd already walked away.

7

The Rabbit And The Eagle

June 7, 2015

APTOS Pharmaceuticals

J oe turned the air conditioner knob to its maximum but still felt hot. He thought wearing a cotton T-shirt and shorts would keep him comfortable; he was wrong. The rocks and trees on the hillside concealed his car from anyone who might look up the hill. Craning his neck, he observed the complex. It was dark and quiet. The van hadn't returned, and he had begun to think Roumoult was wrong. Everyone in the complex minded their own business. He turned and noticed that Ian was fixated on the woods. He picked the radio. "What are you doing?"

"I heard something."

Joe turned the air conditioner down. Silence fell. A few rabbits bounced around in the woods, and bugs hummed softly. "I don't see anything."

"Me neither," Ian replied.

Joe grabbed the book lying on the passenger seat and used it as a fan. His phone vibrated with an incoming call from Roumoult.

"Good evening," Joe said.

"Good morning," Roumoult replied. "How is everything?"

"It's hot as hell, and I've murdered at least twenty flies and fifty mosquitoes. There, there's my confession." Joe laughed. He recalled other bosses getting offended by his jokes. Roumoult was different. Maybe it was because they'd worked together on so many cases.

Roumoult laughed. "I can see you haven't lost your touch. How's it going?"

Joe updated Roumoult and ended the call. Joe appreciated his boss checking on him, but he didn't need a pep talk. He needed a nice bed and a cold beer. He closed his eyes and tried to relax.

"Hey Joe," Ian's voice crackled through the radio.

Joe quickly answered. "What's up?"

"Do you hear that?"

Joe strained his ears. He heard it: a rustling noise.

"Yes."

I think someone's coming,"

"Okay," Joe replied. He withdrew the gun from his pocket, lowered himself in the seat, and peered through his binoculars. His eyes fixed on the bushes, which were about three feet high, stirring as if something, or someone, was moving through them. The rustling became louder. Joe waited. Suddenly, a rabbit jumped out.

Joe laughed. "It's a bloody rabbit."

"Ha! I see it!"

Bored to death, Joe watched the bunny. It was bigger, whiter than other rabbits he'd seen. It remained motionless, looking ahead, ears erect, alert.

Suddenly, there came a loud shriek. Joe peered out of the window and saw an eagle swooping overhead, squealing as it flew over the hill. Joe looked back at the rabbit. It didn't move.

"What the hell?" he grunted, stepping out of the car. The eagle circled above the hill. Joe hoped to scare the bunny into the woods. "Shoo! Go away." But it just sat there. "Hey, stupid rabbit, get the hell out of here!" It didn't move. Joe stamped his feet. Still, it did not move.

Ian laughed. "You've lost it man! Not even a bunny is scared of you."

Joe gave him a dismissive wave.

The eagle shrieked again. Joe turned, and it dove towards him. He quickly stepped aside. From the corner of his eye, he saw the rabbit spring into action. It darted towards the bushes at full speed, jumped on the rock, and launched into the air to attack the eagle. The eagle screeched. Both creatures twirled in the air and fell to the ground.

"Whoa!" Joe cried out, running to the edge of the hill. "What the hell?"

The rabbit and the eagle disappeared behind a cluster of trees. Joe heard shrieks and cries, and then there was complete silence.

Ian joined him. "Did you see that?"

"Yeah, bunny with a vengeance."

"No! Rabbits don't do that! It's not right."

Joe nodded.

"I think we should find it."

Joe eyed him. "Find what?"

"The rabbit. There's something wrong with it."

"No, it's a rabbit with balls."

Ian face turned stern. "It's against laws of nature. Rabbits don't behave like that."

"Okay, fine, go ahead. But watch out for killer rabbits!"

Wellington Heights Apartments

William woke up panting and sweating, frightened to death. He shut his eyes and ran his hands through his hair. In his nightmare, he was locked in the casket again, but this time there was fire everywhere. He sat with his head buried in his hands, steeling himself before getting out of bed and walking into the bathroom.

"I need a distraction," he told himself, staring at his reflection in the mirror.

Trek Apartments, Amsterdam Street, New York

Tom had no choice but to set Andrew Maxwell free; his story checked out. The good news was that they had intel on Ms. Garrison's whereabouts. He stood on the side of Amsterdam Street to wait for William and Roumoult. William had called, and Tom felt obliged to update him. He insisted on coming and bringing Roumoult with him. Initially, he wasn't happy about it, but the last two days had changed his mind. He could see Joan wasn't happy, and she was right. Tom knew he shouldn't indulge them, especially William.

"Look, I understand you care for them, but it could be dangerous. What would the Captain say?" Joan huffed.

"In the case of Cranston and Sterling, he won't say a thing. In the last two days we have gained very little ground. Perhaps we could use the help," said Tom.

Joan glared at him. "Or they could slow us down."

An engine roared. Tom looked past Joan to see a taxi. William jumped out and paid the driver. "Hey!"

"Hey! How are you, doc?" Tom asked.

"I'm good. Thanks for letting me come along with you guys."

Tom and Joan exchanged glances.

"No problem," Tom said.

"How did you find Ms. Garrison?" William asked.

"We got lucky. We checked her credit card history. She took a cab from the airport and booked an apartment for two weeks in this building," Joan explained.

"Mr. Walker, the manager of the building, handled her check in and gave her the keys," Tom added.

Another engine roared. Tom recognized the Audi as it parked behind his car. Roumoult stepped out and came to join them.

"I hope we didn't take you away from anything interesting," Tom teased.

Roumoult chuckled. "Trust me, paperwork on Sunday isn't my thing."

Inside the building, Tom felt much better. The lobby was cold but well-decorated, dimly lit and filled with plants and flowers. They approached the reception, manned by a middle-aged Asian woman. She looked up, eyes sparkling, and welcomed them. Tom introduced himself and showed her his badge.

"Oh, yes, I remember. You called. You're looking for Ms. Garrison. The woman from London."

"Yes."

"Tony gave her the keys. She arrived very late."

"We would like to see Ms. Garrison's apartment," Tom said.

"Sure. Sure. Follow me," said the receptionist. She trotted off on clicking heels.

When they reached the fifth floor, they waited for her to unlock apartment 55B.

"She's not in. I knocked, no answer," she said, holding the door open for them. "Please call me if you need anything."

"Thank you," Tom said.

The apartment had only one bedroom, a small living room, and a kitchen.

"Don't touch anything," Tom said, pulling on a pair of gloves. Their search was brief. He noticed a travel bag in the corner of the living room. The bed hadn't been slept in. The closets were empty, and the towels and toiletries were unused. Tom found the snack tray still laden with biscuits, tea bags, and coffee sachets. "She just left," he concluded.

"Any other relatives or friends?" William asked.

"Nope," said Tom.

"Okay. Three theories. One: she ran away. Two: someone kidnapped her. Three: someone murdered her and buried her somewhere," Roumoult said callously.

Tom stared at him. "Stop!"

"I think she ran away," Joan said.

"Why?"

"The apartment's untouched; there's no sign of a struggle. Did any of you find her handbag?"

"No," Tom said.

"If someone took her against her will, her purse would be here with her passport, money, mobile..."

"So, she ran away," William said.

"But why?" Tom asked.

"Something scared her. Maybe she knew something about Garrison that no one else knew, not even his wife," Roumoult suggested.

"We should send patrol officers with her picture to the airports, bus stations, and train stations. Someone must have seen her leaving the city," said Joan.

"Good idea," Tom replied. His eyes combed the room again, scanning it for missed details. The answering machine grabbed his attention. On the display glowed the number three. "Interesting. She's not here, but she's got messages."

"Maybe Mrs. Garrison called her," William suggested.

"But she didn't know that Ms. Garrison was in New York," Roumoult said, shaking his head.

Tom reached forward and hit the play button.

"You have three new messages," said the machine.

They heard the ring tone, the call was sent to the machine, and then... Nothing. The second message did the same.

"Blank calls?" Tom said. "It doesn't make sense."

The answering machine continued to play the messages.

"Let's get the CSU here," Joan suggested. "They might find something."

Tom bowed and strolled towards the door.

Suddenly, a deep breathing echoed. Tom froze and spun around, looking at the device. The breathing grew louder. Slowly, he took a step forward, eager to listen. He heard a low grunt.

"It's coming for you. You know that don't you?" a scrambled voice croaked. "You are next. You are dead. It's coming for you."

A loud howl pierced the air. Tom stumbled backwards. The cry echoed and died out.

"What the hell was that?"

"A werewolf?" William offered.

"Another threat," Joan said. "But why Ms. Garrison?"

"Maybe she knew something," Tom said. He hit the replay button. They listened.

"Can we trace this call?" Roumoult asked.

Tom shrugged. This case bothered him. Three men murdered by an unknown assailant. The murder weapon vanishes although there is no sign of a break in. Then their bodies are snatched from the Morgue and then sister of one of the victims is threatened and kidnapped. What is this killer after?

Cranston Law Firm

Roumoult and William returned to the Cranston Firm, leaving the detectives with the CSU unit, who were dusting the apartment for prints. Roumoult opened the door to his office and found Angelus waiting for them.

"Hey," said Roumoult.

"Hello," Angelus said grimly.

William took a seat next to Angelus. "How are you?"

"I've been better." Angelus tugged at his hair.

"What's happened?" Roumoult asked, taking a seat.

"I had a chat with Ian and Joe."

Roumoult smiled. "Something happened at AP-TOS?"

"Yes, but it's not what you expected."

"Oh?"

Angelus scratched his head. "It's strange."

"It's been a strange day,"

Angelus told them about the eagle and the rabbit.

"You're joking, right?" Roumoult laughed.

"I'm not."

"And Ian found the dead rabbit and the eagle?"

"Yes."

"Okay. What do you want us to do?"

"Find out why it behaved that way."

Roumoult arched his eyebrows.

"It has nothing to do with the case!" William said.

"We found the rabbit around APTOS," said Angelus.

"So?" said William. "It's a rabbit. I am sure you will find many other animals."

Roumoult knew William was right, but he couldn't ignore his gut feeling. "Can you do an autopsy?"

"I can, but I don't see the point," said William. "There's no link between the rabbit and the case."

"I know it's a long shot," Roumoult admitted.

William looked between Roumoult and Angelus. "You guys nuts," he said, shaking his head.

"Please," said Angelus.

William nodded. "Fine."

When he was alone, Roumoult wondered if he was on the right track. Finding the van to prove Patrick Burns' innocence was paramount, and he still had no proof. The rabbit was interesting, but was it likely to provide him with the clues he needed?

NYPD Precinct

Tom stood in his office frustrated and tired. He was trying to track the call but was having issues with the tech department. "Officer, werewolves don't exist!"

"I know but..."

"Can you trace the call or not?" Tom asked.

"Sorry, we can't."

"Let me guess," Joan said when Tom had hung up. "They can't trace it?"

"No. What about Andrew's boss, Sam?" Tom asked.

"He told me a woman in her thirties, well-dressed with sharp blue eyes and a nice figure, identified herself as Rachael Wagner and paid for the prank."

"How do you know it wasn't Rachael?" Tom pressed.

"He described her as a red-headed woman with blue eyes. Rachael has brown hair and green eyes," said Joan. "It could be another actress for hire."

"I wonder if someone threatened Hawk and Garrison."

"Their family would know,"

"Would they?"

Joan's phone buzzed, and Tom left the office, heading for the kitchen. He needed a cup of coffee. His men were out there, doing their jobs. He wanted to identify the body snatchers, find Ms. Garrison and track down this killer. When he returned, his own phone began to ring. He answered it quickly.

"That's great!" he said down the line. "Send it to me now." He ended the call and turned to Joan. "We have had some luck. The day William disappeared; I asked the tech staff to search for the van using traffic cameras. I gave them a description, a picture of the van, and the time it was seen near the Morgue."

"And?"

"We found it." He double-clicked the email from the tech and enlarged a picture. "And we have the picture of the driver."

Central Park West

Emma couldn't believe how quickly the day finished. She had slept all day, hardly eaten anything.
To make matters worse, Mark had messaged her.
She wondered if she should reply. She decided not to
and got ready for work. As she got dressed, she secretly wondered about Roumoult. It would be nice to
have more friends, she thought.

She stood at the corner of the street, waiting for
a cab. After ten minutes, she finally climbed into one
with a broken, sputtering air conditioner. Peak hour
traffic was starting to clear; she reached the hospital
at nine p.m. She paid the cab driver and stepped out,
pausing when she spotted Tim Larson. He should
have started an hour ago.

Once again, Tim was arguing with the two men
from the cafeteria. But Emma didn't dare intervene.
Chills ran through her body. Yesterday, she'd tried
to talk to Tim. When he found out she had seen him
with two men his face had constricted, his eyes
bulged, and his skin redden.

"You should mind your own business!" he'd
shouted and hadn't spoken to her during the entire
shift.

Whatever was going on, it wasn't worth getting
caught up in. Emma turned away and entered the
hospital.

Cranston Law Firm

Roumoult hit the send button and stretched. It
had been a long day, and he couldn't remember the

last time he'd eaten. He got up and pulled on his coat as William entered the office.

"Why aren't you at home?" Roumoult as yawning.

"I autopsied the rabbit," said William.

"That was quick."

"It was small," William said, easing down into a chair.

"Find anything yet?"

"It was terrible," said William. "I didn't believe Joe, but one look at the rabbit and the eagle changed my mind. The rabbit ripped off one of the eagle's wings and had started on the other. There were a dozen wounds on the rabbit's body. It should have died before it could do that kind of damage. I've sent the blood samples for analysis. I am looking forward to the test results."

After a drink with William, he headed home. Roumoult's head spun as he walked out to his car. He was uncertain where this was going. Was the mysterious van, the stolen boxes, and the rabbit connected?

8

The Darkling

June 8, 2015

Cranston House

T he temperature fell, and a cold wind blew through the streets, moving the trees back and forth and creating a soft, almost rhythmic rustling noise. A full moon glowed brightly in the sky. The Cranston house sat in silence, its windows closed and its occupants sleeping peacefully. A loud buzzing jolted Roumoult awake. He reached for his phone.

"Yes?" he groaned.

"Boss, its Joe."

"Hey Joe," Roumoult sighed.

"Angelus isn't around, so you're my next best bet."

"Where's Angelus?"

"He's in New Jersey. He said he messaged you."

Roumoult couldn't remember. He rubbed his eyes. "What's up?" he asked Joe.

"The unmarked white van is here. Burns was telling the truth."

Roumoult's tiredness vanished.

"Do I follow?" Joe asked.

"No, send Ian. I'll join him."

"We can handle this."

Roumoult pushed the speaker button on his phone. This case fascinated him; more and more unsolved pieces of the puzzle were gradually emerging. Where was the van going? What was it transporting? Why didn't the guards stop it? He had to know. Roumoult switched the lights on, walked to his closet, and dressed.

"Angelus will kill me. It could get ugly boss," Joe said.

"Tell Ian to follow it and keep me posted. I'll leave in a few minutes."

"But—"

"Joe. Do it."

Roumoult drove at full speed towards Long Island. There weren't many cars on the street. The night was quiet and warm. Roumoult's phone rang again; he sent the call to Bluetooth.

"They're coming towards the city," Ian's voice crackled.

"Where are they headed?" asked Roumoult, easing his foot off the accelerator slightly.

"They just crossed Williamsburg Bridge."

"All right. Keep following them."

Roumoult followed Ian's directions and ended up in Lower Manhattan. After parking his car in a secure location, he stepped out onto Lafayette Street. It was well-lit, quieter than usual. A bus chugged down the street; the subway screeched along the tracks. Roumoult kept moving, walking past a Chinese restaurant and soon finding the van on the roadside. He caught a glimpse of the driver: a young, skinny Asian man with dark hair. He kept walking until he reached Ian's black Ford.

"Hey boss."

Roumoult climbed into the car, his nose prickling. The smell of coffee and leftover food was inescapable. His surveyed the dusty dashboard and seats, laden with empty food wrappers and cartons. A GPS sat in a small frame sitting on the dashboard.

"Sorry," said Ian.

Roumoult remained silent. He was used to working with private investigators; Ian's car was better than others.

"What do you think they're doing?" Roumoult asked after a while.

"Takeaway," Ian grunted.

"It's four thirty a.m."

"Early breakfast."

"Unhealthy breakfast."

"I can take care of this," Ian said. "You can go home,"

Roumoult shook his head. "Let's follow them and see what happens."

"Then what?"

"I don't know."

Someone stepped out of the restaurant.

"Here we go," Roumoult breathed out.

The taillights of the vehicle glowed red, and it moved up Lafayette Street. Ian started the car. The gear slipped. It jolted.

Roumoult stared at Ian.

"She gets cold sometimes," Ian said defensively, trying again. The engine coughed to life.

"You should get a new car. Do we have backup?"

"We need Angelus to approve that," said Ian.

They drove toward Park Avenue, maintaining a safe distance from the van.

"What's the protocol?"

"Well, if we plan to shadow it for a long time, we need a second shadow. In case we lose them."

"Did you set it up?"

"I need approval."

"Make the call." Roumoult ordered.

It took Ian a few minutes to arrange it.

"It's done. David Henley will join us in half an hour and be the soft shadow."

"How does this work?" asked Roumoult.

"We're the rough shadow. Eventually, they might spot us, but while we're their focus, they won't realize that David's following them too."

"Sounds good. Are you sure it's enough?"

"It's what Angelus would do."

Roumoult had to settle for that.

"Did they load any boxes in the van?"

"Yep, about ten."

"How were they dressed?"

"Casually with masks,"

"Were the guards around?"

"Nope,"

"Dr. Wheeler?"

"Nope. No one."

"So, they just stepped inside and took them?"

"Not preciously. An hour ago, the guards placed these boxes in the corner of the parking lot. The guards vanished and the van appeared."

"Tell me you photographed everything."

"That's the protocol boss."

"Good," Roumoult said gladly. Patrick was right. But where was it taking the boxes and who was behind all this? He watched the van and presumed that if they stayed on their current course, they'd soon reach Upper Manhattan, but at Gramercy Park, the van took a left, heading toward Chelsea. It stopped at the next red light, and Ian eased his foot off the gas. By the time they reached the junction, the lights turned green. The van raced ahead, and the Ford shot after it. The van turned left again. It was heading back to Lower Manhattan.

"What the...?" Roumoult muttered under his breath.

"Beats me," said Ian. "Looks like he's touring New York."

"What if we're busted?"

Ian glanced at him, tightening his grip on the steering wheel. "Could be, but we can't lose them. We have to give David half an hour."

The van took a right.

"Okay, where does this road go?" asked Roumoult.

"If he follows it religiously, Brooklyn."

"Fine, update David."

Roumoult seethed. It was a quarter to six in the morning, and he was exhausted, slumped in an old, black Ford on the Brooklyn freeway. The van drove towards the exit; Ian changed lanes to follow it.

"I have a bad feeling about this," Ian stated.

"Are you armed?"

Ian reached for his pocket, tapping his 38-caliber firearm.

Roumoult nodded, but it didn't make him feel any better.

"What now?" asked Ian as the van began to lose speed.

Roumoult spotted an intersection. "Could be why," he said, nodding in its direction.

"That's at least half a mile away."

Roumoult didn't reply. A thought popped into his head. He reached for his phone, accessed the video app, and switched it with the GPS.

"What are you doing?" said Ian.

"The van exists. We need proof of it for Patrick Burns. I think this is the drop-off point."

"I think you're right."

The van pulled to a stop.

Ian parked behind a large tree at the top of an incline.

"Ian, we're on top of a hill and exposed."

"We don't have a choice," Ian replied. "If I pass them and stop, we're busted. I can't make a U-turn now; they'll spot us. If I reverse, we won't be able—"

"We're sitting ducks," Roumoult finished for him.

"Boss..." Ian's voice trailed away.

A four-wheeler truck appeared on the other side of the intersection. It turned and stopped in front of the van.

"Now we are in business," Ian said.

Roumoult adjusted the camera to capture both vehicles. A muscular African American man stepped out of the driver's seat of the four-wheel drive. Dressed in a black t-shirt, black pants, and a brown jacket, he towered beside the four-wheel drive as if he owned the world. His set jaw looked heavier under a thick beard. He sauntered towards the van and shook hands with the driver, beckoning for a blond man, his partner, to join him. Soon, the trio walked behind the vehicle, and the driver of the van opened the back door.

Roumoult noticed that a passenger was still in the vehicle.

"Looks like they're done," Ian said.

Roumoult peered into his camera; the men were shaking hands and nodding their heads.

"Okay, Ian can we…" He drifted off. The African American removed a gun and fired at point-blank range.

"Oh, good God!"

"No!" yelled Ian.

The driver's body slumped to the ground.

Roumoult shut his eyes, turning his head away. A loud scream tore through the air. The passenger in the white van hopped out and ran towards a blue car.

"Help, help me! Please, someone, help!" he bellowed.

The African American man calmly moved to the middle of the road and raised his right hand.

Roumoult jumped in his seat as another shot echoed. His heart pounded against his chest and sweat trickled down his forehead. He watched in horror as the passenger bumped against the motor and dropped onto the highway. Hardly able to breathe, Roumoult turned to Ian.

"Ian? Ian!"

Ian stared at him.

"Boss. They're—"

"I know! Call the police," Roumoult choked. He nodded.

The blue car moved backward and began to gain speed. The second assailant opened fire, bullets striking the vehicle. The car swung and tumbled down the road, narrowly missing trees. Roumoult realized that his knuckles were tight on his seat. Tears ran freely down his face. Helplessly, he watched the second assailant jump behind the wheel of the van. The African American turned to the truck.

"We have to get out of here!" Ian cried after finishing the call.

"No!" Roumoult snapped. "They don't know we're here. If we move, we're dead!"

"We should run into the woods..."

Roumoult didn't know. He heard engines and saw the van and four-wheel drive heading for them.

"Too late!" he said. "Hide!"

Roumoult and Ian slid down to the car floor. Revving engines roared past. Shots echoed in Roumoult's ears. Ian let out a long breath and was about to move when Roumoult reached out a hand to stop him. It wasn't safe yet. They waited.

When he was satisfied that the danger had passed, Roumoult climbed back up to his seat, Ian following his lead. He stared at the bodies on the highway. He was a witness, to a horrific crime. A low humming began. Roumoult looked at Ian.

"Oh God," he muttered, seizing his seat belt.

Ian turned the key and slammed his foot on the gas. The Ford darted forward at high speed. Roumoult turned.

"Anything?" Ian asked, eyes fixed on the road.

"No. Keep going,"

The car sped, leaving the bodies behind it.

The Ford crossed the intersection and quickened its pace. Roumoult's eyes remained glued on the hilltop. A black truck appeared.

"Here he comes," said Roumoult, hating himself for being right.

Ian floored it.

"Give me the gun," Roumoult demanded.

Ian handed it over. "I'll try to stay ahead." He pushed the car as fast as it would go.

Roumoult clutched the dashboard.

"Boss, I have an idea," Ian said over the noise of engine. "At the next corner, I'll slow down. You jump out of the car."

Roumoult eyed him. "Not a chance." Their chances of survival were better if they stayed together.

"Boss, please" Ian repeated.

The Ford jolted, pushing Roumoult forward. His seatbelt tightened painfully around his chest and hips. He turned. The back windshield had cracked. The black van circled them and shot off.

"Damn, he's fast!"

Ian gripped the steering firmly, but at the corners, he lost momentum. Another bang, another shudder. The back windshield shattered into pieces, glass raining down. Roumoult's phone popped out of its cradle and slid across the dashboard. Roumoult was just about to grab it when the vehicle shook, sending it sliding to the floor. He clutched his seat.

"He's toying with us!" Ian yelled.

The Ford struggled to take the corner, but the road ahead was straight, which would work in their favor. Roumoult could make out the truck driver's smiling face. He unbuckled his seat belt.

"Boss! What are you doing?"

Roumoult didn't answer. The four-wheeler gathered speed, preparing to hit them again. Roumoult aimed and fired. The bullet careened through the air, piercing the windshield and striking the driver's shoulder.

"Good shot!" Ian shouted.

Roumoult focused and pulled the trigger for a second time. The truck smashed into the car again. He missed. The bullet smashed into the radiator. Ian swayed the car back onto the highway, and Roumoult tried again. Bang! Another shot through the radiator. Smoke emerged. Roumoult pulled the trigger one more time; the vehicle swung and dodged the bullet.

"Damn it!"

The Ford quaked.

"Oh, no!" cried out Ian. He tried changing gears and pushing the accelerator. The car lost momentum. Roumoult had run out of bullets.

"No! No! Don't slow down!" Roumoult shouted, buckling his seatbelt and staring down the bridge.

A hard blow was too much for the car. Roumoult's stomach twisted, and he fell forward. He reached for something to grab onto as the windows caved in. He felt the heat from the radiator on his face. The Ford was rammed against the bridge barrier. The world lurched. Roumoult let out a scream as the Ford fell.

St. George Hospital

Emma removed her mask and walked out of the operating theater. She couldn't remember feeling so overwhelmed. Seeing Roumoult was a shock, but seeing Ian was worse. An MRI revealed that he'd suffered a subdural hematoma. Surgery took two hours, and Emma struggled to stop the bleeding. Ian's vitals were stable, but if he didn't regain consciousness within the next twenty-four hours, he was unlikely to wake again. She stood silently in the corridor, leaning against a doorframe. Five grueling years of medical school were nothing compared to this residency. She wondered if leaving the safety of a smaller medical practice had been a mistake. This incident, maybe because it involved Roumoult, had shaken her. She thought of him, his warmth, and the conversation they'd shared. It had never been like that with Mark. With Mark, it grew slowly and faded fast. Emma took a deep breath and headed for the waiting room.

St. George Hospital

Tom's heart sank when he heard about the highway incident. Two people were murdered, and David

Ruth, the driver of the blue car, was in critical condition. But that wasn't all. Two miles ahead, a group of farmers had seen a truck push a car off the bridge. They'd tried to follow, but the four-wheeler was too fast. They'd hiked down the creek and found Roumoult and Ian unconscious.

Tom stood with Angelus at the door of Room 447 on the seventh floor of St. George Hospital. William and Joan sat in chairs at the edges of the room. Fred Cranston leaned over Roumoult's frame. A square bandage covered the right side of Roumoult's head, and his right arm rested in a sling. Fred turned.

"We didn't want to disturb you," Angelus said, stepping inside.

Tom entered and nodded to Officer Jake, who also stood in the crowded room. It was best to put them both under police protection.

Fred's face had lost its glow; his eyes were swollen and hollow. He sat with his hands clasped together, fidgeting nervously.

"He hasn't woken up yet?" Angelus asked.

"No."

A few rooms over, Ian looked worse. His head was barely visible under the bandages, and purple patches spread over his body. Ian's right leg was elevated and in a cast. Neither William nor Joan had been able to look at him. They stood in the corridor talking in hush voices. Tom noted William brushing his hands against his wet face, and Joan trying to soothe him.

Tom felt helpless. Angelus told him that it was a routine case which had turned deadly. Tom had the names of the two drivers and some intel, and their corpses were being transfer to the Morgue. With no other witnesses, he couldn't track down the murderers; waiting for Roumoult to wake up was his only option.

Roumoult's whole body ached, and someone kept calling his name. Strange voices, blurry visions, and loud noises surrounded him. His eyelids felt heavy, as if something was holding them down. He cried out, his arm throbbing, his skin searing as if splitting apart.

"Roumoult," the voice said softly.

The agony in his skull was unbearable. He didn't want to talk anyone; he just needed the pain to go away. Beeping noises made his head seem to rattle. His eyes slowly opened, and the stabbing sensation in his arm faded.

"Hello," said a familiar voice.

Dr. Matthew stood beside him. He was an old general surgeon who worked in the St. George Hospital and owned his own medical practice. He watched Roumoult through square-framed glasses.

"Hi there," he said. "It's time to wake up."

Roumoult eyes drifted around the room, spotting William, his father, and Jake, who he recognized from their highway search. Sun streamed through the room's small window, and the clock on the wall showed that it was 12.30 p.m. A plastic bag full of yellow fluid hung from a stand above the bed, a tub extending from its base and disappearing under the thick bandage wrapped around Roumoult's left wrist. He wriggled his toes; they worked. He realized that he couldn't feel his right arm. It was wrapped in a bandage and rested in a sling. He looked at the doctor.

"Your right shoulder was dislocated," Dr. Matthew explained. "We put it back in its socket. In addition, your glenohumeral ligament was almost ripped apart. We performed an arthroscopy and put it back together. You'll have to wear the sling for a while, but you should recover."

"I don't know what that means but I'm glad to still have my arm. To be alive," Roumoult croaked.

"The grazes on your temple, right side of the head, and ear aren't bad. They'll heal."

Roumoult wanted to touch his head, but Dr. Matthew motioned for him to remain still.

"I need you to understand, your injuries are extensive. You need to rest. Am I clear?"

Roumoult nodded gingerly. "How is Ian?"

The doctor hesitated. "He's resting. You should do the same."

Roumoult knew the doctor was hiding something from him. He turned to ask his dad, who offered the same non-committal reply.

Fred sat silently, dressed in one his best white shirts and a dark-gray blazer.

"How was your date with Evelyn?"

"It was great until Angelus called me and told me you were in the hospital."

Roumoult made a half-hearted attempt at a laugh.

After Fred and Dr. Matthew left, Roumoult thought about the accident. If he could call it that. It was attempted murder, and nothing was stopping that man from attacking him again. He hated himself for putting Ian in danger, but he couldn't have predicted the shooting. Tom, Joan, and Angelus slipped into the room.

"Hey! I'm glad you are alive," Tom said.

"That makes two of us," Roumoult answered.

"How are you?" Angelus asked

"I'm okay. How's Ian?"

"He's resting,"

"Why is everyone lying to me? He's critical, isn't he?"

"No one's lying to you," Angelus said calmly. "His injuries were worse than yours. He had surgery and is recovering."

"What about the others?"

"The van drivers are dead," said Tom. "The blue car which smashed into the woods belongs to David Ruth. Fortunately, he survived. We need to find the assailants, and we're going to need your statement."

Roumoult eyebrows knitted together. He shut his eyes tight, trying to drive the memories away. "No. Not now."

"I'm sorry," Tom said, sitting at the edge of his bed and pulling out a pen and notebook. "We need to know."

"Tell us what happened," Angelus prompted.

Roumoult opened his mouth to begin but paused before speaking.

"Go on," Tom urged him.

"Where's my phone?" said Roumoult.

Everyone exchanged glances.

"You didn't find it?" Roumoult demanded.

"Why?" Tom asked.

"I used my phone's camera to record the whole thing."

Tom's eyebrows lifted and his lips curved into a smile. "Really?"

"I was gathering proof for my client. I didn't know it would turn into a homicide!"

"That's good." Joan exclaimed. She reached for her mobile and stepped out of the room.

Roumoult was relieved not to have to relive the incident. They waited as Joan made enquiries. She returned looking disheartened.

"What happened?" Tom asked.

"It's dead."

"Are you sure?" Angelus asked. "What about the memory card?"

"It crumpled under the weight of the car."

"Have you shown it to Jack?" Roumoult asked hopefully.

"Good idea," said Angelus. He picked up his phone. "Jack, we need your help; I'm putting you on speaker."

"All right." Jack's voice echoed around the room.

"Jack, we need to retrieve Roumoult's phone's memory. Can you do that?"

There was a momentary silence. "What's he done now?"

Despite the pain, Roumoult grinned.

"It broke," Angelus answered simply.

"Boss? Seriously? Again? What do you have against technology?"

"Can you retrieve the memory or not?" Roumoult asked.

"Where is it?" Jack asked frowning.

"I'll send it over to you," Tom replied.

"Detective Tom? What are you doing there?"

Suddenly, Roumoult felt incredibly tired. His eyelids sagged, and his headache returned. The medicine must be wearing off.

"Jack," said Angelus. "There's a video on the phone, and we need it ASAP."

"That may not be possible because—"

"Jack, just try," Roumoult growled.

"Fine, send it over. I'll look at it, but I make no promises."

Angelus was about to hang up when Jack's voice cracked on the speaker. "Is this your new smartphone?"

"Is it?" Roumoult asked. He couldn't think clearly.

Tom chuckled.

"Your last phone died six months ago. I had a hard time getting your contacts list and data. Then you bought a new black smartphone. Did you buy a new mobile?"

"I don't think so."

"Jack, what's your point?" Angelus asked.

"My point is, for boss's latest mobile, I created a backup system. Meaning it synchronizes everything automatically. The minute he adds a new video or photo, it syncs with the server at the Firm."

"When did you do that?" Roumoult demanded.

"It must be on the server," Jack continued, ignoring him. "Boss, I gave you a user ID and password."

Everybody looked at Roumoult's blank face.

Angelus grinned. "Jack, Roumoult doesn't remember. Why don't you do your magic trick and get us that video."

"Okay."

"And Jack," said Roumoult. "Don't watch it."

Jack grumbled. "Give me few minutes."

As they waited, Angelus asked about the van drivers.

"We got some info from the patrol officers. The drivers of the van were Tim Chen and Jacob Reid. They grew up in the same neighborhood, went to school together, dropped out of college in year two, and started their removal business a decade ago. Their slate is clean. I am going to dig further. It might derail me from the triple murder, but we can't let this trail go cold."

Angelus' phone buzzed. "We've got it."

Everyone gathered around him.

Uneasiness swept over Roumoult. His head pounded, and the sound of bullets firing felt like a weight on his chest. He wished they'd watch the video elsewhere.

"Hold on," said Joan.

"What?" Tom asked.

"The driver. I know him. I've seen him somewhere."

Angelus peered at the screen.

"Oh my God," Tom said.

"Do you know him?" Roumoult asked.

"That's the van driver who attacked the doc!"

"Are you telling me these are the same guys who stole the bodies from the Morgue?" Roumoult asked.

Joan nodded.

"That means the two cases are connected," said Angelus. "Patrick Burns saw the van at the APTOS around the same time Wagner, Hawk and Garrison died. It disappears, and Burns is fired. It is apparent they work for someone at the company. To cover their tracks, they might have hidden the bodies at the APTOS."

"Makes sense," said Tom.

The group continued to watch the video. The entire episode replayed in Roumoult's mind. He was angry and frustrated. He just wanted to sleep or take a pill that would make him forget it had ever happened.

"Any idea who the guy in black is?" Angelus asked.

"None," replied Tom.

"I don't get it. If the van drivers were working for the bad guys, why kill them?" Joan asked.

"To tie loose ends," Angelus concluded.

Roumoult thought aloud. "He executed them on a highway. If I were the bad guy, I'd kill them quietly. Why execute them publicly?"

"Leave this to us," Tom said.

"Do I have a choice?" muttered Roumoult.

NYPD- Precinct

"Are you out of your mind?" shouted Captain Isaac Reed, getting up from his chair. The Captain was a hefty man with a tall frame and silver hair. On his broad nose perched a pair of thick, black glasses.

"Sir, if we put both cases together, five men are already dead, three are in the hospital, and a lady is missing," Tom argued.

"I want the murderer found, but to launch a full official investigation against the entire organization is madness," said the Captain.

"I say we start with APTOS Pharmaceuticals and see where it leads us," Joan suggested.

The Captain sat down. He took a minute to regain his composure, then he said, "Mr. Walter Weldon is a good friend. I'm sure there's been a misunderstanding."

"APTOS might hold the key to solving this case. It belongs to a powerful man; that doesn't mean it's clean," Tom said.

"But the background checks revealed nothing."

"It can't be a coincidence that the men who stole the bodies were the same people who smuggled then boxes from APTOS. Cranston followed them, saw them being murdered, and then Alex Rucker hijacked the van. He tried to kill Cranston and Stanford."

"What do we know about Alex?" the Captain asked.

"He has a long rap sheet. He the kind of criminal we like to keep behind bars, but the system sets them free," Tom said, handing over a folder.

The Captain read through the information. "Fine. Contact Judge Warren. Get a warrant, but don't make public statements until we have hard evidence."

Detective Agency

After returning from the hospital, Angelus got a call from Joe asking about Roumoult and Ian. He updated him on the situation. As soon as he hung up, Jack Calvin entered his office and took a seat in the client's chair.

"Hey man. How are you?" he said, resting his feet on the desk.

Angelus eyed him. Jack returned his feet to the floor. "You saw the video, didn't you?" Angelus growled.

"Yeah. Sorry."

"What have you got?"

"This dude waving his gun around is Alex Rucker." Jack handed over a file to Angelus. "He's forty years old, has a mother. No other family or friends. Man, this guy is deep. They arrested him on several counts of drugs, extortion, and smuggling. He served ten years in prison. Here's the thing: records show that other prisoners referred to him as 'crazy Alex.' Ask me why."

"Because he's crazy?" Angelus said impatiently.

"Crazy is an understatement; this guy is a psycho! He's smart, vicious, crafty, and very, very dangerous. Take my advice man, stay away from this dude. Send the boss back to London. Let the NYPD handle this case."

Angelus remained silent.

"Oh, I see. You don't believe me. Let me give you an example," Jack continued. "Alex got into a fight in prison. That's normal. But this wasn't a typical fight. It was for a piece of bread, a damn piece of bread. Alex started it because he thought it belonged to him. The other prisoner ended up with three broken ribs, two cracked teeth, and his face punched in. He couldn't open his eyes for two days. Alex has a long-standing record of finishing any job he starts, no matter what."

Angelus wasn't afraid. He thought of Ian, fighting for his life, and Roumoult, barely able to move. It was time Alex answered for his crimes. "Where can I find him?"

"The man is a ghost. No one can find him."

"What about his mother?"

"She's in an old age home. He doesn't visit her."

"What about the second man?"

"Marcus Walt, thirty-nine years old, no family or friends, and an expert gunman. He served in the military until 2000. But then he quit. There's a rumor that the army asked him to resign because of misconduct, but there's no proof. He left America and went to Europe for four years. Since his return in 2009, he's stayed under the radar."

"Until now."

"Something changed. We don't know what."

"What about Alex's truck?"

"The plate is registered to Reynolds Anderson," said Jack. "His family buried him five years ago. It's a dead end."

Angelus gritted his teeth.

Jack stood up and put his hands in his pockets. His face turned sullen. "I don't have the courage to see Roumoult."

"I am sure he won't take it personally."

"I-I just can't do it. Can't see him in such a state." He paused and his head slung. "I know it's a bad situation and you're angry and want to punish Alex, but please, let the cops handle it."

"He came after them," Angelus pointed out.

"Yes, let's make sure he doesn't come after anyone else. Someone innocent, like Alice."

APTOS Pharmaceuticals, Long Island

Tom now understood the Captain's reluctance. The Judge was considerate but dubious. It took an hour to convince him and get the warrant.

Tom stepped out of the car and stared at the massive building. Despite its modern design, it looked unpleasant and unwelcoming. APTOS guards approached him and demanded an explanation. He showed them his badge and the warrant. Joan and half a dozen cops came to stand beside him.

Inside, Tom's body went cold. The air smelled strongly of medicine. The floor was well-polished, the walls were white, and the corridors were illuminated by circular lamps. He could hear the low humming of machines. They crossed the narrow corridor. Tom paused. On the other side of the glass wall were three huge cylinders, at least ten feet tall. Several people dressed in white paraded around the area. With a loud click, a long stainless-steel tube shifted and attached itself to the first cylinder. A loud horn echoed. A white powder gushed through the tube and disappeared into the wall. Tom rushed ahead, and he saw that in the next room, the powder was being fed into machines that generated pills. He kept walking, watching the machines fill white bottles out of the corner of his eye.

He walked ahead. The next wide hall was filled with conveyor belts, sealed and green-labeled bottles chugging along them. A huge, silver door opened automatically, and Tom greeted the receptionist.

Soon, a man came rushing through an entrance marked *R&D*.

"Hello. I'm Dr. Allen Wheeler. Is there a problem, Officer?"

"Detective Nash," said Tom.

The man in front of him was of medium stature, with brown eyes and a tired weather-beaten face. He was probably in his late fifties, but the wrinkles and unkempt beard made him look much older.

"We have a warrant to search the premises." Tom said, noting the change in Wheeler's expression.

"What?"

Tom explained to him about the unmarked van and its link to a murder investigation.

"This is preposterous!" Wheeler exclaimed. "I cannot allow this! You'll have to wait for Mr. Weldon."

"Do you think you have a choice?" Joan sneered.

Dr. Wheeler fell silent. Tom nodded to the search party, and they split in different directions.

"We have nothing to hide," said Wheeler.

"Then there should be no trouble," Tom remarked.

Tom could sense Dr. Wheeler's unease as he led his team into the R&D department.

It was close to eleven p.m. when Tom had had enough. They'd interviewed all the employees. No one knew about the van. They thought Patrick Burns had been fired because of misconduct. Many of them didn't even know he existed. The guards denied seeing the van. The medicines were genuine, and the employees' records were clean. Company documents, financial accounts, and management files were up to scratch. There was no security footage of the white van. When Tom asked about Burns. Dr. Wheeler claimed that he was a troublemaker and a liar, that he'd been a risk to the company's reputation. Tom knew he was hiding something, but without proof, his hands were tied.

St. George Hospital

Roumoult eyed Officer Jake, who was enjoying a Knicks game. He couldn't focus. William stopped by and told him everything about his day until he was bored to death. There was only one thing he cared about. The police had searched APTOS Pharmaceuticals and found nothing. When Angelus visited, Roumoult could sense his anger and urged him to let the cops find Alex. He told him to continue watching APTOS, something told him there was more to come. Angelus agreed to keep Joe on the job and partner him with David. Sluggish and tired, Roumoult sent his father home and stared at the ceiling.

The door open and Emma looked in. "Hi!"

"Hi," Roumoult replied, thankful for the distraction. "What are you doing here?"

She strolled in with her hands in her apron pockets. "I came to see how Mr. Stanford was doing, and I thought I should drop by to see you too."

"You work here?" Roumoult asked, realizing his ignorance. He tried to recall if she'd mentioned that she was a doctor. No, she hadn't. Roumoult fidgeted with his blanket. Sure, he'd wanted to see her again, but not like this.

"Yeah," Emma replied, glancing at the officer, whose attention was still very much focused on the game. "I work downstairs in the ER."

"So, you're a doctor?" said Roumoult.

"Yep. The paramedics brought you and Ian to the ER last night."

"Well, thanks for looking after us."

"You're welcome. So, are you working on Tom's case?" Emma sat gently at the foot of the bed.

"How do you know that?"

"Wagner was my patient."

"Oh, I see. I'm sorry," he said, struggling to think. "I think you should stay away. It's complicated."

"I like complicated."

Roumoult smiled and told her what he knew. Emma stayed for a while. After she left, he thought about her. She made him feel something he wasn't quite ready to admit.

"Cute doctor," Officer Jake mocked. "Girlfriend?"

Roumoult laughed. "No."

9

Creatures Of The Dark

June 9, 2015

Lower Eastside, Manhattan

T he alarm buzzed and Tom opened his eyes. Turning the alarm off, he stared at the roof of his bedroom. He groaned, still feeling unrested. Outside his bedroom window, the city was already awake and noisy. His neighbor spoke loudly on the phone on the fire escape. The bakery underneath his apartment was making croissants, the scent drifting in and mingling with spices from the Indian sweet market across the street.

Tom stood and looked at himself in the mirror. Again, he remembered what his ex-wife used to say: "Tom, you drink too much beer. Stop now, or you'll turn into a barrel of beer."

He smirked; he looked like a cola bottle, just a bit curvy around the middle. He could live with that.

He went into the bathroom and examined his tired face, struggling to remember the last time he'd felt truly happy. It had been two years ago. Before

Claire, his ex, left him for refusing to put their relationship before his work.

Tom showered, shaved, and walked into the kitchen. He made bacon and eggs, and he listened to the latest score on the Knicks replay. But his mind wandered back to the case. Had he missed anything? He couldn't be sure. He had to follow the trail of clues.

City Morgue

William was overwhelmed with emotions and had cried himself to sleep. Just too much was happening. Jonathan had come to his office twice asking if the case files were ready to be submitted. They weren't, because William was struggling to catch up. He was constantly thinking about Roumoult and Ian. He blamed himself. A tapping noise distracted him, and Juliet walked in with a file.

"How are you doing?" said William.

"Good," replied Juliet. "How's your head?"

"It's all right."

"I heard about Roumoult. I'm sorry."

"I've gotten us in trouble again."

Juliet smiled.

William shrugged. "I didn't mean to."

"I know. You have a knack for it. Here you go." She handed him the file.

William was confused. Had he overlooked something?

"Now tell me, where did you find Mr. Rabbit?"

William laughed. "What did you find?"

"Remember, this may have nothing to do with the case."

"Okay."

"I did all the tests I would normally do for humans," Juliet said. "At first, I thought maybe this rabbit was sick, but I was wrong. He was a test subject, but not for a disease."

"Oh?"

"Someone dosed this rabbit with a dissociative drug."

"A hallucinogen?"

"Phencyclidine, or PCP," Juliet replied.

William sat back in his seat. "Wow!"

"The rabbit inhaled it. I detected it in its hair and blood."

"That's interesting."

"Yes, it is. PCP was developed as an anesthetic, but in the 1960s, it was withdrawn from medical practice."

"Because of the side effects." mentioned William.

"Yes. In the early 1960s, research studies showed that it caused delusions, severe anxiety, and irritation in patients recovering from surgery. Doctors stopped using it, but the damage was already done. Due to its euphoric effect and detachment from the world, it soon emerged as a popular recreational drug. Every user has a different psychological response. Low doses are detrimental, but a high dose can kill you. Side effects range from erratic, violent, and dangerous behavior to complete loss of touch with reality. Usually, it causes mania leading to violent attacks, murder, rape, and suicide. It's classified a schedule II drug and hardly used in its purest form."

William scratched his beard. "What about the rabbit's brain?"

"I found several damaged brain cells, especially in cerebellum and medulla oblongata, as a result of long-term exposure to the drug. Your Mr. Rabbit was so stimulated, he might have been in a delusional state."

"That could explain why it attacked the eagle," William thought out loud.

"What?"

"Never mind."

"Did you detect any PCP in the bloodstream of the three victims?"

Juliet looked him in the eye. "Find me the bodies and I'll let you know."

City Morgue

After Juliet left, William took another pill. The headaches still bothered him. He suspected he'd need a refill. He worked for the next two hours, then he picked up his jacket and walked out of his office. Outside, a warm breeze greeted him. The streets were active and full of life.

He had lunch with Roumoult but didn't tell him about the PCP or the rabbit. An idea lurked in the back of his mind. He left the hospital, bought two coffees and a few doughnuts, and took a taxi to the police station.

NYPD Precinct

"You've never bought me coffee before," Tom commented, looking at his cappuccino.

"He has a theory, and he doesn't want us to say no," Joan said knowingly.

William beamed, and their eyes met. He wondered if he should ask her out for dinner. Too much: maybe a coffee. Tom's voice interrupted his thoughts.

"This is a bribe?"

"Consider it a gesture of good will," William responded, taking a seat in front of the detectives. "I want you to keep an open mind."

Tom chewed his doughnut. "Doc, I think we can take it."

William explained what he'd learned about the rabbit and the PCP.

"The rabbit did what?" asked Tom, setting his coffee aside.

William described again the rabbits encounter with the eagle.

"That's some rabbit."

"That's a delusional rabbit," William corrected.

"How is this linked with the case or APTOS?" Tom asked.

"The rabbit's erratic behavior made me think. It's possible someone doped our three so-called suicide victims with PCP before their deaths. Look at the big picture. Each one of them had everything to live for. Their lives weren't perfect, but they had no history of grief, or sudden loss, or depression. They were healthy and happy. Why did they kill themselves? What if the killer didn't want the murders to be obvious, so he doped them with such a high dose of PCP, they did the dirty work themselves."

"That's a good theory, but we need proof," said Tom.

"To dispense the drug, he would have used something,"

"You mean the murder weapon," said Joan.

"It has to be something very... simple. No one would dream of it as a murder weapon and it could still be at the crime scene."

Tom looked thoughtful. "You got all this from a rabbit?"

NYPD Precinct

Tom got a lead on Marcus Walt and rushed off with an officer. Joan stayed with William as they tried to figure out the murder weapon.

William stood beside Joan, looking at two whiteboards. "Ready?"

"What are we doing?" Joan asked.

"We're making an inventory of everything found and photographed at the crime scenes," William replied, finishing scribbling items onto one of the whiteboards before recapping his marker.

"What are we looking for?" Joan asked.

"Something present at all the crime scenes, something links the three deaths." William was hoping the killer had left a trail. It had to be unconventional. It had to be something seemingly non-threatening. He scrunched up his face, thinking hard.

"I don't see it," said Joan.

"Let's begin with Wagner's apartment," William proposed. "Six torn books, three broken vases, one broken glass table, and three smashed designer mirrors. One landscape painting, three cracked photo frames, and one smashed flat TV. Four blue lamps..." He paused to look at Joan, who was comparing the items.

"Nothing jumps out."

William continued to read. "Two small angel-shaped figurines, five plants, two swords, and a set of Russian dolls."

Joan shook her head.

"On the carpet, the CSI found glass pieces from mirrors, the glass table, and LED lights. The rug was wet—and covered in coins, soil from one of the smashed pots, torn paper, roses, a china teapot, and two cups with saucers." He paused. "Unopened mail, keys, a Rolex watch, a tie, prescription glasses, a cigar, a marriage ring, a working smartphone..."

"Wait." Joan held up a hand to stop him.

"What?"

"What did you just say?" she asked, staring at the board.

"Uh, smartphone."

"No, before that."

William read the list backward. "Smartphone, a marriage ring, a cigar, prescription glasses..."

"That's it!"

"Prescription glasses?"

"No, not that," Joan replied, and circled the words *cigar box*. "Is there a cigar box on your list?"

"No. The inventory mentions a cigar." William picked up Wagner's case file. Joan grabbed Hawk's file. They combed through the crime scene photos.

"It was in Hawk's penthouse," Joan said, passing the photograph to William.

William shuffled through Wagner's file and stopped when he found a picture of a cigar lying on the carpet. They compared the two photos.

"Did Garrison get it?"

He picked up Garrison's file and looked through the photos. "There!" He jabbed his finger down forcefully. The picture showed a silver box on the coffee table.

"Why didn't we find it at Wagner's place?" Joan asked.

"Because he trashed it," said William. "It could still be there."

"How do we know it's the murder weapon?"

"Only one way to find out."

Joan drove William to the crime scene. The traffic was horrendous, but William didn't mind. Time on the road was time spent with Joan. He discovered that they had a lot in common. She'd had to transfer because of a case involving a crook lawyer. The Captain had wanted him alive, but Joan had taken matters into her own hands. Her partner was shot in the crossfire and died in hospital. Since then she had struggled. Joan told William that she wanted to be a good cop but didn't feel supported. She struggled to work with Tom; she suspected he didn't trust her.

"He takes his time," William defended him.

"He's different with you, and even more so with Roumoult. With him he's…"

"Competitive? Yeah, Roumoult does that to people."

"Why would Tom compete with Roumoult?" Joan asked.

William shrugged. "Roumoult, unknowingly takes over and Tom hates that. For once, Tom wants to beat him and solve a case like this."

Joan parked the car, and they stepped out of the vehicle. "I don't understand men," she said.

"Most men don't understand women," William countered.

She blushed. "I think you do."

"I am a little above average; I have some leverage,"

Joan chuckled. "A little?"

"I'm modest."

Wagner's Apartment, Park Avenue, Manhattan

They entered the lobby of the building and took the elevator to the fifth floor. Joan unlocked the apartment. William pulled on a pair of gloves as Joan began searching.

"There!" Joan pointed out the cigar between the shattered glass table and the lounge. She carefully placed it in the evidence bag.

"Where's the box?" William asked.

"It could be anywhere in the apartment."

William examined the objects on the carpet, while Joan searched the living room. "If I was Wagner, drugged and hysterical, how would I behave?" William wondered aloud.

Joan faced him.

"Maybe I found the box at my door, or maybe it came by post as a gift." William walked toward the door. "Following my routine, I stepped inside the apartment and put the unopened mail on the table," he continued, moving to stand by the table. "I took off my watch and put it in the bowl with my keys." He pointed at the silver bowl on the floor. "I picked up the small package and walked to the couch. I sat down and opened the box."

"Something happened," Joan interjected.

"The drug was released," said William nodding. "I screamed in terror!"

"And the box fell out of my hands!" Joan finished for him.

William dropped to his knees. "Aha!" he cried, finding the box under the couch. He stood up and was about to open it, but Joan stopped him.

"Don't open it. It could be dangerous." She put it in another evidence bag.

William was thrilled. They were finally getting somewhere.

Just then, Joan's phone rang. She answered it, and a broad smile appeared on her face.

"It's our lucky day," she said. "We found Marcus Walt."

23rd Street, Bronx

Three patrol cars stopped on the street. Cops jumped out and ran. A few spectators watched from a distance. Two cops separated from the group and cleared the area. The group slowed down near the gates of the third building.

Tom paused and looked at his partner. She nodded. Wearing a bulletproof vest and armed with his gun, he opened the rusty gate and stepped inside the premises of the building. He pushed the main door open and stepped into a dim and silent lobby. His eyes settled on the narrow staircase. The group crept to the fourth floor. Tom stopped and checked the hallway. It was clear. As he moved forward, he read the numbers on the doors: "*4A, 4B, 4C.*"

Joan and the squad followed behind. They reached the door marked *4E.* Tom leaned against the wall, and Joan positioned herself opposite to him. An officer rushed forward with a battering ram and broke the lock. The team spread throughout the apartment. As they searched, Tom studied the uneven carpet, fallen cushions, and a broken beer bottle.

"Detective Nash!" called out a voice.

Tom rushed into the room and paused. A faint metallic odor caught his attention. Tom didn't like this part of his job. He felt his throat tighten as he moved past the squad, following a trail of blood across the white carpet. His pulse rose. Marcus lay in the pool of blood, which had spilled from the stab wounds in his chest. His eyes were wide open, staring without seeing.

"Okay," Tom called. "Get the CSI unit."

"Detective, you should see this."

Everyone turned.

"What is it?" Tom asked warily. He stood next to the officer and looked into the dark closet. A red light blinked rhythmically. A timer glowed: *20*, *19*, *18*.

"Get out! Get out!" Tom yelled.

The squad rushed out of the room. Tom wondered if he could disable it, but there was no time.

"Tom!" he heard Joan shout.

He didn't move.

"Tom!"

The timer kept blinking: *16*, *15*. He had to go. Leaving the body behind, Tom ran out of the room.

Joan waited for him at the door. "Run! Don't stop, no matter what!"

He saw the last man of the SWAT team disappearing down the stairways. Joan was a few paces ahead of him. Boom! A horrific explosion shook the floor. An immense fireball blasted through the wall and spread out across the corridor. Tom rushed down the stairs. He was pushed forward by the enormous force. His feet left the ground, and he smashed into the wall.

APTOS Pharmaceuticals, Long Island

David Hensley opened his mouth and yawned. He glanced at Joe, who slept in the passenger seat. David was older and heavier than Ian, and his specialty was surveillance. He ran his hands through his ash-brown hair and stretched, then he glanced at his notepad. Since the police raid, several cars had visited APTOS. He'd noted their time of arrival, departure, and the number plates, if he could see them. Angelus updated him and warned him to expect anything. David heard him, but he didn't believe it. Looking up, David admired the cloudless sky, the moon casting a white glow over the vicinity. The night was quiet, except for the buzzing mosquitoes in the bushes and the soft hoot of an owl hidden somewhere in the woods. David reached over and tapped Joe on the shoulder, waking him. "It's time."

"Yep," Joe replied groggily.

"I've got you a flask of coffee and doughnuts," David said, gesturing to the backseat. David picked up his binoculars and surveyed the area. He began with the complex. A few lights glowed, and two employees worked on the first floor. They'd been there all day. He observed the parking lot, the guard tower, and the open ground. He eyed the trees surrounding APTOS.

"You should go home," said Joe. "Your shift is over."

But David didn't listen. He wrinkled his brows and kept watching the forest. In the soft glow, he thought he saw something move.

"David?" Joe asked.

"Shush," David whispered, continuing to observe. He adjusted his binoculars and waited for a few minutes, but nothing stirred. "Probably a small animal."

"I hope it's just another rabbit."

David smiled, then something else caught his attention. The woods fell deadly silent. No humming, buzzing, or hooting.

"What?" Joe asked observing the change in his demeanor.

David threw the binoculars and pulled Joe down.

"What? What's going on?" Joe spluttered.

"Shush," David hissed. "There's something out there."

They sat still and quiet. The air turned chilly, and the wind died out. Both men lifted their heads tentatively. Under the glow of the moon, David saw a tall, dark bipedal creature with long claws gliding through the forest. It paused for a second, and its head slowly twisted towards them. Joe ducked immediately, but something drew David toward the unworldly creature. He watched intently as it turned and disappeared into the darkness.

10

The Cigar Box

June 10, 2015

St. George Hospital

Emma couldn't wait to begin her day shift. Working nights was getting on her nerves. She pressed her sore arm to ease her pain. It had been a busy night. Paramedics had brought in Tom Nash. He was fortunate. The blast could have killed him, but he'd escaped with nothing more than a sprained wrist and a few bruises.

Emma thought her heart was foolish. It cared for people who kept things from her. Like Mark and Tim. Tonight out of the blue, Tim asked her for a favor. After he was so rude to her, he wanted her to cover for him while he took care of some personal business. She thought it would be an hour, but it was now three a.m., and he still hadn't returned. The ER staff were more than qualified to handle emergencies, but when Dr. Lox came looking for Tim, Emma got worried. She didn't say much to her boss, but she decided to check if Tim had returned. She looked in the cafeteria and at the reception, and she checked with staff members. No one had seen him. She went to the staff room for a bite to eat and found Tim standing near his locker.

"You're back," she said.

"Yes, I am. Sorry I'm late. I'll cover for you sometime."

"It's all right," Emma said. "Dr. Lox was looking for you."

"What did he want?"

"I don't know. He said he wanted to speak with you," said Emma.

"What did you say to him?" Tim quizzed her.

"I didn't say anything."

"Did you tell him I went out?"

"No."

"Are you sure? What did you tell him?" he asked, half yelling.

"I told you, I said nothing," Emma said. "What the hell is wrong with you?"

"What did you say!?"

"Nothing! Where have you been?"

"That's none of your business!" Tim snapped before storming off.

Tim's reaction puzzled Emma. She felt like she didn't know him anymore. Disheartened, she shoved her hands in her apron pockets. She spotted something on the floor—a tag. She picked it up and flipped it. The words *Don Wagner* stared back at her.

APTOS Pharmaceuticals, Long Island

When his phone rang at one a.m. Angelus thought it was just another routine call. He was utterly wrong. His investigators were hysterical claiming that there was a creature in the woods. They had armed themselves and were urging him to call the police. He rushed to the scene hoping to settle things. After listening to their ordeal, he didn't know how to react. First, it was the crazy rabbit. Now, it was a monster. "That's absurd!" he exclaimed.

"It is, but we saw it!" said Joe.

"It was there, and then it vanished!" said David.

Angelus looked Joe in the eye. "Did it leave any tracks?"

"No tracks."

"What exactly did you see?"

Joe described the scene.

"Was Roumoult expecting this?" Joe asked when he finished.

Angelus raised his eyebrows and shook his head. "I believe his expectations were more...earthly."

NYPD Precinct

Tom and Joan wore chemical suits with masks and thick gloves. Tom rubbed his wrist. Once again, Joan offered to examine the cigar box. He shook his head. Ignoring his fatigue, he focused on the cigar boxes on the table in the containment room. The square, steel-walled room was designed to contain explosions and gas leaks. Tom pulled at the sticky material of the chemical suit and turned his attention to the box. The box was extraordinary, with a teal-colored freehand design printed on a silver background. Tom chose the middle cigar box, rotated it in his hands, and examined the bottom. No names, initials, or any sign of a manufacturer were visible. His fingers ran over the smooth surface. He couldn't see any hidden compartments. Tom took a long breath, his heart drumming as he set the box down on the desk and gradually opened it. He waited. Nothing happened. The box was lined with red velvet and housed five cigars. Pressing his fingers against the lid, Tom checked under the lining. He used his magnifying glass to study the interior. Then he slowly lifted a cigar.

Puff!

Tom stumbled back. Joan gasped. Next, they heard a click, and a small compartment sprung open on the left side of the box, followed by a soft hissing noise. A tiny green cloud rose into the air. The secret compartment remained open for a few seconds before closing.

"Wow," Joan muttered.

"Unconventional indeed!"

The drug testing took time, and Tom used it to talk to the patrol officers looking for Ms. Garrison. Still no word. He feared he might have lost her. The description of the fake Rachael Wagner was a dead end, and Alex had vanished into thin air. He went through the pictures of the crime scenes, making sure he hadn't missed anything. An officer popped by his office and handed over a folder.

Tom read the toxicology report. "Joan, they found traces of phencyclidine in the secret compartment of all cigar boxes."

She turned to face him. "The killer delivered the cigar boxes to each of the victims. They opened them and were exposed to a high dose of PCP, which lead to the hallucinations."

"And the hallucinations lead to the suicides," Tom picked up from where she left off.

"Then the killer targeted Marcus and the van drivers to cover their tracks."

This, Tom realized, was no ordinary killer. He was shrewd, but then why hire an assassin who liked to kill people in broad daylight?

"Are you ready?" Joan asked. "I found five shops that sell custom-designed cigar boxes."

Tom nodded resolutely. "Let's go!"

June 11, 2015

NYPD Precinct

Tom's wrist was better, but his mood was not. They'd spent the entire day scouting gift shops, asking the owners if they recognized the cigar box, Alex, Marcus, or any of the suicide victims. Their search revealed nothing. Tom hunted for traces of Ms. Garrison. There were none. If she'd taken a cab, it had been unregistered, or she'd paid in cash. At the end of the day, Joan went home, but Tom couldn't give up. He stayed back and wracked his brains for anything that might provide an answer.

11

The Lady Below

June 12, 2015

St. George Hospital

R oumoult remained silent throughout his sponge bath. The nurse changed his blankets and set his pillows. One side of his butt was sore from the injections, and he tried in vain to settle comfortably into the chair. His arm was still in a sling. Dr. Matthew slipped inside and greeted him.

"How are you feeling?"

"Fine," Roumoult grunted.

"The exact words I wanted to hear," Dr. Matthew replied, turning to the nurse, "What about the head dressing?"

"Not done yet," she responded.

"Ah, good. Perhaps I can have a look."

Roumoult's head stung less now. He waited patiently for the doctor to unravel the dressings, trying to ignore the feeling of his skin being pulled and suppress the anger bubbling inside of him.

"No showers for a couple of days," Dr. Matthew ordered. Then he added with a smile, "Looks like you're ready to head home."

Roumoult's anger vanished. "What?"

"Your father will be here to pick you up soon. Now listen. Your arm must remain in the sling, and you need to take your medicine on time. No work, no alcohol, and plenty of sleep and fluids. You're on some strong medications, so don't drive. I'll see you back here in two days. Understood?"

"Yes,"

The hospital paperwork took far too long, but finally, Roumoult climbed into the car with his father and Jim. Fred sat beside Roumoult, discussing a deal with a client over the phone.

"Dad, can I use your phone?" Roumoult asked after Fred had finished his call.

"Why?"

"I need to talk to Angelus."

"About?"

"The case. He hasn't given me an update."

"I told him not to,"

"What?" Roumoult spluttered.

"You just got out of hospital!" Fred responded.

"I just want to know what's going on."

"It's not your case anymore. I want you out."

"Dad, please."

Fred stood his ground. "I want you off the case, end of story. Do you understand?"

Cranston House

After Fred had left for work, Roumoult contacted Angelus, who provided him with no update on the case but did tell him the tale of the monster. He didn't know what to make of it. Roumoult told Alice to get him a new phone and asked about cases at the Firm. Same answer: "Everything is great, and you need to rest." Then, he got hold of William, who said the NYPD were working on it and told him to stay at home. Roumoult was stunned. His dad had gotten to everyone.

The NYPD detectives arrived at the door. He was a bit surprised. Roumoult invited them into the living room.

"We thought we should check on you. How are you feeling?" Tom asked.

"Better, thanks," said Roumoult. "Enough about me. How did that happen?" He gestured to Tom's injuries.

Tom told him about the explosion before moving on to tell him about the cigar boxes and the PCP.

"The three cigar boxes are identical, and each one had a secret compartment loaded with PCP. As soon as someone moves the first cigar, the gas is released," Joan said.

"Do you think the trigger mechanism is a part of a custom design?" asked Roumoult.

"I don't know," Joan replied. "There are no fingerprints or initials. We've been searching for the last two days. We identified shops that sell these cigar boxes and confiscated surveillance tapes from the shops to see if Alex or anyone related to the case bought a cigar box."

Roumoult nodded. "Great work!"

"How is everything going at APTOS? Any leads?" Joan asked.

Roumoult remembered Angelus' phone call and laughed. He described the events of the monster in the woods.

Tom's eyebrows slowly lifted, and a smile pulled at the corner of his lips. "You know what? Right now, I have my hands full of 'worldly' issues. I'll let you handle the monster."

Cranston House

Roumoult laid on the couch and stared at the ceiling, listening to the TV. His arm wasn't painful anymore. His mind wandered back to the case, and he reminded himself that the detectives were making progress. Fred was right; he'd done enough. He watched TV to kill time, and then he read the paper. But he couldn't shake the nagging feeling that he had missed something. He shut his eyes and let his mind flow. A thought popped into his head. He rushed upstairs and found Patrick Burns' number on his laptop.

"Hello," said a tired male voice.

"Mr. Burns, Cranston here."

"Oh, hello,"

"Is everything okay?"

"Yes, yes."

"Is this a bad time?"

"Oh, no. I'm surprised, that's all. I haven't heard from you since our last meeting."

"I have been busy, and your case is progressing. Alice will give you a complete update once it's over."

"Okay."

"What happened to the containers you found?"

"Dr. Wheeler told me they were contaminated and destroyed."

"How? Where?"

"We send them to a warehouse for processing and proper destruction following safety protocols."

"Do you know the batch number of the containers?"

"I do."

"Great, could you give it to me?"

"Let me find it."

Roumoult put the call on speaker and picked up a pen with his left hand. Patrick returned to the phone and read out the number. "Where is the warehouse?" Roumoult took down the address.

Morris Avenue, Bronx

Roumoult snuck out of the house while Charles was busy and insisted that Jim drove him to the Bronx. He called Angelus, who said he'd only come if it meant dragging him back to bed.

When they arrived, Jim parked the Audi, and Roumoult grabbed a torch and stepped out. It was a warm evening. A handful of people walked down Morris Avenue. Several cars passed as Roumoult marched toward the building. He felt his pulse rise and looked up and down the street.

"Is it important to find that box now?" Jim asked.

"If the killer thinks he's a suspect, he might get rid of it."

"What if we're too late?"

"Let's find out."

The streetlights cast a yellowish glare over the road. Soon, Roumoult and Jim came to a halt in front of a brick building with four large windows covered in muck. The front wall bore large cracks, and the white paint had withered away. Roumoult couldn't believe his eyes and rechecked the address. They were in the right place. Roumoult tried the door; it was locked. He made sure no one was watching them and reached for his set of skeleton keys.

"Are we breaking in?" Jim asked.

"Yep," Roumoult muttered, trying to insert the key with his left hand. The third key did the trick. The door opened with a loud crackling noise. The beam of light from his torch cut through the blackness. They stood in a small room with several fractures in the ceiling and large patches of light-green paint chipping away from the walls. He noted an old dusty table, a wooden chair, and three file cabinets.

"This was an office," Roumoult whispered.

"That closed a long time ago," Jim added, opening a drawer of an empty cabinet and peering inside.

Across the room, they were met with another door. Roumoult tried the doorknob; it was unlocked. He walked through and found himself in a large open space. He covered his nose with his shirt. A strong pungent smell dominated the air. He tried to breathe through his mouth. In the dull light, he noticed grime and cobwebs coating the windows and walls of the warehouse. The hall was at least ten feet high and approximately two hundred square meters. The windows were barred and bolted.

"Are you sure this is the place?" Jim asked.

"Yes," Roumoult insisted.

"Maybe your client had the wrong address."

Roumoult looked at the pile of boxes on both sides. He marched forward, flashing the torch into gaps between the stacks of boxes. He spotted a loading door and a forklift leaning against the wall. He walked in a circle, and he came to a stop beside Jim, near the door.

"Anything?" said Jim.

He shook his head and slowly walked towards a window. He peered through and noted a small, unkempt courtyard. Turning his attention to the boxes, he tried to find the batch number. He stood on his toes and tried to reach for a box. It was too big. Jim appeared and grabbed the box, placing it on the floor. "We open it?" he asked.

"Hold on." Roumoult angled the beam of light to shine on the label and read the batch number. It was different.

Jim opened the large cardboard box and threw out the packing material. It was filled with several white containers. Jim pried one of the containers open, revealing a white, strong-smelling powder. Roumoult gave the batch number to Jim, who quickly searched the rest of the warehouse. None of the boxes matched the number.

"Maybe this was a wild goose chase," Roumoult admitted.

Jim's mobile rang. "Angelus is here," said Jim as he headed for the door.

Standing alone in silence, Roumoult wondered if Dr. Wheeler was lying to Patrick Burns. With a heavy heart, he switched off the flashlight and strolled towards the door. He'd hoped to find the stolen van or the green containers. A low-pitched noise echoed through the warehouse. A ringing, a muffled bang. No, it was something else. It was a faint ringing sound. What Roumoult heard next melted his heart. It was more than a cry; it was the desperate sobbing of a woman who had lost all hope. Roumoult wanted to call out to her, but he didn't know if she would be able to hear him. He ran to the door, and it slammed shut. He froze. From the darkness, a familiar face emerged.

"You!" Roumoult spat venomously.

Alex stood in front of him with his hands on his hips.

"Well, well, well,"

Roumoult stepped back, determined not to show fear. Alex grabbed him and pushed him to the ground.

"What are you doing here?" said Alex.

Roumoult threw a punch with his left hand, but Alex caught it in mid-air and twisted his wrist. He yelled out.

"What are you doing here?" Alex repeated.

When Roumoult refused to answer, Alex struck his shoulder. Excruciating pain shot through his arm, and Roumoult yelled out in agony.

"Talk! Did you come for her?"

Roumoult felt dizzy. Alex made him stand and twisted his arm behind his back. "If you don't talk, I swear to God, I will break your arm."

Roumoult felt breathless, shaky. The door flew open with a tremendous bang. A powerful light shone on their faces. Roumoult shut his eyes. He thought he heard footsteps, but he wasn't sure.

"Get that bloody light off me!" Alex shouted. He grabbed Roumoult's neck, and Roumoult felt cold steel press against his temple. "Turn the light off or I will shoot him!" The light remained on their faces for a moment, then slowly moved toward the floor.

Roumoult's vision returned to normal. Angelus' six-foot frame emerged from the shadows, a gun in his hand.

"Let him go, and we will talk," said Angelus.

"No," Alex replied.

"Angelus, just shoot," Roumoult pleaded, trying futilely to free himself.

"Don't move. He won't shoot. I've got you." Alex laughed.

"Damn you," shouted Roumoult. He heard a dragging noise and looked up. Before he could yell out, dozens of boxes fell on them. A loud bang echoed. He lost his balance and fell hard. He opened his eyes, and pushed the boxes off him.

The lights flickered on.

"Are you okay?" Jim asked, giving Roumoult a hand.

"Yes," he said gratefully.

A loud pounding echoed. A large cloud of dust dispersed into the air. Alex stepped out from a cluster of boxes. His right arm was bleeding. Like a tiger,

Angelus sprang on him and pushed him to the ground. He gripped Alex's throat with both hands.

"Stop him," Roumoult told Jim.

"Me?"

"Angelus, stop! Angelus! He has a hostage. We have to find her! Stop now!"

Alex punched Angelus in the face, but Angelus did not relinquish his grip. Alex's face turned pale, covered with sweat, and his eyes bulged.

"Angelus, please," Roumoult shouted.

Unexpectedly, Angelus let go of Alex, grabbed his shirt, and pulled him to his feet. "This is for Ian," he spat and punched him in the face.

Alex fell with a loud thud.

Angelus gave Roumoult a frosty look.

Roumoult gulped. "Thank you."

Angelus glared at him. "What part of don't leave the house didn't you understand?"

The Bronx

Tom was more than happy to shove Alex into the back seat of the patrol car. He slammed the door shut and watched the car drive away. Now they had a murder weapon and a suspect, he could take the police detail off Roumoult. He nodded to Officer Jake, who had been following him since he left the hospital. Unfortunately, tonight he lost the Audi in traffic. Tom returned to the warehouse. Roumoult sat against the wall, holding his arm. His face was sweaty and pale. Angelus and Jim stood beside him.

"You should go home," said Tom.

"Jim got me my meds. I'll be fine. Find her. She's here."

Angelus grumbled. "She's not here!"

A dozen cops were searching every inch of the warehouse.

"Are you sure you heard her?" Tom asked patiently.

"Yes, I am," Roumoult insisted.

Tom waited for the men to finish their job. "How did you find him?" he asked, tilting his head.

"Trust me, I wasn't looking for him," Roumoult answered darkly.

"I had the entire squad looking for that maniac," Tom continued. "Apparently all I had to do was wait for you. You're like a magnet for trouble."

Angelus stepped forward; arms folded across his chest. "This happened because you didn't do your job."

"Cut it out!" Roumoult groaned. "It's no one's fault."

Angelus grumbled and left.

The police search was unsuccessful.

"Are you sure?" Tom asked almost pleadingly.

Roumoult got to his feet, nodding. "Yes, and it was quiet."

Tom told everyone to be silent. They walked to the center of the warehouse and waited. A siren sounded in the distance. Then they heard the subway speeding along the tracks. A few more minutes passed, and Tom strolled towards the south wall, Roumoult following. Tom put his ear against the wall and closed his eyes. There it was—a soft tapping, followed by a sharp dragging noise.

Tom stepped back from the wall and pointed to a thick pipe that disappeared into the ground.

"Someone's down there," Tom said.

Light from the warehouse streamed out of a window to the right of the pipe, reflecting over the dirty lawn. Tom unlocked the window, pushing it open with a heavy cracking noise. Behind it was a small courtyard with an old, rusty fence that was partially covered with tree branches. The grass was uncut and covered in cans and pieces of paper.

Tom climbed up and out of the window. Water splashed over his pants, and his feet froze. He looked down at the pothole. "Crap!" he shouted.

Joan laughed. For a moment, she perched on the window frame, then she jumped over the pothole.

"It's just not my day," Tom whined.

A door opened, and Roumoult entered the courtyard, flanked by police officers. They used their flashlights to search the grounds. Weeds poked up through the uneven ground, littered with empty and broken pots, and two wooden frames. Tom flashed the torch toward a patch of soil. He stepped closer, crouching down and brushed away dirt with his right hand.

"What is it?" Joan asked, kneeling beside him.

"Someone's moved the soil." He handed the torch to Joan and dug, not stopping until his fingers made contact with something cold and hard. Sweat dripped from his forehead as he removed the rest of the soil and uncovered a metallic manhole. He clambered back to his feet and pulled open the hatch. A narrow staircase disappeared into the dark void.

"Okay," said an officer.

"Ready?" another asked.

Tom nodded.

Two cops began to climb down the ladder. The detectives and Roumoult watched as the light from the flashlights descended.

"How deep is this?" asked Joan.

"My guess is ten to fifteen feet," Tom replied. He unbuttoned his cuffs and rolled up his sleeves. "Cranston, you're staying here."

Roumoult nodded. Peering over the pothole, he said, "The flashlights are gone."

Tom looked down and was met with complete darkness. He was about to call out when a bright light flickered to life.

"There's electricity down there?" said Joan.

"That's convenient," Roumoult said.

Gradually Tom, followed by Joan, climbed down the ladder. Roumoult watched them, worry creasing his brows. Tom felt anxious too. This case was volatile. He had survived a bomb blast, and Roumoult and the others had suffered a lot. Who knew what he was climbing down to next?

Two officers waited at the bottom of the ladder, which was the only sign that the cavern at the base of pothole was anything other than an ancient cave. The air was stale, full of the stench of garbage. A small light bulb hung from the roof, suspended from an electricity board by a loose cord. The pipeline clung to the wall, turning and disappearing behind a door.

One of the cops unlocked the door, and several flashlights pierced the darkness. In the gloom, Tom could make out a bed, a desk, a chair, a fan, and a small stove nestled in a corner. There was no one in sight. The lights turned on, and a second door grabbed his attention. He nudged it open. From the depth of darkness, he heard a sob. A feeble figure rocked in the furthest corner.

"Hello," Tom said, slowly walking forward.

The woman screamed. She pressed herself forcefully to the wall.

"NYPD," Tom said, putting his firearm away. "It's okay, you're safe. It's okay."

The cops cleared the area, and Tom stepped closer to the woman. Her head moved, and a pair of big eyes stared widely at him. He recognized her immediately. Those gray eyes, the heart-shaped face with its sharp chin. Her skin was pale and clammy, her eyes sunken, and her clothes torn and dirty. Her hair had frizzed and filled with dirt and cobwebs.

"Ms. Garrison," Tom breathed. "I'm so glad we found you."

She trembled but allowed Tom to approach her. When he made it to her side, she slumped in his arms, and he held her close, fighting back his own tears.

12

Family Secrets

June 13, 2015

APTOS Pharmaceuticals, Long Island

Another night in the wilderness bored Joe, but he wasn't one to leave a job unfinished, and this one wasn't done yet. He sat in the car with his eyes glued to the complex. He didn't need to watch the woods; that was David's job. A static humming captured his attention. Two steady headlights moved toward complex. Joe grabbed his binoculars and watched. The gates opened gradually, and a sedan drove toward the parking lot. Joe saw a lanky figure step out of the car. It moved toward the main gates.

"What are you doing here?" Joe wondered aloud.

Mark Weldon cast a furtive glance around him before unlocking the main door and disappearing into the building.

St. George Hospital

Emma left the ER quickly. Reaching for the tag in her pocket, she wondered if she was making the right decision. Tim and six other doctors were busy in the ER, and she'd already completed her hours for the week. For the first time in the last twenty-four hours, she had the opportunity to check if Wagner's body was hidden in the hospital. Don Wagner's remains weren't in the storage room, and the only other place they could be was the mortuary freezer.

Palms sweating and heart racing, she waited for the elevator to reach the basement. She stepped into the dim corridor and glanced back to make sure she was alone. She marched down the passage and then through a door and switched on the lights. A dozen clean metallic beds were crammed into a medium-size hall. Six cabinets stood on one side. Emma approached the small, square doors that housed remains scheduled for burial. Trembling, she opened the first compartment: empty. The second compartment smelled strongly of formaldehyde; a lifeless gray face lay still on the tray. Emma pushed the tray back into the chamber and shut the door, moving on to check the next compartment.

Emma wanted nothing more than to run away, but she couldn't abandon Wagner. If he wasn't in any of the compartments... Her eyes settled on the big door to her left.

The sign said *Authorized Personnel Only*. Behind that door were donated or unidentified remains that had been assigned to medical students for dissection. Dismissing her doubts and the fear rising in her throat, Emma stepped inside. The fog blinded her for a moment, and she quivered in the sudden cold. When the mist cleared, she saw several figures wrapped in plastic, lined up neatly in four rows. The bodies were stiff, naked, and crooked. Faces were frozen in grimaces. Wrapping her apron around her, Emma moved forward.

Emma leaned over one of the bodies and lightly pressed the plastic on the shoulder, reading the tag. It wasn't Wagner. She bowed and moved on. She bent over and checked the next corpse's ID. There wasn't one. The body was male and fit the dimensions of Wagner. Emma took a breath in and carefully unzipped the bag. The smell was almost too much, but she gently removed the cover, revealing a bald, skinny man with sunken eyeballs. A sense of sadness overtook her as she covered the body and urged herself to keep going.

NYPD Interrogation Room

Tom believed it was his duty to understand the reason behind the crime. He wasn't a psychologist, but understanding criminals often helped him catch them, and over the years, he'd developed a good knowledge of criminal behavior. Twice, Tom had saved convicted criminals and faced heavy criticism. The perpetrators had acted out of pure rage as a result of their circumstances, and while others believed they would never rehabilitate, Tom had encouraged the Judge to reconsider. But he had no mercy for Alex. He was a felon who expressed no sentiment or regret for his crimes. Still, Tom knew that Alex was a pawn, and he was determined to find the real culprit.

Alex's left eye followed Tom's every move. His right eye was black and swollen. His face was battered, his upper lip bruised, and his lungs wheezed as he struggled to breathe. The consequence of Angelus's anger and Tom wasn't surprised.

"Well, well, well, if it isn't Detective Nash."

"It's good to see you too," said Tom. "I like you in cuffs. I plan to keep you that way."

"I make my own plans."

"Is that so? You have a history of three assaults and drug trafficking charges. In 2003, you were a prime suspect in two murders, but the charges didn't stick because of lack of evidence. In 2005, you were caught red-handed for drug trafficking, smuggling, and assault. You were put away for ten years."

"Prison life was interesting."

"Looks like you want to go back there."

Alex said nothing.

Joan placed the pictures of the drivers on the table. "You killed two men in cold blood. Then you and Marcus shot an innocent passer-by, almost killed Mr. Cranston and Mr. Stanford, and kidnapped Ms. Garrison. I'm sure you murdered Marcus."

Alex shrugged indifferently.

"We know you're not working alone," Tom said, placing the bank statement on the table. "We found your accounts under a pseudo-name. Where did you get the money? You were bankrupt six months ago." Tom picked a black duffle bag up from near his feet and put it on the table.

Alex's eyes locked on the bag.

"I understand this belongs to you. Fifty thousand dollars in cash. We found it in your secret hideout under the warehouse."

"It seems you have enough to put me away," said Alex.

"Yes. But we need some answers. Who hired you?"

Alex's swollen lips spread into a broad smile. He said nothing.

"Why did you kill them?" asked Joan.

Alex peered at her through his left eye. "It's just a job."

Tom asked again, "Who hired you?"

Alex looked away.

"Who hired you?" Joan repeated.

Alex turned to face her. "I don't know. Never met the guy. I don't care."

"How does he reach you?" Joan enquired.

"Phone, email, text?" said Tom.

Alex did not respond.

"How did you get the job?" Tom pressed. "Answer me!"

Alex looked at him. "When he needs something done, he hangs a red flag on a light pole in front of my building."

"How did you find him?" asked Joan.

"I didn't. After I left prison, he found me."

"How?"

"One day, I got a package with a note, a deposit, and a job. I completed the task and got the rest of money."

"When did he contact you?"

"About eight months ago."

Joan sighed. "Do you recognize Mr. Garrison, Mr. Wagner, and Mr. Hawk?" She put their pictures on the table.

Alex remained apathetic.

"Did you kill them?" Tom asked.

"He tells me, I do it," said Alex. His lips peeled back, revealing a crooked smile.

"Twenty-five thousand dollars appeared in your account three days ago. What was the job?" Tom asked. "Who was your target?"

Alex looked away.

"It doesn't matter," said Tom when it was clear Alex had no intention of revealing anything more. "You lost, and the money is worthless to you. You are worthless to him."

Alex glared at Tom.

"You failed," Joan said leaning forward. "You failed at your job."

"You're a dead man walking," Tom added.

Alex looked from one to another and smiled wickedly. "I'll do my job," he said confidently.

"You can't, you are going to prison." Tom replied.

"I can. I'll kill Cranston for free."

Tom laughed out loud, but Joan got up from her seat, walked calmly around the table, and swung her fist. It collided with Alex's jaw.

"No!" Tom yelled.

Alex slid off his chair. Tom restrained Joan, whose fists flung wildly, trying to reach him.

"Ha, ha, ha!" Alex laughed, his one good eye glowering at them, laughter turned into a monstrous cackle. Two officers entered the interrogation room and grabbed Alex. He screamed at Tom, "You fucking bastard! Who do you think you are? Don't you know who I am? I'll kill you all! I'll kill you! All of you!"

The door banged shut and his shouts drowned out.

St. George Hospital

Roumoult was living a nightmare. As soon as Tom had found Ms. Garrison, he'd collapsed in exhaustion and pain. His memory was foggy. Dr. Mathew told him they'd brought him to the ER in an ambulance. When he opened his eyes, he was back in a hospital bed, loaded with antibiotics, painkillers, and fluids. The doctor was livid and told him he was lucky that his shoulder hadn't popped out of its socket again. Fred said nothing. He probably felt that Roumoult had suffered enough.

Roumoult woke up to find that he'd been transferred to the first floor. The strong smell of disinfectant irritated his nose. He sensed someone beside his bed. He turned his head and saw Emma.

"Hey."

"Hi," he said, glad to see her.

"I heard you were back. Are you okay?"

Roumoult replayed his ordeal with Alex in his head. She didn't need to know the details. "I was in a lot of pain," he said. "Thought it was best to come in."

"Are you feeling any better?"

"Yeah, I am." He waited for her to say something, but she just looked at her toes. "Are you okay?"

Emma's face constricted. "I don't know what to do. I'm...confused."

"About what?"

"I shouldn't bother you with it. You're supposed to be resting," she said anxiously.

"You're not bothering me. Tell me what happened."

"I don't know what to do," Emma repeated.

"About?"

Emma cast a glance around, checking that there was no one else nearby. "All right, I'll tell you, but you have to promise not to make a scene."

Roumoult nodded.

"I found Don Wagner's body tag."

"What!?"

"Shh..."

"You found the body tag? Did you find the body?" Roumoult choked.

She shook her head.

"How? When?"

Emma told him about searching for the body, rifling through drawers, unzipping body bags. "Emma," Roumoult rubbed at his face. "Why did you put yourself in unnecessary danger? You should have called the police."

"I-I couldn't," Emma choked.

"Why not? Do you realize what this means? Someone in this hospital is stealing evidence. Hell, it might be the murderer!"

Emma fell silent.

"Did you find Wagner?" Roumoult pressed.

Emma shook her head with dismay.

"And you don't know who dropped the tag?"

"No."

Roumoult watched Emma's face solely and couldn't shake the feeling that she was hiding something. "Emma, please don't lie to me."

"I-I don't think he had anything to do with it."

"You don't know that."

"But—"

"Emma, you are risking—"

"He's harmless!"

"You could be wrong!" Roumoult spluttered, trying hard to keep his voice from shouting.

"I knew it! I knew this was how you'd react. I should have never told you!"

"Emma, I didn't mean to..." It was no use. She turned on her heel and marched out the door.

St. George Hospital

Jenny Garrison sat on a chair, staring at the wall. Bruises covered her neck and face, but she looked much better.

"Hello, Ms. Garrison. How are you?" Tom asked, softly closing the door behind him as he entered the room. He felt blood rush to his face.

"I'm well, thanks to you," she replied.

"I can't take all the credit," said Tom. He and Joan settled into the chairs by Jenny's bed. "Do you have everything you need?"

The lady nodded.

"Once you are released, we would like to keep you in a safe house. I am sorry this is an active investigation and we can't let you return to London yet."

Ms. Garrison looked disappointed.

Tom leaned forward, "We will try to wrap this up quickly so that you can get on with your life."

"That's the thing. How?"

"Well, you begin with talking about it. I can help you out if you like." He offered.

Their eyes met.

"Are you ready to talk with us?" Joan asked changing the topic.

Jenny's eyes dropped to her hands, which fumbled with loose threads in her blanket. She nodded slowly. "I don't know how much I can help, but I'll try my best." She drew in a long, steadying breath. "I live in London, and I work at a finance company as a consultant. I'd been planning to visit New York for some time; I wanted to see my nieces. The week that Clark died, he called me. That was odd. He never called. He told me not to come to New York, but he wouldn't explain why. I got frustrated and hung up on him. Two days later, he was dead. Oh, I felt miserable! I flew to New York immediately. I'd just arrived at the apartment when the phone rang, and I heard that horrible voice on the other end of the line. I was terrified! It rang again, and I let it go to the answering machine. There it was again: the threat, the creepy voice, and the howl. I left and took a taxi to the police station. Suddenly, I started to feel dizzy and dozed off." Jenny paused. "I woke up in the dark room and realized that he'd kidnapped me."

"Alex," Tom clarified.

"Yes, Alex. As soon as I could talk, he started harassing me, threatening to kill me. And every night, he would come in and make threats." Jenny gulped. "He thought I knew something about Clark."

"Did you?" asked Joan.

"No. We didn't talk much."

"Why not?"

Jenny shrugged. "We just didn't."

"Jenny, why did you and Clark stop talking?" Tom asked.

Blood drained from Jenny's face, and in her white hospital gown, she looked like a ghost. "Because Clark was... He was... Let's just say, I'm not surprised he knew Alex."

"Jenny, what happened between you and Clark?" Tom pressed.

"It doesn't matter now."

"It might," said Joan gently.

Jenny looked between them and then cast her gaze back down to her fumbling fingers. "If you insist. Ten years ago, I lived Minnesota with my brother. My parents died when I was ten; our aunt took care of us for a while, but then she fell ill. By the time I turned sixteen, I was completely depended on my brother. I was always aware of his short temper and how overbearing he could be, but it wasn't until I started dating that I discovered my brother's true possessiveness. I was finishing college and in love with Timmy Carter. Cute guy, a mechanic, and an orphan. Clark didn't like him and kept interfering in our relationship. He was always taunting, passing comments, and kept telling me I was worthless, and Timmy would get tired and dump me. It went on for a year. The day I graduated, Timmy proposed, and I said yes. I was on top of the world, and I shared my joy with my brother." Jenny swallowed thickly. "And he just turned into this jealous, screaming monster. It is heartbreaking when your only family, someone you trust, treats you that way."

"What did he say?"

Jenny looked at Tom. "He called me a whore, slapped me and then shoved me to the floor. He said if I married Timmy, he'd kill him."

Tom's heart sank.

"I wept for hours. I begged him to let me go. To leave me alone. But he was adamant and ruthless. That night, I planned to run away with my fiancé. Before dawn, I packed my bags and left home to meet him at the bus stop. An hour passed, and he never showed. I went to his house, and the front door was locked. He wasn't at the garage, and none of his friends had seen him. After a week, his body washed up on the riverbank. They told me he drowned. The police thought he'd gotten drunk, fallen into the river, and died. Timmy wasn't a heavy drinker. I know he didn't fall into the river. He was pushed. Detective Tom, I hated my brother because I think he killed my fiancé."

"How do you know?"

"Since the day Timmy disappeared, Clark had that look in his eye, that crazy look, just like Alex. He was overjoyed and kept telling me I had no choice but to live with him for the rest of my life. I would be his slave, his servant, and he would never let me go. There was no point in arguing with him; he was mad. I booked a ticket to Washington, and the next day, I left without a word to live with my friend. I survived there for three weeks. It was horrible. The threats, the calls... My friend began to worry and wanted to report Clark to the police. I didn't want him in my life, so I pulled out all my funds, borrowed money from my friends, and traveled to Europe. I spent a year traveling before I settled in London. Timmy's death still bothered me. A year later, when I had enough savings, I hired a private detective who consulted a medical examiner. It wasn't helpful. The medical examiner confirmed the death was by drowning and that it was possible someone had pushed him, but there was no evidence of foul play. I had to let it go. A few years passed, and Clark gambled away our parents' and my aunt's money. The only reason he stopped gambling was because he met Amanda, and she got pregnant with their first child. He married her and got a job in a filtration company. Things have been normal since then."

"I'm sorry," Tom said kindly.

Jenny smiled. "Detective, I don't know how this helps you. Alex was afraid I knew something. He worried that Clark had told me a dark secret. But he hadn't. He just didn't want me to come to New York."

June 14. 2015

Cranston House

Once again, Roumoult found himself in the car heading home from the hospital. Fred hadn't said a word, and that meant trouble. Roumoult tried to speak to his father; it was no use. Fred dropped Roumoult at home and left without a word, leaving the house quiet. Roumoult decided not to pull any more stunts; he'd focus on work. But working with his left hand wasn't easy, and his mind was clouded with thoughts of the case, Fred, and Emma. When he came downstairs for lunch with Charles, Roumoult spotted a tall, muscular man in a suit standing on the lawn.

"Charles! There's a man outside!"

"Oh, yeah," Charles said casually. "That's the bodyguard."

Roumoult was astonished. "For me?"

"Yes. To keep you in the house and keep Alex out. There are two more, but I don't know where they are right now."

"Is that really necessary?"

Charles eyed him. "Given last night's events, yes, I think it is!"

Roumoult felt like a prisoner in his own home, and it was entirely his own doing. As the day progressed, he grew weary. When Tom called in the evening, Roumoult was thankful for the distraction.

"Back home, I see? How are you?" said Tom.

"Home is much better than the hospital. I'm doing better."

"I think you should rest."

Roumoult ignored him. "Did we find out who bought the cigar boxes?"

"Not yet," said Tom. "On the upside, we'll have the last six weeks of surveillance footage from these gift shops soon. Let's see what happens."

Roumoult couldn't help but think that it was a long shot. "Did you get anything out of Alex?"

"He's an ass."

"What happened?"

Tom explained what had happened in the interview.

"Well, that's not surprising," said Roumoult. "Did you find anything else, other than the money?"

"Alex was carrying coins, cash, keys, a mobile phone, a compass with a magnifying glass, and a blank Bible."

"A blank Bible?"

"A book with freehand design and the words *Holy Bible* printed on the cover. But all the pages were blank. I don't understand. Alex isn't religious, so why carry it?"

"I guess it means something to him." Roumoult shrugged.

"Nothing means more to Alex than money."

"Could you take a picture and send it over?"

After he'd hung up on Tom and spoken briefly with Alice, Roumoult was worn out. By the time he got to Tom's email, he'd had enough. He wearily examined the book cover in the photo, decorated with a sparkling, golden freehand design on a black background. It could wait until tomorrow. Roumoult ate a quick dinner, took his meds and then slept.

H.G Ahedi

13

There Are No Coincidences

June 15, 2015

Cranston House

R oumoult couldn't stop thinking about the pocket bible and its intricate cover design. He watched the pacing bodyguard through the window as he poured himself a cup of coffee. Then turned his attention to the arching, swirling design of the tablecloth against the wooden surface of the dining table.

"What are you thinking?" asked Fred.

"No, nothing."

"It's something."

"Just thinking about patterns. Do they mean anything?"

Fred looked thoughtful. "Depends."

Suddenly, Roumoult had a thought.

"Oh, I know that look," said Fred.

"See you later Dad." Roumoult stood, poured out the rest of his coffee, and hurried upstairs.

He turned on his laptop and opened the picture of the book cover. He magnified and studied it. His eyes widened, and his jaw dropped.

"Wow!" he whispered.

He grabbed a pen and wrote as quickly as he could. When he was done, he had a ten-digit number. He called Tom.

"Good morning Cranston."

"Hi, Tom. I might have something for you."

"Oh?"

"The cover design has hidden numbers in it," said Roumoult. "I'm marking the outline and sending it to you."

"How many digits?" asked Tom?

"Ten."

"Bank accounts?"

"I think so."

"Only one?"

Roumoult froze. He hadn't thought of that. "Wait," he said. He squinted and made out the twisting patterns of thirty other numbers. Four account numbers.

"Roumoult?" said Tom after several minutes of silence.

"Tom, I have four account numbers. Can you check them?"

"Wow! Of course, email them through," Tom said. "I'll see what I can do."

"These could lead us to Alex's boss," Roumoult suggested.

"Maybe, let's see. How did you know?"

"It was you. You gave me the hint: the money. The book kept bothering me. Why carry a blank one?

It's got to be important. Plus, I asked myself, why would Alex carry around a compass? I'm sure he wasn't planning to sail. He didn't need the compass, but he needed the magnifying glass attached to it."

"To read the numbers," said Tom.

"Exactly."

NYPD Precinct

Tom couldn't control his excitement. The banks had called him back and provided him with all the information he needed including the video surveillance tapes. Alex had opened these four accounts six months ago under false names and social security numbers. For the first two months, the accounts remained inactive, but in the third month, Alex had deposited twenty-five thousand dollars in one account, which was withdrawn again within forty-eight hours. Tom put the statements aside and sunk into his chair beside Joan, who was checking that it was Alex who'd deposited the money.

"Got it," Joan said, playing the video clip. "What time was the first deposit made?"

Tom consulted the bank record. "Ah, 11:15 a.m. on March 31, 2015." Tom waited.

Joan forwarded the clip and stopped at 11:10 a.m. Both detectives stared at the monitor.

"There!" Joan pointed to the man entering the bank.

Tom smiled. "It's Alex, I knew it!"

They watched the next ten minutes of footage, which showed Alex depositing the money.

"Okay. Then what happened?" asked Tom.

"Two days later, someone withdrew the cash at 2 p.m."

Joan found the video clip for April 2, 2015 and fast-forwarded, stopping at 1:50 p.m. People could be seen walking in and out of the bank; children played near the exit. Men and women sat on benches, waiting. The cashiers were busy; the bell chimed. "Oh my God!" Joan cried out, hitting pause on the video.

"I don't believe this!" said Tom. Clark Garrison appeared clearly on the screen. "Play the rest of it." Garrison withdrew the money before leaving the bank.

Joan paused the video and turned to look at her partner. "The money, it's the connection between Garrison, Wagner, and Hawk!"

Tom got to his feet. "Four accounts allocated to four people. Alex makes the deposits, a payment. They all work for the same man!"

"This is incredible."

"How much did Garrison earn?"

Joan checked. "There were three deposits of twenty-five thousand, five thousand, and twenty thousand dollars."

"Fifty thousand dollars? His wife thinks they have no money!"

"Mr. Garrison was a man of secrets," said Joan.

"The other accounts could be for Wagner and Hawk."

"Let's check."

Tom waited for Joan to find the next clip and hit play. They watched with keen interest. Tom almost jumped out of his chair when he saw Hawk enter the bank. His excitement grew as Hawk withdrew fifty thousand dollars. "Any other activity?" he asked hopefully.

"No, just one deposit and withdrawal."

"Well, if we're on the right track, the third bank account was Wagner's. Let's see if Alex makes the deposit and Wagner withdraws it."

Tom and Joan skipped through video after video, and as the footage progressed, Tom's theory withstood. Alex had arrived at the bank and made the deposit. The money had remained in the account for a week, and then Don Wagner had shown up and withdrawn the money.

"Okay, let's look at the fourth bank account," said Joan.

Tom pulled out the statement. "This is odd."

"What?"

"Alex put money in the fourth bank account last week; it hasn't been withdrawn yet. Can you check it online?"

Joan's fingers danced across the keyboard. "The money is still there," she confirmed. "So, the fourth account belongs to a fourth person who hasn't withdrawn it yet. Why?"

"Maybe the job's not complete," Tom proposed.

"Or he hasn't had an opportunity."

"Call the bank; ask them to flag this account. When this guy comes to get his money, we'll be waiting!" Tom felt excitement pulsing through his body. "We have to tell Roumoult!"

The Golden Goose, Lower Manhattan

Roumoult was happy with his day. His shoulder pain was almost gone. Even the case was coming together. He was eager to help Tom crack this case and speaking to his father lifted his mood. He longed to speak to Emma and ask if she had found Wagner's remains. He couldn't call her—what if she was still mad?

After sunset, William called Roumoult and suggested they go out for dinner. Roumoult spoke to his father, who allowed him to leave the house on one condition.

William glared at the man in the suit. "So now you have a driver and a bodyguard?"

Roumoult didn't respond. They sat at a corner table in the large dining hall. The restaurant was on the ground floor of a five-star hotel, and tonight it was quieter than usual. Soft jazz music filled the air. The lights were dim, and the French windows offered a spectacular view of the city.

"How's the case going?" William asked.

"It's still a puzzle."

"Any ideas?"

"A few," said Roumoult.

"Tell me."

"William," Roumoult started. The bell above the restaurant door chimed, and Tom and Joan walked in. "What the hell are they doing here?" said Roumoult.

"Joan texted me and I told her where I was," William explained.

Roumoult rolled his eyes.

Tom walked over to the table. "Would it kill you to invite me for dinner?" he said.

Roumoult eyes drifted past Tom to where his guard stood, muscles tense. "It's okay," said he. "These are NYPD detectives."

"What's going on?" said Tom, turning to eye the guard.

"Is that a bodyguard?" Joan asked.

"Dad's idea."

Tom didn't comment and pulled up a chair beside Roumoult, while Joan squeezed in between William and Tom.

"Roumoult, guess what," said Tom. "The numbers were a major clue. Alex opened the bank accounts to pay the victims." Tom explained what they'd discovered about the accounts. "This case finally makes sense."

"If they were working for Alex, why did he kill them? If he killed them," said Roumoult.

"Well, he claims he did," Tom replied.

"But you don't know. Alex is not a discreet killer, and the murders of Wagner, Hawk, and Garrison were well-planned."

"My guess is Alex was the middleman used to hire the three victims. When the job was done, he delivered the cigar boxes that lead to their deaths," Tom suggested.

"There are still so many unexplained aspects. The werewolf, the boxes in the van, Patrick Burns, and the stolen bodies," William pointed out.

"Why kidnap Ms. Garrison?" Joan added.

"I don't know about werewolves, but maybe Alex and his team used the two drivers to steal something from APTOS and Patrick saw them," said Tom. "The stolen bodies may have nothing to do with this case. As for Ms. Garrison? Alex must have taken her under orders from his boss."

Both William and Joan fell silent.

Roumoult picked up the butter knife and began playing with it as he visualized the puzzle unraveling in front of his eyes. He wasn't paying much attention to Tom.

"What do you think, Roumoult?" Joan asked unexpectedly.

"Sounds like a reasonable theory,"

"Oh, I know that tone," said William.

"Go on, what do you think, Roumoult?" asked Tom.

"Tom, you have a good theory," Roumoult said slowly.

"I know I'm right, and you can't admit it, can you?"

Roumoult gritted his teeth. "What if you're right and wrong?"

Tom crossed his arms. "Go on."

Roumoult caught sight of a chessboard on one of the other tables. "Excuse me," he said, leaving the table to get it. He carried the chessboard back over and dropped it onto the table. Roumoult placed the black king on the left side of the board. "Let's say that this chessboard is our case. The black king is Alex's employer, and Alex is the black knight." He placed the black knight beside the king. "This black knight does all his boss's dirty work, including handling his money, and killing and kidnapping people." Roumoult picked up three black pawns. "Imagine these three pawns are Garrison, Hawk, and Wagner. Now, let's imagine that there is another king, and he hates the black king." He placed the white king opposite to the black king. "The white king also has a knight." Roumoult put a knight next to the white king. "We don't know his identity, but let's assume he's like Alex, only more cunning and elusive. Now, let's say he has two people working for him." He placed the pawns on the board.

"The van drivers," said William.

"Right," said Roumoult. "The black king has an agenda, a mission. He has Alex and these three men working for him. This could be a gang, who knows how big. They might be involved in drugs, trafficking, assassinations..." He paused. "Now, let's say the white king orders his knight to kill the black king's pawns, and he tells him to make the murders untraceable." Roumoult knocked down the three black pawns one by one. "The black king finds out and gets angry. He needed his pawns; they were important for his project. In revenge, he sends Alex, his knight, to kill the white king's pawns, and Alex executes the van drivers." Roumoult knocked down the white pawns. "Now, the black king doesn't want to take any chances, so he tells Alex to kidnap Ms. Garrison," Roumoult reached for a bishop to represent her, "to find out what she knows. We should remember, the white king has his own plans. The unknown shipments in the middle of the night, the dismissal of Patrick Burns when he suspected something, and the use of PCP. Let's not forget the werewolves and phone messages."

William eyed Roumoult. "You said the black king's team was a gang. Why?"

"The way they operate," Roumoult answered. "The money and the execution. Look who they hired."

"What about the white king's team?" Joan asked.

"They're smarter, more strategic, and more dangerous. The black king will make a mistake, and we'll catch him. But the white king is shrewd."

They sat in silence. Soft music played in the background. Roumoult looked at his friends. "Guys, it's just a theory. We need proof."

Tom glowered at him.

"But it's the first theory that makes complete sense!" Joan said.

"Oh, you always have to be right! Don't you?" Tom fumed.

Joan and William exchanged mischievous glances.

"You asked for it!" said Roumoult.

14

Hunter

June 16, 2015

NYPD Interrogation Room

Tom sat with Joan. Today, Alex looked more human. He could open his swollen right eye partially, and the bandages around his head were less obtrusive. Tom felt his pulse quicken. This was the part of his job he enjoyed most, laying the trap and catching his prey.

"Where's the van?" Tom asked, killing the silence in the room.

Alex brows knitted together.

"The van you took after murdering the drivers," Tom clarified. "Where is it?"

Alex didn't open his mouth.

"This guy you're protecting. Your boss? He's using you to do his dirty work. You are just another tool. You go away, and he will find another one."

Alex sat still and silent.

"You say you killed Wagner, Hawk, Garrison, and Marcus Walt," said Joan, trying a different angle.

"Yeah, don't forget the van drivers," Alex replied proudly.

"Okay. How did you kill Wagner?"

"I slit his throat."

"You didn't kill him, did you?" said Joan.

"I did," Alex insisted.

"No, you were on the same team," Joan said.

"What were you planning?" Tom asked.

Alex gave the detectives a cold grin. "I don't have to tell you anything."

Joan got up. "Oh, you will. You'll tell us everything."

Alex's face set, his jaw jutting out. "You can threaten me, torture me. You will fail!"

Tom smirked and walked to the corner of the room. "While you've been rotting in your cell, my boys have been searching your secret hiding place with a comb. We found something. Something you wanted to bury so deep that no one would ever even realize it was hidden." Tom opened an envelope and tilted it. A Blackberry phone fell out onto the table with a clunk. Its screen was cracked, and its keyboard was badly dented, as if crushed by a hammer. "I wonder why you destroyed it. We had our tech people examine it and guess what we uncovered? Text messages, lots of them."

"You lied to us," Joan said, coming forward. "You were in direct contact with your boss."

"We extracted dozens of texts, even ones you'd deleted," Tom stated. "He told you to take out the van drivers and Marcus, transfer the money, and kidnap Ms. Garrison."

Joan moved to Tom's side. "I wonder, what makes a man hit his phone with a mallet?"

"Something he fears..." said Tom, "or someone." He placed his mobile on the table beside Alex's. "We found a message hidden in your phone, a voice mail. From the devil himself," He pressed the start button on the recording.

"It's your turn..." said the intense mechanical voice they'd heard in Ms. Garrison's apartment. "You have lived long enough, and you will die a coward, like your friends. I'll hunt you, and soon I will find him. I will find you and send you straight to hell!" A howl sounded.

Alex's face paled. His lips pressed into a thin line.

"He took the words right out my mouth," Tom said.

"You didn't want to hear that voice again, did you?" asked Joan. "Every day, you got the same message. We found at least fifty of them on your phone. He scared you to death."

"You didn't want to live Wagner, Hawk, and Garrison's nightmare," Tom continued. "Their past haunted them. Wagner couldn't look at himself in the mirror, because he saw the devil in himself, so he smashed every mirror in his apartment. But he still couldn't take it, so he shot himself!"

"Hawk went mad and killed himself in his penthouse. Garrison was probably the toughest man on your team. But this guy got to him. At first, he scraped and scratched himself until his skin bled. It maddened him until he stabbed himself to death," Joan said.

"He haunts you, doesn't he?" Tom leaned in close to Alex's face. "He's after you. You are next on his list. Being in custody is the only thing keeping you alive and sane."

"You're safe here, for now," Joan added.

"So long as we don't leave your cell open," Tom said. "You have a chance. Help us. This is a one-time offer. Tell us everything, and we will protect you. If you help us, hell, I will speak to the D.A. But it's your choice."

The room fell silent. An entire minute passed.

Joan looked at Tom. "The man has made his choice."

Tom grimaced and closed the file.

"Wait, stop!" Alex shouted; his voice strangled. "Stop! Okay, fine!" Alex yelled. "I'll tell you what I know!"

Tom felt a wave of excitement wash over him.

"Where is the van?" Joan asked.

"I took it to 24th Westchester Avenue in the Bronx and left it there unlocked."

"What was in the van?"

"Some boxes. Apophis thought it was important."

"Apophis?" asked Tom.

"That's what he calls himself," Alex replied. "It's the name of an Egyptian God."

"He thinks he's God?" Tom said.

"No!" said Alex. "It's a handle. The Apophis symbolizes terror, darkness, and death."

Tom made a note of it in the file.

"Did you deliver the cigar boxes to Wagner, Hawk, or Garrison's houses?" Joan asked.

"No. I'm no delivery guy."

"Did you kill Marcus?"

"I had to," Alex admitted. "He had no control over his mouth or his pocket. Apophis wanted him out."

"You didn't have to kill him," said Joan.

Alex shrugged his shoulders.

"Why did you blow up the apartment?" Tom asked.

"Apophis likes to be dramatic."

"How many people are on your team?" Joan countered.

"I knew of Marcus, Wagner, Hawk, and Garrison. That's it."

"Then why did you open a fourth account?" said Tom.

"For a new team member. I don't know his name. I opened the account and deposited the money."

"There is still money in it."

Alex shrugged. "That means he didn't finish the job."

"Why hire the fourth man?" said Joan.

"No idea."

"Why kidnap Ms. Garrison?" said Tom.

"Apophis thought she knew something. Garrison called her before he died, and Apophis wanted to find out why."

"What did she say?" Joan asked.

Alex shook his head. "She kept saying Garrison didn't want her to come to New York."

"But you didn't believe her," Tom said.

"The Apophis thought Garrison spilled his guts, but he was wrong."

"Then why not let her go?"

"It wasn't in my hands."

"Why did you shoot drivers of the white van?"

"They were two-timers."

Tom raised his eyebrows.

"They were freelancers," Alex explained. "They worked for anyone who paid them. I knew, and I understood. It's a job. We had a few deals last year. I trusted them. I knew they'd stolen the bodies and the boxes from that company for another party. I didn't care. But Reid sold us out. He blabbed about Wagner, Hawk, and Garrison's project involving the Apophis. He was an informer. Apophis got angry and ordered me to get rid of them and hijack the van."

"Why did they steal the bodies?" Tom asked.

"Beats me."

"What were you doing at the warehouse?"

Alex cursed under his breath. "It's a perfect hiding place. Reid and Jacob stacked their goods in that warehouse from time to time. I thought I could hide until my trail ran cold."

"Okay, now the ultimate question," said Tom. "What's is the Apophis planning?"

"I have no idea, man!" said Alex. "I was just doing a job. Get me a good deal, and I'll testify."

NYPD Precinct

Tom willingly completed the paperwork for Alex's transfer. The district attorney wasn't happy about indulging a criminal. It took twenty minutes for Tom to convince him that he planned to use Alex to catch the murderer. Reluctantly, the district attorney agreed. He pressed the enter button on the keyboard and closed the file. Tom leaned back in his armchair, rocking slightly. He wondered if he should call his former partner, John. This case was getting bigger and more interesting by the day.

Cranston House

Sitting on his balcony, Roumoult sipped his coffee. He touched his right arm—still in a sling, no more pain. Today he was supposed to go to the hospital and meet Dr. Mathew. Work was far from his mind; he'd started enjoying his time off. The more time he spent on his own, the more he thought about Emma. He had to get in touch with her soon. Fred joined him.

"Hey Dad."

"Good morning," Fred said, making himself comfortable in the other chair. "It's a beautiful day." He looked up from his newspaper. "I should take Evelyn out for lunch."

"Good idea."

"What's bothering you, besides the case?"

"Nothing."

"Don't lie to me," Fred said.

Roumoult sighed. "Have you ever said something and regretted it?"

"This must be my lucky day. Finally, my son asks me a sensible question."

"You're the only person I can ask. William falls for every woman he looks at; I can't take his advice. And I can't speak to Angelus about things like this. Alice and Jack..."

"Should stop beating around the bush," Fred completed his sentence.

Roumoult looked at him in surprise.

"I'm not blind. You are my only son, and your friends are like my children. Alice likes Jack, and vice versa, and you have feelings for Emma."

"How do you know?"

Fred laughed. "Because you have never asked me for relationship advice. But you're doing it now means that she's important to you. For her sake and yours, just go talk to her."

"Dad, don't put ideas in my head."

"I already did."

NYPD Precinct

Tom sent Ms. Garrison to a safe house. He tried to contact John, but his phone was unreachable. Following his instincts and Roumoult's theory, Tom figured that Dr. Wheeler could be the white knight. He pulled up Wheeler's file; he had no criminal background. He was an excellent researcher and a good manager. Over the course of his career, he'd won two best scientist awards and three leadership awards. But that was before his wife's death. In the last two years, his fame had faded, and so had his contributions to research. Dr. Wheeler had developed most of the products manufactured and sold by AP-TOS. Tom knew it could be a dead end, but he felt

talking with Wheeler was necessary. He called AP-
TOS and found out that the doctor was away on business.

In the afternoon, Joan went for lunch with William, and Tom spent the time scrutinizing the surveillance videos from the gift shops. He couldn't help
but wonder about Joan and William. He was happy
for them, and he felt envious. He was on his own,
alone.

In the video, a bell rang, and Tom watched a
customer enter the shop. He browsed for a few
minutes, picking up items and putting them back,
then leaving without buying anything. All the clips
were similar. Tom thought about the task at hand.
He didn't even know when the killer had bought the
cigar boxes, and his chances of finding the footage
were getting slimmer.

Cranston Law Firm

Roumoult came to work but within an hour wondered if he had made the right choice. Fatigue made
it difficult for Roumoult to complete the brief Alice
needed done. Alice kept reminding him that Fred and
the board members of Cranston Enterprises were
waiting for it. Fred planned to drop by later to sign
off on it. It was too much. Roumoult struggled to con-
centrate, thoughts of Emma clouded his mind.
"Think," he told himself, trying hard to focus.

St. George Hospital

Don Wagner's body was still missing, and Emma felt responsible. Every spare moment she got, she searched the hospital, including the patient rooms. She stretched her legs, thinking she should ask for Roumoult's help. Would he understand? She didn't want to put Tim in danger. She continued her work, absentmindedly bandaging a teenage boy's arm. Her phone vibrated. She checked her messages and gave a bitter laugh.

"What does he want?" she muttered skeptically.

NYPD Holding Cells

Alex wiped the sweat off his forehead. Sunshine streamed through a narrow window near the ceiling, casting a dim yellowish light. A tired ventilator coughed out dusty puffs of cold air. Alex sat in his cell alone, tired and cursing his decision to stay in New York. He hadn't realized he was being shadowed until he received those messages. Changing his mobile number had given him peace for a while, but then the threats began again. He wasn't the only one, but when the other victims died within forty-eight hours of each other, he knew he was next.

A guard walked past Alex's cell; his face barely visible in the dim light. Alex glanced at the wall clock. It was ten to four in the afternoon. He clenched his fist. He'd never failed. Triumph was his middle name. But this unseen hunter and Angelus had gotten him. How could he let it happen? How could they have beaten him? Alex clenched his teeth.

"If I ever get the chance," he told himself, "I'll kill them." The deal was just an excuse, something to buy him time. He knew they would transfer him, and he knew they needed him to testify. They didn't know the Apophis needed him, that he'd get him out. Then he'd finish the job he started. He wouldn't hide anymore. He would become the hunter.

A door banged shut and hurried footsteps crashed down the hall. Alex sat up straight. Slowly getting off the bed, he came to stand at the corner of his cell. The guard had vanished. The steps grew louder. Alex moved back. He was here. He was here for him. The detectives had promised to protect him. Alex's heart raced. He waved frantically at the camera, hoping to warn the cops. The lights flickered out. Alex felt his anger vanish and all he wanted was to stay alive. He stood against the wall, hiding in the darkness. Hardly breathing, he prayed, hoping to be left alone. The footsteps stopped. Silence returned.

Alex shook his head, cursing himself for overreacting. "It must be another guard." He poured himself a glass of water and turned around. Breath left him. His mouth opened, and the glass dropped from his hands, and shattering into pieces. The ventilation fan rattling above him halted. Alex sized the faceless figure. It had to be at least six feet tall. A set of large lifeless eyes stared at him. Dark. Steady.

The clock on the wall chimed once at four p.m.

"Who are you?" Alex demanded.

"Your worst nightmare." The tone of the voice was familiar.

The clock chimed twice.

"Guard! Guard!" Alex yelled.

The clock chimed three times.

"I've enjoyed our little game, and now it's time for the final act," said the figure.

The clock chimed for the last time.

"Goodbye."

Whoosh! Green gas rushed into the cell. Alex yelled at the top of his lungs. "Help! Help! Anyone?" But no one came, and the gas engulfed him.

NYPD Precinct

A clap of thunder sent a shudder through the building. Tom's chair tremored, and he slid out of it, falling flat on his face. Joan screamed as a cabinet above her tumbled. She rolled away just in time to avoid being crushed. The tremor died out.

"What the hell was that?" Tom asked.

"Earthquake?"

Fire alarms blared. Water gushed from the ceiling.

"We've got to get out," said Tom.

Cops rushed down the stairs. The Captain ran with the fire warden.

"What happened?" Tom asked.

"There was a blast on the fourth floor. Evacuate now!"

Tom followed Joan downstairs and left the building through the emergency exit. They gathered half a block away from the building. Smoke drifted out of the windows of the fourth level. Loud sirens filled the vicinity. The fire brigade rushed into the street and came to a screeching halt. A shadow swooped overhead: a chopper. The word was out. Tom could already picture the headline of tomorrow's newspaper: *Bomb at the NYPD Precinct*. "Looks like everyone is out," he said noticing the fire brigade closing the main entrance.

"Oh, no," cried Joan. "Not everyone."

Tom heart sunk.

St. George Hospital

Somehow Roumoult finished the brief and reluctantly went to the hospital. He felt instead of calling he should go and speak with Emma. First, he saw Dr. Mathew, who once more gave him a lecture about his health. The good news was he didn't need to wear the sling anymore. Then he asked around and found Emma's office. He was just about to knock when heard voices.

"Let's talk," a man said.

"Mark...I don't think we should." Emma replied.

Roumoult took a step back.

"We were fantastic together. I want you back," Mark said.

Roumoult felt his blood boil and his cheeks flush. He spun around and saw Tim Larson smiling at him.

"Mr. Cranston!"

Roumoult wished he would lower his voice.

"Good to see you're getting better."

"Thank you. I am feeling better" Roumoult replied, hoping Emma didn't hear them. No such luck. Emma and Mark emerged from her office.

"What are you doing here?" Emma asked, moving to stand beside Tim.

"I was looking for Dr. Matthew. I guess I took a wrong turn," Roumoult bluffed.

Emma looked at him disbelievingly.

"I'm glad you've recovered," Mark said.

Roumoult managed a bleak smile. "Thank you. I should leave." He pointed behind him. "It was nice seeing you all."

NYPD Holding Cells

The bomb squad cleared the building. The fire was out. With gas masks hanging around their necks, Tom, Joan, and two officers moved toward the cells. Tom slowed his pace when he came to the gloomy corridor where Alex had been held. The red lights blinked on and off. Tom peered through the small glass window and saw the green mist. They put their masks on. He waited as an officer unlocked the door and shoved it open. Tom stepped in and swallowed hard. He felt as if he'd stepped onto an alien ship. The green mist was everywhere. His breathing became shallow, and the mask limited his view. Alex could be anywhere.

Tom walked to his left and kicked open the first holding cell. An officer marched inside and shoved the bed aside. There was no one there. Tom moved to the next one, Joan close behind him. Empty. Tom surveyed the area. The group reached what had been Alex's cell. Tom's throat went dry. The door had been bashed in, the lock broken, and the iron bars bent. His blood ran cold. A devilish laugh echoed in the darkness.

Tom scanned his surroundings frantically as an enormous shadow loomed over him. He raised his head. Hanging onto the bars of the cell was Alex. His eyes bulged, red and bloodshot, and his face dripped with sweat. He sprang on Tom, sending him crashing to the floor. He snatched the gun from Tom and began to fire, shooting the officers. Next, he aimed for Joan and fired. She disappeared behind the wall.

"No!" Tom shouted. Alex swung a fist knocked him out cold.

Cranston Law Firm

Fred arrived at the Firm to sign the brief that Roumoult had prepared. He decided to remain in Roumoult's office while Alice took care of the rest of the paperwork. He knew Roumoult had left for his appointment and wondered if he had spoken to Emma. Alice stepped in, "I have sent it off." She said.

"Thanks, I think I will wait here for Roumoult to return."

She nodded, "Great, I am heading off. See you later."

Ground Floor, Cranston Law Firm

Angelus' drive from Long Island was long and boring. Joe and David had seen nothing, but they suspected that Dr. Wheeler had spotted them at one point. Angelus entered the lobby of the Firm and found Alice and Jack.

"I'm going home. What is it?" Alice asked.

"Okay, I'm sorry. I realize you wanted me to come to the party. Anyway," Jack stuttered, "It's too hot today. If you're thirsty, I can buy you a beer, or lime juice, or ice cream, anything you want."

Angelus smirked.

"A yes or no is fine. Preferably a yes," Jack muttered. At that moment, he caught sight of Angelus.

"Don't let me interrupt," Angelus said. "I'm just heading to my office."

"No!" Jack called. "Don't leave."

"I think I should."

Jack grabbed his arm.

"This has nothing to do with me," said Angelus.

Alice folded her arms, looking annoyed.

"But Angelus—" Jack started.

"You messed this up. You sort it out!"

Alice let out a high-pitched scream.

Angelus spun. Alex charged towards him with a knife, eyes wide and rabid. Angelus dove, trying to stop him, but Alex was too strong, and Angelus was too late.

"No!" Alice wailed.

A shooting pain tore through Angelus' skin. He looked between the knife and Alex, who smiled wickedly. "No one beats me." He sneered.

Jack screamed in anger, shoving Alex away from him.

Angelus tumbled and fell. He could hear Alice sobbing. "No, no," she cried.

Angelus eyes fluttered closed. "Alice," he whispered. "Run."

"I am not leaving you!"

Angelus saw Jack throw a chair at Alex, who lost his balance and stumbled backward out of the Firm's door. A thud echoed.

"I locked him out. Alice, call an ambulance," Jack said, kneeling beside Angelus. "Tell me what to do! Tell me what to do!"   "Jack." Angelus looked down at the knife, feeling strangely disconnected.

"There's a gun in Angelus' drawer," said Alice.

A shot rang out. Alice cried out, spreading her arms to shield Angelus. The glass cracked. Angelus saw Alex's figure, a gun clutched in his fist, pointing unshakingly at the door. Then suddenly, Alex turned away.

"What happened?" Alice asked.

Jack looked over. "Oh, God, no."

Using all his remaining strength, Angelus forced himself to sit up. The glass door was cracked, but Alex had disappeared. "Alice, Jack, leave now!" he yelled. The pain was too much. He heard a gun click.

Cranston Law Firm

Roumoult opened the car door. Sirens blared in the distance. For the last two hours, he'd been walking in the park in an attempt to drown his sorrows, ignoring phone calls. He'd needed time to himself, to think, to try to forget. Emma cared for Mark, he reminded himself over and over.

"Wait here, I should be back in half an hour," he told Jim before stepping out onto the street.

The Audi glided up the street and made a U-turn. Roumoult saw a taxi stop and Emma hopped out. He frowned.

"Where have you been?" she asked. "We need to talk."

"No, we don't. Everything is clear as day to me!"

"Oh, is it?" said Emma. "You know nothing! Why haven't you been answering your phone?"

"What are you doing here?"

"Why did you come to the hospital?" Emma countered.

"For nothing!" Roumoult stalked off in the direction of the Firm.

"You drove twenty blocks for nothing?" she asked, grabbing Roumoult's arm.

He faced her. "Look," he said. "I came because I thought you might need help. Maybe I was too blunt, but I..." He drifted off mid-sentence and studied her face.

Emma reached out and grabbed Roumoult's coat, pulling him towards her. Then he saw him, Alex. Blood covered his face. His eyes were red and filled with rage. His torn left sleeve was dangling around his thigh. He looked as if he had crawled out of a horror movie.

Roumoult took a deep, shuddering breath.

"I'll enjoy this," Alex muttered.

Spotting a knife in Alex's hand, Roumoult took a step back, shielding Emma. Suddenly, an engine roared. Roumoult shoved Emma roughly out of harm's way. The Audi raced toward Alex and rammed into him. Alex's body bounced up onto the bonnet, rolled over, and fell on the pavement. The Audi continued over the flower beds before losing momentum and coming to a stop.

"Oh my God!" Emma yelled, running to help Alex.

Roumoult caught her. "No!"

"Roumoult, he will die,"

"You don't—" Roumoult was interrupted by the sound of Alex groaning. "You have got to be kidding me."

Blood poured profusely out of Alex's mouth. Grimacing in pain, he staggered to his feet. Roumoult didn't want to tackle him; he couldn't. The best thing to do was run. Alex withdrew a gun and pointed it at Emma and Roumoult with a shaking hand. Emma's grip tightened on Roumoult's arm.

"Alex..." Roumoult said.

"You do not get away," he said. The weapon shook in his unsteady grip.

"Alex...please," Roumoult said.

A loud bang resonated. Blood splattered over Emma and Roumoult. Emma cried, still not relinquishing her grasp on Roumoult's arm. Alex fell to his knees, nursing his bleeding arm. "Ah!" he wailed in anger.

Before Roumoult knew it, Fred stood beside him. "Dad?"

Rage flashed like a fire in Alex's eyes. He reached again for the gun. Fred lifted Angelus' shotgun.

"No!" Roumoult shouted, reaching for his father. It was too late. The bullet tore through Alex's head.

Roumoult couldn't move. Alex lay dead on the roadside. He realized he was holding his breath. Emma stood by his side, shock rushing through her body in waves.

"Dad," said Roumoult.

Fred turned to look at him, horror creasing every line of his face. Roumoult saw Tom. He stood a few paces away, flabbergasted. Joan stood on his side glaring at Alex's dead body. A scream brought him back to reality with a jolt. Roumoult knew that voice.

"Alice!" He ran.

Roumoult halted at the door of the Firm, where he could see Angelus lying unconscious on the floor, his white shirt soaked in blood. "No! No!" Roumoult dropped to his knees, and he let his tears fall freely. The sirens and screams around him died out.

Emma bent down and pressed her ear against Angelus' chest. She said something but he couldn't understand. She reached for his hand, placing it firmly against Angelus' wound. More sirens sounded, and the medics rushed in. "He is still breathing, the cut is deep, I need gauze!" Emma shouted.

Roumoult felt someone grab him. It was Tom. He pulled him away.

"Roumoult, he'll be fine," Emma said distractedly, all of her focus on Angelus.

Isn't that what they always say? Roumoult stared blankly at his blood-soaked hands.

Once the paramedics had loaded Angelus onto a stretcher and driven away, Alice collapsed into Roumoult's arms. They supported each other. "I am so sorry," he muttered.

Alice sobbed. Jack stood in a corner hiding his tears.

Jim drove them to the hospital. Roumoult's mind was blank. Words did not come easily; condolences made his heart ache more fiercely. Numb and in shock, Roumoult walked through the overcrowded corridors of the hospital. Everyone stepped into the waiting room in grief-stricken silence. Roumoult's eyes kept drifting toward the blue door, expecting Emma to step through at any moment and announce that Angelus was gone. Minutes ticked slowly.

Finally, the door flung open. Emma hurried out. "He's fine," she said.

"Don't lie to me," Roumoult choked.

"I'll never lie to you."

An invisible weight lifted from his shoulders.

"Roumoult, you need to sit down," Fred suggested.

He obliged.

"The wound was approximately seven to eight inches deep on the right side of the umbilicus," explained Emma. "Fortunately, it missed most of the main arteries. It ruptured his intestine, leading to massive blood loss. We have stopped the bleeding, and he needs a blood transfusion. His condition is serious, but he will live."

NYPD Precinct

Tom felt miserable. He had never seen Roumoult in shock. They had never been in such a grave situation before. Angelus was lucky, he survived and had people looking after him. He was concerned about Joan. She was alone and wasn't asking for help. He felt guilty for letting her down. He was a disappointment. After Alex had knocked Tom out, he'd attacked Joan and tried to strangle her. The only reason Joan was alive was because the Captain showed up, forcing Alex to retreat. The bruises on her face and neck were becoming darker and she walked with a limp. Tom was worried and kept asking her to see a doctor. She refused.

The media blamed the NYPD for the chaos Alex had left behind. And they were right. Four officers had been attacked, and Angelus and Roumoult had almost been killed before Alex was shot dead by Fred. Now Tom had to face the music. This was the first time in his career that he'd been under such public scrutiny, and he couldn't help but feel he deserved it.

"I have to say, I am disappointed," said the Captain. "Not only was someone able to infiltrate the Precinct and drugged that lunatic, but because of you two, he escaped. You put yourself in unnecessary danger and got two officers shot!" The Captain slammed his fist against the desk. "Thank God they were wearing bulletproof vests."

"But—" Joan started.

"I'm not finished yet," the Captain spat. "You are senior officers. I depend on your good judgment! You endangered the lives of NYPD officers and put innocent bystanders in the line of fire!"

Tom hung his head.

"I could take you off the case. I could fire you! But that won't do any good. You messed this up, and you are going to clean it up. Remember, I have my eye on you two. No more mistakes!"

St. George Hospital

Once stabilized, Angelus was transferred to the fourth floor. He'd regained consciousness for a few minutes and exchanged words with the doctors. Now, he was sleeping. Roumoult made sure Jack and Alice got home safely. Fred went with the cops to give a statement, and William volunteered to tag along. Roumoult still couldn't speak. His tears had dried out, and his mind remained frozen in time. Images of Alex dying, Fred holding the gun, Angelus bleeding to death, and Alice crying haunted him. He told himself they were safe now, but he had a hard time accepting it.

After eight p.m., Fred stepped in and took a seat beside Roumoult.

"How was it?" Roumoult asked.

"As expected, Tom doesn't think they'll charge me."

Roumoult nodded. "You didn't speak to them without your lawyer, did you?"

"No. The lawyer made it on time."

"Good. I trust Tom but I wanted to be on the safe side."

Fred scorned, "He let Alex out."

Roumoult said nothing. He blamed no one, except himself.

"Are you okay?"

"No, I 'm not. I-I can't cope with this."

Fred said nothing.

Roumoult continued. "Everything was fine this morning, and..." His words melted. The shots still echoed in his head.

"I'm sorry," Fred said sincerely.

"It's not your fault, Dad, it's mine," Roumoult replied.

Fred looked down at his hands, unable to meet Roumoult's eye. "I killed a man," he said in a hollow voice.

Roumoult turned to look at him.

"I just acted. I'm so sorry. It was horrible. I saw Angelus dying, Alice crying... Alex was attacking you and Emma... I just... I pulled the trigger," he said. Fred's shoulders began to tremble, and soon his entire body was racking with sobs.

Roumoult couldn't watch his father cry. He placed an arm gently around his shoulder and tried, silently, to comfort him.

15

Ortiz

June 17, 2015

Ortiz's House

O rtiz Stalin sat in the dark, staring blankly at the TV. He couldn't believe it: Alex Rucker was dead. Pictures of the crime scene flashed on the screen. He cursed. It was all going to hell!

Ortiz stepped under the dim overhead light. He was a short, obese man in his mid-fifties. His large nose bulged out of the thick gauze that covered his face. Brown eyes peered beadily through the two holes in the bandage.

Ortiz had always lived in the shadows. Born and brought up in a poor and dangerous neighborhood in Queens, he understood the cruelty of the world all too well. His mother was a prostitute who'd left when he was young; he never knew his father. With nowhere to go, he'd lived with Pitt Garcia, a local bookie for a gang. By the age of twenty-five, he'd become Vincent Corner's favorite protégé, and then he

schemed to murder Vincent, and took over his operations. He was smarter than his predecessors and
disappeared from police radar.

In 1975, Ortiz shifted his attention to third
world countries, where corruption was easy and life
cheap. His gang invaded and looted ships, careful to
leave no traces. But then things got ugly. He lost one
of his best men, Van Gerkins, and the rest of his
team on the Nefret. His Egyptian informers believed
that God had put a curse on Van, turning him into a
maniac who killed everyone else on the ship. Ortiz
didn't believe in such things, and even after Van's
death, his business thrived. The conflict in the Middle East served him well, and he supplied arms to
both sides, earning high profits.

But then things changed. Six months ago, Ortiz's
shipments stopped. Just disappeared. Gone! His men
vanished too. Soon, he found out that someone was
intercepting his goods. Police raided his warehouses
and killed two of his finest men. His illegal trade with
the army collapsed. He lost millions, and the FBI was
behind him; he had to escape.

Though he was out of Egypt, Ortiz was still in
danger. He had to disappear quickly. He fumbled
with the bandages on his face. Just one more job to
do, he thought.

St. George Hospital

Roumoult sent Fred home and stayed back with
Angelus. Yellow sunrays poked through the curtains,
and dust particles danced in the light. Roumoult
thought about what to do, listening to the low tones

of chatting nurses and beeping machines. After some time had passed, Roumoult sat up and saw Alice sitting beside Angelus. When had she slipped in? The clock read 8:45 a.m. Roumoult made his way to the bathroom and brushed his teeth. When he returned, he found Emma talking with Alice.

Alice agreed to stay with Angelus, and Emma insisted that Roumoult joined her for breakfast. He pushed his food around his plate, only half listening to Emma talk about work. After breakfast, Jim drove Emma home and Roumoult to work. The idea of sitting at home and mourning daunted him. He needed to fix things. Working was better; it resolved things; it kept him busy.

Roumoult called everyone involved to make sure they were okay. Fred was agitated and furious at Tom. Roumoult told him to rest and let it go. William was miserable, blaming himself for being the person who'd reopened the case. Roumoult advised him to go to work, but he refused. Tom seemed disturbed, but he handled himself better than the others.

"Oh no," muttered Jim as they neared the building.

Reporters were waiting near the entrance, and there was a crowd of spectators. Jim changed their route, took them around the block, and drove into the parking lot.

Roumoult didn't step out. "Did I thank you?"

"You don't have to, Sir," said Jim.

"You saved my life and Emma's."

Jim twisted around in the driver's seat. "I couldn't just stand by."

"You could have," Roumoult insisted.

"No, I couldn't."

"Thank you," Roumoult told him earnestly. "I'll never forget what you did. If you ever need anything, anything at all, let me know."

Jim beamed.

Roumoult and Jim got out of the car and headed for the lobby. It was swarming with men dressed in white suits, clicking pictures and taking samples. The blood on the carpet sent nausea rippling through Roumoult's stomach. He turned away.

NYPD Precinct

The blast hadn't damaged much of the structure of the building, but now there were more cracks in the walls, the plumbing wasn't working on the second floor, and there was no electricity on the fourth level. Everyone tried to adjust to their new circumstances. The Captain was busy relocating staff and handling calls from the media, the police commissioner, and the Mayor.

Tom focused on the bomb and the bomber. The killer had hidden the device in the tearoom on level four and created the perfect distraction. It was a contained explosive used in mines, mainly made of ammonium nitrate, triggered by a remote detonator. It had knocked off two cops and set the entire room on fire.

A cylinder was hidden inside a ventilation shaft in one of the holding cells. Tom stood by as the bomb squad made sure it was safe and moved it. He watched silently as they dusted it for prints, but something told him it was a dead end, just like the cigar box. Leaving the CSI to do their jobs, he returned to his office and updated Joan.

"Are you sure?" she asked. Her voice cracked with fatigue and hopelessness.

"A cylinder with no identifying markers. Anyone could have purchased it."

"And the gas?"

"PCP and plenty of it, everywhere. I sent the samples to William. Hopefully he can find something. Did you find who drugged Alex?"

"It's maddening," said Joan, "I've backtracked the video recordings. The perpetrator is not on them."

"Are you sure?"

"He had a lot of guts coming into the NYPD, planting the bomb, drugging Alex... I don't understand how that it's possible. Unless..." Joan drifted off.

"Unless what?"

"He's one of us."

"No! No. That's not possible."

"He knew where Alex was located," Joan pointed out. "He knew where to place the explosive. It is possible."

Tom felt uneasy, but he couldn't deny the possibility that Joan was right.

Wellington Heights Apartments

William hated himself. He'd drunk every ounce of whiskey he had, then Joan had come over to chat with him, and he'd blamed her and Tom for letting Alex out. She'd stormed out of the apartment.

Hungover and bleary-eyed, William woke to the sound of his phone ringing over and over. He finally sat up. "I'm going to…" he muttered, picking up the phone. "Yes?"

"Good afternoon to you too," Juliet said.

"What is it?" William asked.

"Can you come in today?"

"No."

"Dr. Chandler wants you to finish Alex's autopsy," Juliet continued, pretending not to have heard him.

"What?" William rubbed at his eyes, all remnants of sleep fading. "Why?"

"It's your case. And Tom sent some new samples."

"Juliet, not now!"

"William, stop it. I will only say this once: you started this, now finish it!"

Cranston Law Firm

Roumoult felt pain in his arm and stopped typing, waiting for it to settle. If he thought he could handle everything, he was wrong. Charles called him repeatedly to remind him to take his meds. Still, he had the feeling that he'd forgotten something, or someone. Joe! He picked up his phone and dialed. "Are you okay?" he asked.

"What's going on there?" said Joe. "I haven't heard from you or Angelus for over twenty-four hours!"

"Sorry, it's been crazy," Roumoult replied.

"Tell me something I don't know."

"Angelus is fine. Everything is fine."

"No, it's not," Joe argued. "Nelson updated me. Boss, I can help. I can handle the Agency."

"And leave David alone?"

"He can handle himself. Everything's normal here," Joe replied casually. "People are working late at night. Dogs are barking. Guards are taking their rounds. No more rabbits. Someone was giggling in the woods... I think I heard wolves howling. But everything is cool"

"Really?"

"I've seen worse."

For the first time all day, Roumoult smiled. "Fine," he said. "Take over the Agency and ask David to watch APTOS. Send him back up if necessary."

Already, Roumoult felt better. Joe knew Angelus' business inside out, and Joe's help would free Roumoult up to take care of everything else. Still, he was sure he was missing something. "Oh my God," he cried, springing out of his seat. He left the Firm and walked straight into the lab. Jack was sitting on a chair, mopping half-heartedly as its wheels dragged tracks across the wet floor. "What are you doing?" Roumoult asked, noticing a few bottles of beer scattered over desks.

"Sorry, coffee wasn't helping."

"Check on Alice," Roumoult sighed. "Then go home and rest. Okay?"

Jack hung his head. "Okay." He drew in a breath. "He nearly killed Angelus."

"Jack..."

"I wish I could have done more."

Roumoult gave what he hoped was a reassuring smile. "Jack, you did your best."

"I feel awful."

"Me too. We'll get over it. We have to."

Roumoult turned to the monitor where security cameras showed Angelus sprawled out on the floor, blood pooling beneath him, Jack and Alice standing over his writhing frame. Roumoult's heart sank. The video played through, then skipped to the next clip. Roumoult had had enough. He stepped forward to switch it off, but something caught his attention. He paused and peered at the screen.

"Boss?" Joe asked.

"Move over," said Roumoult.

"What did you see?"

"Something important we missed."

NYPD Precinct

Tom followed his instincts and drove to Long Island to find out more about Dr. Wheeler. The truth was, he needed some fresh air. He returned to Precinct in the late afternoon and hurried into the office.

"There you are," Joan said.

"Sorry I'm late. Any luck with the explosives?"

"Yes. The cleaner says there was nothing under the sink last week, so I pulled up all the surveillance tapes. Jake and I tried to identify as many people as we could. Most of them were cops. The people we didn't know, I searched for in the police database. All of them were authentic, except one." She handed a photograph to Tom.

Tom sized the man. He was in his late thirties with a grim face and a well-built body. He wore dark sunglasses and an NYPD uniform.

"I checked the badge number. It doesn't exist."

"Great work!" said Tom.

"I'm running the photograph through the database. Let's see what happens. Did you find anything on Dr. Wheeler?"

"Yes. I visited his neighborhood and knocked on a few doors. According to his neighbors, he's a kind, helpful man. He's lived in the neighborhood for twenty-six years, but six months ago, he changed. The neighbors say he started behaving strangely, that he seemed preoccupied and turned into a loner. Then they heard cries, screams, and howls coming from the house."

"What?"

"At first, they thought Wheeler was watching horror movies, but it continued every night for two weeks. An uneasiness swept over the neighborhood. People confronted Wheeler, and when he didn't listen, they considered reporting it to the police. But the noises stopped." Tom paused. "So, they left him alone. One of his neighbors, Mrs. Thompsons, told me she saw him talking to himself."

"She saw him?" said Joan.

"The design of her house is such that the window of her kitchen faces the living area of Wheeler's house. It gives her a clear view inside. She claims she saw him arguing."

"With whom?"

"With himself," said Tom. "There was no one else there. She said she saw a man visit him twice a week ago. Can you guess who?"

Joan shook her head.

"Mark Weldon."

"What?"

"Yep. Now here's the problem: no one has seen Dr. Wheeler for the past forty-eight hours."

"Of course," said Joan.

"I went to APTOS; he isn't there. According to his colleagues, that's not like him. He never misses a day of work."

Tom's phone buzzed. Roumoult was calling him. He hesitated.

"Answer it," Joan said.

Tom smiled at his partner and clicked the green button.

NYPD Precinct

"We come in peace," Roumoult announced, entering his office.

Tom's anger was long gone. "It's okay. I'm not proud of what happened."

Roumoult nodded. "Neither am I."

"What have you got?"

"We checked my Firm's security camera footage and noticed a man who seemed out of place." He put a photo down in front of Tom.

"That's the same man," Joan said, comparing the still to the pictures she found of the man who'd allegedly placed the bomb.

"We tracked him on six news channels," Roumoult said, showing them the pictures, "and traffic cameras."

"You have access to traffic cameras?" Joan asked.

"I'm resourceful."

"That means someone in the traffic department owes him a favor," Tom explained.

"The thing is this guy followed Alex!" Jack spoke up. "He was watching everything. Like it was a TV show for him."

Roumoult produced a map, placing it beside the photos. "He got into this black sedan parked three blocks from the NYPD, then he drove to the Firm at East Avenue, arriving at about five p.m. That's when Alex attacked Angelus and me. He lingered until we sent Angelus to the hospital. Then he took the subway, and we tracked him to Astra Place subway station. After that, we lost him."

"If he was at Astra Place at a quarter to six p.m., maybe we could we pick up the trail," Tom suggested to Joan.

"Do you have an ID?" Roumoult asked.

"We're running it now," said Joan.

"How long will that take?" Jack asked.

"It depends," she answered. "If he has a criminal background, we might find him. If not, our next choice is the DNV database."

"We'll try our best," Tom said.

"It's worth a shot," said Roumoult. "He could be the white king."

"Speaking of the white king," Tom replied, "Wheeler might be the white knight, and Mark Weldon might have something to do with the case."

16

Organic

June 18, 2015

City Morgue

Reluctantly, William performed Alex's autopsy. It was not a pretty picture. He pulled a bullet out of his shoulder and another from his brain. The ballistic reports showed what William had expected: both bullets were from Angelus' shot gun. The toxicology report was no surprise. Alex had inhaled a heavy dose of PCP. He estimated above thirty milligrams. If Fred hadn't killed Alex, the PCP would have. William's phone beeped, and he glanced at a message from Juliet.

He took the elevator down to the basement. The pathology lab wasn't glamourous. It was a plain white room with three long benches. Below the benches were huge compartments filled with assay kits, test tubes, gloves, and laboratory glassware. On them sat microscopes, centrifuge machines, a fingerprint development chamber, a fuming chamber, and an automated DNA sequencer. Juliet was peering into a microscope.

"Hey," William said.

"Hey!" Juliet stepped back from the microscope to look at him. "Are you okay?"

"Not really." William shrugged.

"Is it Alex or Joan?"

"Both."

"Well, it'll get better," said Juliet.

William shook himself off. "What did you find?"

"The PCP residue," Juliet said, referring to her notes. "Dyed with a green color. It's one of the finest and purest forms I have ever seen. But one thing was unusual." She stepped aside, inviting William to look into the microscope.

Several green crystals and dark spots marked the slide. William zoomed in and could see circular black spots, out of which tentacles emerged. "What is that?" he asked.

"I don't know, it looks organic."

The Vintage, Lower Manhattan

Roumoult didn't want to go home, so when William invited him out for a drink, he welcomed the distraction. To his surprise, he wasn't the only one.

The Vintage was a bar sandwiched between two tall buildings at the corner of Mercer and Broome Street. Its walls were cream, and two large oak counters stood opposite each other. Well-polished wooden shelves held a variety of liquors and drinks. The bartenders were busy taking orders and serving drinks.

People milled around in groups at the edges of the small dance floor, shouting over the loud music.

Roumoult was thankful that the media was leaving him alone for now. He grabbed his fourth drink and returned to the table. Joan and William were still arguing. Tom was trying to handle the situation without success. Roumoult had given up trying to help them. Jack and Alice sat close; hands linked. Emma was more drunk than Roumoult, giggling loudly as they spoke about everything but the case. Though it was past midnight, no one wanted to leave.

After two a.m., Roumoult stood outside Emma's apartment. She leaned on him, mumbling incoherently. He was attempting to unlock the door with Emma's key and wondered if someone had spiked his drink; he'd never felt so out of control. He unlocked the door, and they entered the apartment.

"This is not my home," Emma said, barely able to keep her balance.

"Okay. Now go to bed."

She smiled and flung her arms around his neck. Their eyes met, and Roumoult thought he was losing himself. "You are making this extremely difficult," he said.

"Don't go," Emma whined.

"I have to. Otherwise—" He paused at the glint in her eyes. Reaching up a gentle hand, he brushed his fingers through her hair and then across her cheeks. "I need to go," he said, feeling blood rush to his face. Before he could step away, she pulled him closer and sealed his mouth with a kiss.

17

Blue Lily

June 19, 2015

Museum of Natural History

W illiam and Juliet waited impatiently, William's mind ticking over his night out with Joan. They had a fight, forgave each other and then had a good time. Unfortunately, he ended up with a headache. He had taken an analgesic and it helped a bit. He tried to focus on the job, to identify the material found in the PCP. It was biological, and fortunately, they had abundant dry sample from the cylinder to conduct several tests. But their journey hadn't been easy. Juliet had separated the anomaly from the PCP by sending the sample through a mass spectrometer. The device broke down the compound and identified its contents. Of all the components, the ratio of carbon 14 isotope was very low. This sparked another branch of the investigation that landed them in Dr. Payne's office at the Museum of Natural History. Dr. Payne recommended they do carbon dating, a test to identify the age of the sample. As he waited for the results, William looked around.

This lab was very different to the ones William was used to. On the other side of the glass wall, counters were lined up. Most of the tables held a microscope, yellowish samples in glass containers with dusting brushes, and empty containers. He spun and looked at the accelerator mass spectrometer, the machine that measured radiocarbons in a sample. It was a monster. He surveyed the long, hefty tube of approximately one hundred centimeters radius, which disappeared into a hefty semi-circular segment. At its mouth was a small opening used to feed the sample. The hefty part of the equipment was the electromagnet used to deflect the ions in the sample. It emerged on the other side and was bolted into a steel amplifier and a chart recorder.

Dr. Payne looked unblinkingly into the microscope. The slender man had a rigid, expressionless face. His dark eyes remained fixed. His most distinct feature was his large shiny forehead, with a thin layer of hair tickling the tops of his ears and the back of his neck.

"Well?" William asked tired of waiting.

"It's peculiar," said Dr. Payne. "This sample had limited exposure to the atmosphere."

"Meaning?"

"It could have been stored in an airtight container."

A bell rang. The carbon dating was complete. Dr. Payne jumped with excitement and hurried to collect the report. Scanning it quickly he said, "I was right, I was right! It's over five hundred years old!"

"What?" William demanded. "How could that be?"

"When an animal or plant dies, it stops exchanging carbon with the environment, and from that point onwards, the amount of C-14 undergoes radioactive decay and decreases. The older the sample, the higher the level of decay. This organic material is around five hundred years old."

"But it was in PCP," said William.

"PCP was synthesized in the 50s. This organic material is ancient."

"So, someone deliberately mixed it with the PCP?" William asked.

"It appears so," said Dr. Payne.

"What is it? A bone? Ancient tissue? What?"

The doctor twisted his jaw. "Hmm, now we need a DNA sequencer."

William's headache returned with a vengeance.

Central Park West

The loud ringing of a phone pulled Roumoult out of his slumber. His head was throbbing. He reached over and answered the call. "Hello?"

"Roumoult, where are you?" Fred demanded from the other end of the line.

"Dad? Oh…"

"Did you forget again? There is a trustee and board members meeting at midday at Cranston Enterprises. You have to be there!"

"Dad, slow down. You're too loud. I have a headache."

Fred hesitated. "Are you hungover?"

Roumoult's annoyance grew. "No," he said defiantly. "I'm in bed. I'll be at the meeting. Just give me a few minutes, okay?"

"In bed? Are you sure?"

"Yes."

"Well, if you're in bed, it's not yours!"

Roumoult rolled over onto his side. A woman slept beside him. "Oh my God."

"What did you do?" said Fred.

"Dad, I've got to go."

"Just tell me where you are."

He couldn't remember.

The woman muttered something and turned. Hair fell across Emma's face. Roumoult relaxed.

"Are you with someone?" asked Fred, still on the line.

"I'll call you later," Roumoult answered. He ended the call. Roumoult tried to get his thoughts together. Emma snuggled closer. He had to get out of there. Trying not to wake her, he gently removed her hand from his waist. She rested it back on his chest and mumbled, "Mark...don't go yet."

Roumoult's face reddened. He climbed out of bed quickly, waking Emma up.

"Hey?" she said drowsily.

Roumoult reached for his coat on the chair.

"Good morning," she said.

He managed a bleak smile.

"Roumoult?"

"Look, I'm leaving. We—"

"Why?"

"We'll talk later."

Emma studied his face. "What happened?"

"We'll talk later. Okay?"

"What happened?"

"Why did you force me to stay?"

"Because you wanted to stay," she said.

"Do you remember what happened last night?" Roumoult asked.

"Yeah, we're good."

"No, we are not!" Roumoult exclaimed. "If you still have feelings for your ex, go back to him!"

Emma looked like she was going to argue, but Roumoult didn't let her. He marched out of the bedroom and the apartment without looking back.

NYPD Precinct

Tom sipped his coffee as he checked his emails. He'd had a fun night, but he'd gone home alone. Everyone around him had someone in their lives. Someone to care for, someone to love. He was alone; he didn't even have a cat. His mind drifted to Ms. Garrison. He wished he'd had the chance to get to know her better.

Joan stepped in and wished Tom a good morning. She looked better today, and he knew she had finally spoken to Emma and got some meds for her injuries.

"Good morning," Tom replied glumly.

"What's wrong?" Joan asked.

"Oh, nothing. No luck with the cigar boxes, and the bank hasn't called, which means the money is still there. The bodies are still missing, and Wheeler's disappeared. We can't trace the bomber."

"Something will pop up," Joan said. "What's the matter? You look sad."

Tom scowled.

"You can tell me," Joan urged.

"It's just last night."

"Was it me?"

"Oh, no," Tom replied, waving his hand dismissively. "You were with William. Emma was with Roumoult. Jack was with Alice. I woke up this morning on the couch. On my own. I don't even have a cat."

Joan's smile widened. "Ms. Garrison is nice," she said.

Tom couldn't hide the color that rose in his cheeks. "She is nice," he said. "And involved in this case."

"She's not a suspect," Joan countered.

"I don't think it's a good idea."

Joan crossed her arms. "Look, you'll never know until you give it a shot."

Tom hesitated.

"Or maybe we could get you a cat?"

The phone rang and Tom couldn't believe his ears. Someone had withdrawn the money from the fourth bank account. To Tom's surprise, it was Dr. Tim Larson. He had him brought to the Precinct for questioning.

"How did you get involved in this?" he asked.

"Because I'm stupid,"

Tom studied his face, his sallow skin, his dark under-eye circles. "What do you take?"

"Ecstasy,"

"Are you an addict?"

"I was close. For the past year, I've been going to this club in Chinatown to meet my dealer. He calls himself Mario. I don't know his last name. I didn't tell them who I was. But two months ago, they found out I was a doctor."

"He wanted something from you," said Tom.

"Yes. I thought he needed prescription drugs. But no... He wanted something else. I used to assist plastic surgeons. I completed the training and was ready to start my practice, but at the last minute, I decided to pursue emergency medicine."

"They needed you for a surgery?" Tom asked.

"Yes."

"Do you have a license for that?"

"I do," said Tim. "Mario wanted me to do a surgery. I said no, but the man didn't stop calling! Then the threats began. He told me he'd tell my boss I was using drugs. I was scared I'd lose my job, but it felt wrong. I said no. Then they targeted my family. One day, while I was at work, my wife called, terrified. A man had broken in, attacked her, and shoved her down the stairs." Tim paused. "The fall wasn't bad, but it immobilized her. I called Mario and told him to back off. Things were quiet for a couple of days, and my wife recovered. But one night, I heard a loud crashing noise and screams. My daughter..." He stopped for a moment, as if gathering his thoughts. "I ran upstairs and grabbed her and my son. I left them with my wife and came back to my daughter's room with a baseball bat. It stunk, blood everywhere! Nausea took over me, and I threw up." He hung his head. "It was pig's blood. It took two days to clean it up, and I can still smell it. My daughter doesn't sleep in that room anymore." He looked pleadingly between Tom and Joan. "Please understand. I had no choice."

Tom nodded and motioned for him to continue.

"Finally, I said yes. Mario said he'd let me know when he needed me. Two weeks later, he called and told me to take a day off work for the surgery."

"I'm guessing a face," said Joan.

"Yeah. Remove all identification marks. Change it as much as possible. I couldn't risk my children's lives, so I agreed. Mario promised fifty thousand dollars. I didn't want the money. Trust me, I just wanted the nightmare to end. I took the deposit of twenty-five thousand dollars and put it in my daughter's college fund. Then I received my instructions. On April 29, I was to take a taxi to the corner of Madison Square and wait. A black car was supposed to arrive and take me to a fully equipped surgical room. I wasn't supposed to chit-chat with anyone, I was just there to give instructions."

"Did you do it?" Tom asked.

"That's the thing," said Tim. "I remember getting the text, taking the taxi, and waiting at Madison Square, but after that, I remember nothing!"

"Nothing?" asked Tom.

"Nothing!"

"That's absurd," Joan declared.

"I'm telling the truth!" Tim said frantically. "They deleted my phone memory. There is no trace of Mario ever calling me. I can't remember the surgery, but I know I did it."

"How is that possible?" asked Tom.

"That evening, I woke up in an alley twenty blocks from my house. I got home and told my wife everything. I thought they must've doped me, so I tested myself. There were traces of LSD in my blood."

"And?" Joan pressed.

"It doesn't suit me," Tim said simply. "The last time I took it, I lost two days of my life."

"And Mario knew that?" said Joan.

"Yes. After two weeks, he called. I was furious. He told me it was for the best and informed me my patient was recovering. He said I could withdraw the rest of the money. At first, I didn't want to take it, but I changed my mind. After that millionaire shot that criminal, Alex, Mario disappeared."

"Dr. Larson," said Joan. "Please try to remember."

"I wish I could! But I don't."

"What else can you tell us?" Tom asked, hoping to gain more information.

"Mario and his stupid men. You know what they say: once you make a deal with the devil, you belong to him."

"What happened?"

"His men wanted to hide bodies in the hospital."

Tom eyes widened. "Who?"

"How many?" said Joan.

"I don't who, but there were three of them," Tim told them.

"Three bodies?" Tom asked. "You hid three bodies at the hospital?" He got to his feet. "Did you look at them?"

Joan placed photos of the Van drivers on the table. "Are these Mario's men?"

"Yes!"

"Where are the bodies now?" Tom asked.

"I told them to take them away. They said that they needed to keep them for a night because their freezer broke down."

Tom covered his face with his hands. "And you let them?" His blood boiled. "Someone murdered these three men, and you helped..."

"Whoa! What?" Tim's eyes darted back and forth. "They told me they were fam... Oh, gosh, I never thought..."

"Where did they take the bodies?" Joan asked slowly.

"I don't know."

"So, you hid evidence for the crooks and performed illegal surgery. Now you can't remember anything of any use?" Tom said. "That's just fantastic. What should I do with you?"

"Maybe I can help."

Tom sized him. "Maybe you can. How do we find Mario?"

Long Island

Tom appointed Officer Jake to search for Mario. Once he got the warrant to search Dr. Wheeler's house, he headed for Long Island. A handful of people watched as the group of cops entered Wheeler's home. Three cops moved toward the backyard. Tom advanced to the front door. As a courtesy, he knocked.

"Dr. Wheeler, NYPD. Open up!"

As expected, there was no reply.

A cop broke the lock and busted the door open. The police entered the house. The living room was small and empty. Tom's nose wrinkled as he picked up a nasty odor coming from the kitchen. It was a mess. Dirty dishes and boxes of food were everywhere. Coffee mugs sat on the dining table, still half-full of stagnant dregs. Tom ran up the stairs to the first floor. The cops checked the bedrooms. Wheeler was nowhere to be found.

Cranston Law Firm

Roumoult was not the master of his emotions today. The trustee's meeting went well. Most of the members just wanted to make sure that the bad media didn't affect the company's performance. Of course, money was more important that the President's mindset. Roumoult assured them that their investments would be safe, and that Fred wouldn't be prosecuted. Fred kept pressuring Roumoult to tell him about his morning. He didn't break. After checking in on Angelus, he was glad for the reprieve of work.

Roumoult pushed his chair away from the desk and walked around the office. He could hear Alice talking on the phone. He stood near the window, admiring the skyline. The sun had set, and the city glowed under the dark sky. Again, his mind wandered to Emma. He felt he'd been too impatient with her.

Two taps sounded against the door. Tom and Joan walked into the office. William must be late; he wasn't with them.

"How was your day?" asked Roumoult.

"Oh, don't ask," Tom said. He moved to stand under the air conditioner, letting cool air ripple through his hair. "We've been hunting for Wheeler," Tom said. "He has disappeared into thin air. And I have to tell you about Dr. Larson."

Roumoult listened to Tom talk for the next ten minutes, with occasional interruptions by Joan, who had collapsed into the client's chair and now slumped lifelessly, her eyes closed and her jaw set.

"They hired him to do a plastic surgery, and he can't remember doing it?" Roumoult asked.

"Yep. And he hid the bodies in his hospital for a night," Tom replied.

Roumoult bit his lip.

Tom studied his face. "You knew!"

"Not exactly," Roumoult said.

Tom knitted his brows. "Your girlfriend knew, and she told you."

"She's not my girlfriend!" Roumoult snapped.

William arrived, and the situation diffused. "Hey, how is everyone?" he asked happily, obviously not picking up the tension in the room.

"Roumoult, the least you could do is offer me a drink," Tom said. Roumoult left and returned with lemonade for everyone.

"I had the most exciting day of my life!" said William.

Tom gulped down his lemonade.

William produced a picture of green crystals and black dots. "We found an anomaly in the PCP," he said.

"Those black dots?" asked Joan.

"Yeah. They're organic. We did every test possible but couldn't identify them. Juliet ran it through a mass spectrometer and found out it had a low carbon 14 intake."

Blank faces stared back at him. Tom turned to Roumoult. "Do you have anything stronger than lemonade?"

"I might have some scotch."

"Good," said William. "We should celebrate!"

Roumoult got up and returned with a bottle of scotch and glasses.

William continued to explain. "When a living organism dies, it stops taking in carbon. From that time onwards, the levels of carbon drop. The older the sample, the higher the rate of carbon loss. We consulted an archeologist and did a carbon dating test."

"So how old is this sample?" asked Roumoult.

"It's five hundred years old! Isn't that exciting?"

Everyone looked at each other. Tom tilted up his glass, draining it.

"How does it help us?" Joan asked.

"Once we knew it was ancient, the next step was to identify it," William said. "To do that, we did DNA sequencing." He pulled out two papers and put them on the table. "Its genome matches Nymphaea Caerulea!"

"What's that?" Tom asked candidly.

William produced another paper.

"A flower?" Tom said with disappointment in his voice.

"Not just any flower," William replied. "It's Nymphaea Caerulea. Also known as the blue lily, a flower indigenous to Egypt."

Roumoult sat back.

"Don't you see?" William asked. "We found the remains of Nymphaea Caerulea, blue lily, mixed in the PCP, and its five hundred years old!"

"So, it's an old flower," said Tom.

William shook his head in exasperation. "Dr. Payne says the blue lily was one of the most important ritual flowers in ancient Egypt. It was valued for its beauty, lilac scent, symbolism, and intoxicating effects."

"It's another drug?" Tom concluded.

"I don't think adding it into the PCP was to increase intoxication. PCP itself is quite potent," William explained.

"Then it's a signature," Roumoult suggested.

"Indeed," William agreed.

"How does that help us?" asked Tom.

Roumoult turned to Tom. "It means our murderer is someone who has access to historical artifacts, maybe someone who works at the museum. That, Detective, narrows your suspect list."

"I'll shorten your list even further," William added. "Our archeologist friend says the Weldon's have investments in Egypt. Walter Weldon, who is Mark's uncle, runs a number of projects in Egypt."

"But why Egypt?" Joan asked. "There are plenty of excavation sites elsewhere. Why not South America?"

William nodded. "I asked the same question. The archeologist said there were personal reasons."

Everyone fell silent.

"And of course, there's a myth," William said playfully.

"Ah! I got this one!" Tom said. "There's a curse."

Joan gave a short laugh. Roumoult grinned.

"There are dozens of theories. In ancient mythology, the blue lily is a symbol of rebirth. If we apply it to our case, the murderer could be someone who's risen from the dead."

Roumoult threw his head back and let out a loud laugh.

"Great! Fantastic! How do you suppose I get a warrant to arrest a mummy?" Tom mocked.

APTOS Pharmaceuticals

Tom enjoyed teasing William, but he couldn't discount the lead he'd provided. He started compiling a list of people who could be linked to the case and historical artifacts. Weldon's name popped up everywhere. It was late, and Tom was just about to head home when an urgent call changed his plans. He picked up Joan and drove to Long Island. He parked behind Roumoult's Audi. When he couldn't see him, he called him.

"Where are you?"

"Come into the woods."

Tom and Joan approached the woods cautiously. The bushes reached up to their knees. The dense trees blocked most of the moonlight. It was eleven p.m., and the air was humid. An owl hooted somewhere not far away, and Tom saw a cluster of bats flying east.

"Charming," Tom muttered. He spotted a light six yards away and increased his pace. "What the hell are you doing here?" he called out.

"Where's the backup?" Roumoult asked. Joe stood beside him.

"It's on its way to APTOS?" Tom answered.

Roumoult motioned for Tom and Joan to join him at the edge of the hill. Together, they kneeled and watched. Tom's vision took time to adjust to the moonlight. Roumoult handed over the binoculars, and he surveyed the landscape starting from APTOS. A group of men hopped out of a van and moved toward the complex. He shifted his focus to his far right and noticed a steep, narrow opening that stretched from the woods to the plains near the company. Roumoult tapped on his shoulder and pointed to the rocks. Tom zoomed in. A figure emerged.

"Your monster?" Roumoult whispered to Joe.

"Yes, it's Wheeler," Joe said.

"What?" Tom turned to him.

"It reappeared last night," said Joe. "David followed it and recognized him. Before he could catch Wheeler, he disappeared into the trees surrounding the company. When I came on duty tonight, I heard giggling in the woods and saw him hiding in the shadows. I immediately called the boss."

"He's hiding in the company?" asked Joan.

Joe shook his head. "I don't know... He just appears and disappears."

Tom watched closely. Wheeler hid behind the rocks then moved maliciously forward, like a mythological creature, dark and fierce. "We're following him," he told Roumoult. "You stay here."

"Agreed." Roumoult answered.

Tom and Joan darted through the woods, approaching the steep opening. Tom reached the edge and looked down, then he broke into a jog. They huffed and puffed on their way down the hill. It had been ages since Tom had had to run after a suspect. He came to stop and fought to catch his breath. Joan stopped a few paces ahead. Tom called Roumoult to ask for intel.

"He's headed for the plantation."

There wasn't a moment to lose; they ran. The plantation was a mix of oak, Sherman, red maple, and pine trees. Tom and Joan shot down the slope and soon reached the other side. Wheeler had vanished.

"Where did he go?" Joan wheezed.

Tom stared at the ten-foot high cement wall. Again, Tom called Roumoult, who confirmed that Wheeler had not doubled back.

"Maybe he climbed the wall and jumped over," Joan suggested.

"I know he's high, but he's not superman," Tom said. He leaned to his right, resting against something solid: a large green dumpster, too tall for him to reach its lid. "What's this doing here?" he muttered. He spotted a three-legged chair resting against its side. He grabbed it and set it in front of the dumpster.

"Don't do that," Joan said.

Tom ignored her. He stood on the chair and opened the lid. A distinct rotting smell crept up his nose. He shone his phone's flashlight inside. Paint was chipping, and the dumpster walls were coarse. It was almost completely empty. Tom's eye caught a small, black knob at the bottom. He held his phone in left hand and tried to reach it. The hefty lid weighed on his back.

"Joan push the lid up," he said.

"No."

"Just do it."

Tom felt the lid's weight lift off of him, and he leaned forward and pushed the knob. A loud clack surprised him. His feet slipped, and his phone slipped out of his hand. He tried to grab it in midair. With a loud hissing noise, the floor of the dumpster lowered. Tom's mobile slid over it and disappeared. Then the exit closed. "Wow," he breathed.

Tom instructed the squad to keep searching the pharma. He and Joan sat inside the dumpster and pushed the button. For a moment, their bodies suspended in air. Then they landed on something almost soft.

The mattress was old and too hard for sleeping. Clutching his back, Tom got to his feet.

Joan stood in the dark tunnel. "Where are we?"

"An old tunnel under the company," Tom answered. A howl startled him. Two large cages sat in a corner of the small space. Inside, white wolves pawed at the ground and barred their teeth.

"They are real?" Joan squeaked.

"Yeah," Tom whispered. "Let's get out of here." He spun around and was confronted by an iron door. Tom unlocked it and swung it open. Bright light blinded him for a moment. He stepped into the well-lit, white-furnished laboratory. Machines beeped, and colorful liquids were lit by flickering flames. Four long workbenches held glass beakers, papers, files, and test tubes of different sizes. Tom saw boxes nestled in a corner, similar to the ones that had been in the van. He reached into one and extracted a glass ball filled with bright green gas.

"What is that?" said Joan.

Tom put it back carefully. "A bomb."

They heard a rattle. Tom armed himself. A door burst open, and Wheeler stormed in. He jabbed Tom sharply in the stomach, and Tom fell hard. Joan booted Wheeler, and he landed on the floor.

"Stay down!" she yelled.

Tom grabbed his weapon. He had to look carefully to make sure he had the right suspect. The Wheeler they'd met had long since disappeared. This man was sickly. His eyes bulged, and his skin was pasty and pale. He glared at them with an animalistic hunger. Filthy white clothes hung limply off of him.

"Dr. Wheeler, you are under arrest," said Tom.

Dr. Wheeler growled.

Suddenly, a second door opened, and an armed officer entered the lab. Wheeler leaped, knocking over Joan. Tom tried to act, but he was too late. Wheeler snatched Joan's weapon and rested his finger on the trigger.

A deafening bang resounded. Blood dripped steadily to the floor. Tom looked at Joan, sure that he would find it trickling from a wound in her side. She was fine. Wheeler fell to his knees and then keeled over onto his stomach.

"No!" Tom flipped Wheeler onto his back. "Dr. Wheeler! Wheeler!"

"Call an ambulance!" Joan cried.

Wheeler wheezed, and blood bubbled at the edges of his mouth. His lips fluttered, but he could not answer.

"Who did you work for?" Tom asked. "Was it Weldon? Is it Weldon?"

Dr. Wheeler's eyes rolled, his pupils dilated, and the final breaths of life left him. He body sagged.

Tom's throat clenched. This case was a disaster. This was the second suspect he'd lost this week. He wondered who was next and what he could do to stop it.

H.G Ahedi

18

The Weldon's

June 20, 2015

NYPD Precinct

At dawn, Tom found himself in the Captain's office again. Joan stood beside him. The Captain strolled back and forth, hands running up and down his jawline. "Let me get this straight," he said. "Two detectives, six well-trained officers, and Wheeler is still dead?"

Tom nodded. "He was targeting Detective Chase, and the officer pulled the trigger."

The Captain rubbed his temples. "Who made those green bombs?"

"Wheeler. They are made of glass with a highly potent strain of PCP, along with the murderer's signature," said Tom. "The green gas is a dye used to create smoke bombs. Sir, Dr. Wheeler was just a tool. The white king was using him to create chemical bombs. There might be more of them."

"One step at a time. The good news is we've uncovered the secret lab and seized the chemical

242

bombs. Close ATPOS Pharmaceuticals until further notice. Get a warrant and question the Weldon's. Let me know if you find anything. Keep up the good work."

"So how are we doing?" Tom asked Joan, returning to the office with two large cups of coffee.

"Tim Larson, his family, and Ms. Garrison are all in safe houses," she said.

"Good. We'll have to wait for the warrant, but there's nothing stopping us from questioning Mark Weldon."

"Agreed," said Joan.

"What about the precinct bomber?" Tom asked.

"You'll love this. Roumoult tracked him to Astra Place. Our people checked all the train station cameras for that train until its last stop."

"He wasn't on it?"

"He boarded it but never left."

"Unless..." Tom started.

"He wore a disguise, got rid of it on the train, and disappeared into the crowd," Joan finished.

"Oh, I love this case," Tom said sarcastically. "What about the cigar box?"

"Another dead end."

"Fine," said Tom. "Let's go through the list of people working with historical stuff, starting with the Weldon's."

The media were tailing the NYPD and Weldon for their stories. Tom did all he could to avoid them. Tom spent his day focusing on the Weldon file. No one in the family had a criminal background. The Weldon's denied any knowledge of Wheeler's activities or his lab. For now, evidence pointed to Mark and his uncle,

Walter Weldon. Mark was often involved in fundraisers. Walter had a keen interest in archeology and ran several humanitarian projects, including campaigns for the Indian Ocean earthquake in 2004, Hurricane Katarina in 2005, an earthquake in Pakistan in 2005, and the Haiti earthquakes. Tom raised his eyebrows. The family had helped rebuild schools, hospitals, and houses in affected regions. Their projects were ongoing. Though he was now sixty-three years old, Walter had traveled to several dig sites, helping to search for buried treasures and retrieve artifacts, which he'd then donated to local governments. He supported young and aspiring archeologists and funded expeditions to Egypt, Mexico, Central America, Amazon, and even the Antarctic. Walter and Mark had power, influence, and money, but Tom could find no plausible motive for murder.

Cranston House

Roumoult sat on the balcony sipping tea. Today, he'd canceled his appointments, and decided to work from home. He'd used his time to catch up on paperwork and sleep. Tonight, both Fred and Charles had plans, leaving Roumoult alone in the house. He relaxed on the chair and closed his eyes. The gates opened with a clang. An engine groaned, and a car backfired as the driver pushed it to its limits. Roumoult ran downstairs and opened the door.

"Hello!" William chirped.

"Do me a favor. Fix your car."

"Why?"

"Because it's about to die."

"No, its not. Its perfect."

Roumoult changed the subject and offered him a beer. He returned to the balcony, William following behind him.

"How are you?" William asked, taking a seat.

"I'm just tired. My shoulder pain has returned, and I wanted to think."

William sipped his beer. "About?"

"The green gas and the blue lily. They feel symbolic. I think it means something."

"To the killer?" William asked. "I agree. He could have chosen any color. He chose green. And he deliberately mixed blue lily into the PCP."

"I wonder," said Roumoult, "what if he did come back from the dead?"

William stared at him.

19

The Ship Of The Dead

June 21, 2015

St. George Hospital

Emma returned to her small, messy office at the end of a challenging morning. Tim had told her everything. He'd apologized to her, which she didn't think was necessary. She drank her coffee and thought about her breakfast with Joan. Joan thought that Roumoult had overreacted and that Emma had just made a mistake. Emma looked at her phone; no missed calls. She closed her eyes and wished that she'd never asked him to stay.

Cranston Law Firm

Roumoult spent his morning looking for incidences, blasts and massacres involving gases. The problem was, he found too many. He'd underestimated the horrors of human history. When thought of explosion-related deaths, he thought of bigger conflicts, like wars. But it amazed him to read of the amount of deaths that had resulted from small explosions and gang attacks. After two hours of searching, he'd gotten nowhere, so he handed the task over to Jack. He knew that Jack could use keywords and search strategies much more effectively than he could. He had another important task. He had to pick Angelus up from the hospital.

Cranston Law Firm

Roumoult rubbed his temples. Aches in his arm and back stopped after he took his meds. He'd completed his legal work, and now he was looking at the big bundle of papers. Jack was thorough and collected thousands of stories, categorizing them according to country and year. The murderer's signature was a flower native to Egypt, so Roumoult thought it was best to start there. He found several interesting stories in newspapers, magazines, and books. One by one, he scanned through the articles. Most of them were on local gangs and terrorist attacks. He was so engrossed in his work that he didn't realize it was getting dark. A tap on the door distracted him.

Emma rocked on her heels. "Hi, am I disturbing you?"

"No, no," said Roumoult, getting to his feet. He turned on the lights and invited her to sit in the client's chair.

"I can come back later," Emma said.

"No, it's okay," Roumoult replied, taking a seat.

Emma looked at his desk. Papers were strewn all over it, making it a jumbled mess.

"I'm trying to figure something out."

She smiled.

Roumoult felt his heartbeat quicken. "What can I do for you?"

Emma smiled feebly. "I'm sorry. I didn't mean to hurt you."

Roumoult bowed his head. The truth was his anger was long gone. Too much else had happened to soften it. "I'm sorry too."

Emma looked astonished.

"I just stormed out of there," Roumoult continued. "I never gave you a chance to explain. I reacted badly."

"I just wanted to see you," said Emma.

Roumoult didn't know what to say. He chewed on his lip.

"I think you're busy," Emma said. "Maybe we'll catch up later."

"Sure thing." Roumoult stood up and looked at her. Emma lowered her eyes. He felt his heart race.

"Bye," she said. She left abruptly, leaving Roumoult wondering if there was something else, he was supposed to have said.

After Emma left, Roumoult couldn't focus. He sat in silence, swaying back and forth in his chair. He left the office and returned with a glass of scotch and decided to push on. Flipping through pages and pages of history, Roumoult felt distressed. Too many people had perished unnecessarily. He sipped his drink as he read one story after another. Then something caught his eye. He sat back and looked at the newspaper clipping. A picture of a medium-sized ship caught his attention, and so did the title: *The Ship of the Dead*. Roumoult peered closer and read the small print: *Mysterious slaughtering onboard the Nefret in Cairo, Egypt in 1975*. It was published in the New York Times. Roumoult checked the internet for related articles and found nothing. He printed the clipping and stared at it. "Why was it called the ship of the dead?" he wondered aloud.

June 22, 2015

National Public Library of New York

As soon as he woke up, Roumoult had to drive to the Firm to meet with a few clients and approve briefs. He left the Firm at lunch time and parked his car on East 41st street, walking back toward the Library. He rushed up the stairs, entered the vast hall, and walked straight to the information desk. The queue was long, and he had to wait. He explained he was looking for a newspaper article and the librarian provided him with directions.

The Microform Reading Room was on the first floor opposite the Library's shop. Roumoult used the computer to search the catalog for articles published in 1975. Unfortunately, he couldn't find any. He returned to the reception. The librarian, an older woman with cat-eyeglasses, looked annoyed. "You again?" she said.

"Yes," said Roumoult, handing over a printout of the newspaper clipping. "I'm looking for an article, but I can't find it."

The woman merely glanced at the print and turned to the computer. "Because it hasn't been digitalized."

"Okay. Could I see it or get a copy?"

"Fill in the request form and submit it." The librarian slid a clipboard across the desk.

"Can you make an exception?" Roumoult pleaded.

Her eyebrows knitted. "I can't leave the counter to go hunting for a newspaper."

"Well, can I look for it myself?"

"No. These are old papers and probably the last copies. I can't let you play around with them. You'll have to wait."

Roumoult stood in a corner, watching people walk past him. His phone rang again; he silenced it. He glanced at the Librarian, who glared at him occasionally out of the corner of her eye. In the late afternoon, he finally followed her back to the first floor.

"You're lucky," she said. "We had a couple of requests from the archives, and I just added yours to the list."

"Thanks." Roumoult waited as she disappeared into a cramped office and returned with an envelope. "Is this it?" she asked pulling out a copy of the article.

"Yes." Roumoult peeked in curiously. "Can I—"

"Yes, you can keep it."

"Thanks!"

NYPD Precinct

Roumoult couldn't miss his appointments; he had to return to the Firm. He called Tom to ask him to stay back. At eight p.m., he found himself in the elevator. It stopped on the third level; he stepped out. The place looked deserted. He marched along the corridor and knocked on Tom's door. As expected, Tom, Joan, and William were waiting for him.

"I really need to eat," Tom said.

"This won't take long," Roumoult promised, handing each of them a copy of the newspaper article.

"'Ship of the dead'?" William asked.

"It's a copy of an article published in 1975 by Raker West. It describes an incident, actually a massacre, involving sixty people in Egypt on a ship called the Nefret. The article says that the locals believed that a green demon possessed a tourist, who slaughtered everyone else on board."

"A demon?" Tom asked rolling his eyes.

"Let me finish," said Roumoult. "Raker West didn't think it was a demon and spoke with the police investigating the crime. The police told him that two locals found the ship adrift and boarded it. The deck was painted with blood, and there were human remains everywhere. They freaked out and called the police. The cops noted something particular: a green substance was spread through one of the cabins and on the deck. They inspected the bodies and retrieved bullets belonging to an AK 47. The passengers died before their bodies were mutilated. Police traced the murders to the man they found in the Captain's chair. He'd shot himself in the temple."

"That's dreadful!" cried Joan.

"According to the manifest, there were only forty-six people on the Nefret, and nine crewmen, including the Captain. But they discovered over sixty bodies," said Roumoult.

"Why?" asked Tom.

"The police thought the Apophis raided the ship but something..."

"Apophis?" both Joan and Tom interrupted him.

Roumoult sulked. "I don't think an Egyptian God…"

"No, no, it's a handle. Alex told us his boss called himself the Apophis."

Roumoult arched his eyebrows. "That means Apophis could be the black king?"

"Exactly," said Joan.

"So Apophis, a.k.a. the black king, planned to loot the Nefret, but something went wrong," Roumoult continued. "The green dust might have been a hallucinogen that drove everyone nuts. Especially the guy who murdered everyone and chopped up the bodies."

"Could the green gas be PCP?" Joan asked William.

"Or something like PCP?" Roumoult suggested.

"Okay, forty years ago, Apophis raided the Nefret, and a green gas was released that turned one man into a maniac who killed everyone. How is it linked to our case?" Joan asked.

"The green gas, Egypt, the blue lily… It all means something to our killer," said Roumoult. "Perhaps someone's loved one was brutally killed on the Nefret, and he wants to get back at the Apophis. He could be the white king."

"Ahh… I see, the white king's motive is vengeance," Tom concluded.

"Sounds logical," Roumoult said.

"Where is the ship now?"

"I don't know. There are no more articles about it. It's as if it vanished into thin air."

Tom sulked. "Let's suppose someone wants to take revenge. How do we find this guy?"

"Let's start with our primary suspects," Roumoult said. "Weldon."

"Very rich, very powerful, no motive." Tom ticked items off on his fingers.

"What about their link to Egypt?" asked Joan.

"Mostly expeditions and humanitarian projects."

The room fell silent.

"There's one way to find out," Roumoult said quietly, "Work out if any of the Weldon's were on that ship."

Tom slowly put his hands on his waist. "Now, how do you suggest we get the passenger list of a ship that probably sank over four decades ago?"

NYPD Precinct

Tom felt like climbing to the top of the Empire State Building and screaming at the top of his lungs. On the other hand, the case was beginning to make sense. Now there was potential for a motive: the white king wanted revenge, and the black king wanted wealth. He contacted the tech department to see what else they could find out about the Nefret. Officer Jake entered his office and handed him an address. He studied it, and thought it was worth a shot.

Cranston Firm

Roumoult's day passed quickly. He told Jack to find out more about the Nefret and set to work rifling through old media reports and dealing with clients. To make matters worse, he was scheduled to attend an afternoon project meeting with his father and Paul in Jersey. He resented the time wasted on the long drive. He liked action and getting things done, not participating in long and boring discussions. He was tempted to make up an excuse not to go, but one look at the agenda told him that he was needed.

City Morgue

Files, books, loose papers, and newspaper clippings were scattered all over the floor of William's office. His mobile buzzed.

"Hello?" he said.

"Hi, William. This is Emma."

"Hi," William said uncomfortably.

"Don't worry, I'm not calling to gloat. I need help."

"With what?"

"Wagner left me a clue."

Emma did not take long to arrive. William invited her into his office, and she handed him a half-torn piece of paper with something messily scribbled on it.

"It was posted to me,"

"Why?" William asked.

"Maybe because I believed him. And in the same envelope, I found this access card." She withdrew a small plastic card from her pocket and gave it to William. "I wonder what it opens."

William cleared some space on his desk and took a few minutes to set up his electric magnifying glass. He carefully placed the piece of paper and turned on the light.

"What is it?" Emma asked.

"From its thickness, possibly a piece of a business card," William replied, carefully flattening the paper using tweezers. "This," he gestured to the scribble, "looks like a symbol."

"Did someone draw it?"

"No. It looks printed. The symbol has three spirals in bold, black ink, interlocking with each other, making a triangle. We can only see part of the triangle."

"Do you know anyone who could identify the other part?" Emma asked.

William smiled.

After sending Jack all the information, William and Emma got busy organizing. Secretly, William wondered why Emma hadn't gone to Roumoult. His thoughts were interrupted by a return call from Jack. He put the phone on speaker.

"I found what you asked. It's a symbol of Celtic origin called a Triskele."

"Anything to do with religion?" asked William.

"Depends. I'm sending you the complete picture of the symbol. The Triskele is one of the oldest Irish symbols in existence. It appears on entrance of Newgrange kerbstones from as early as 3200 BC."

"Okay, how does that help us?" Emma asked.

"Well, it's a logo of a company," said Jack.

"Wagner's company? I am sure Tom checked those." William said.

"No. It's under Racheal's name. We've been checking Wagner's finances, properties, apartments... Suppose there was something he paid for, but Rachael owns or runs."

"That makes sense," Emma said.

"This symbol was used as a logo for Angel Garments, which was a company registered in Rachael's name. It's located on Staten Island. I'm sending through the address."

Statue of Liberty

William rested his weight on the balcony of the ferry and admired the statue. It never failed to amaze him. Staten Island drew closer. William welcomed the fresh air. Working around corpses all day and in an office under dim light, he sometimes forgot the fresh beauty of real life. The city lights dazzled. Emma sat on a bench and played with her phone. William wondered whether he'd done the right thing in bringing her along.

Wagner had led a prosperous life, launching several major business pursuits, including businesses in his daughter's name. In 1999, he had started a manufacturing factory called Angel Garments. It had eight production lines and used only top-of-the-range equipment. It had been a successful venture until an incident had killed two people. The Wagner's took it badly, and the company shut down. Based on Jack's information, William presumed that Angel Garments was located about three miles beyond the theater, past Fort Hill Park on Staten Island. To get around quicker, William booked a rental car. He called Joan, but she said she and Tom were busy chasing up another clue to join them.

New Jersey

Roumoult strolled toward his car, rubbing the back of his neck. After two hours of discussion with Paul, Fred, and other board members, the meeting was finally over. He got behind the wheel and rested his head back against the seat. Immediately, his thoughts were consumed by Emma. Why had she just left? His phone buzzed.

"Hello William, how are you?"

"Great," William said.

"Are you home?"

"No, I'm heading for Staten Island."

Roumoult laughed. "Why?"

William explained.

"How did you get the business card?"

"Wagner sent it to Emma."

"Emma?" Roumoult asked. "Is she there with you?"

"Yeah."

"What's she doing there?"

"Her idea, not mine," William said defensively.

"Did you call Joan?"

William pretended not to have heard him. "You should come," he said.

"William," Roumoult growled. "She shouldn't be there."

"Are you coming?"

"NO!"

"I'll text you the address anyway."

Roumoult shook his head. "Goodnight."

Staten Island

William drove, passing the theater and the park, houses, churches, and residents strolling down the streets. Three miles ahead, the houses became sparse, replaced by dense trees and bushes. There were hardly any streetlights, which made it difficult to navigate, and all the buildings looked alike. William and Emma decided to search on foot. They climbed out of the car and began to walk up the street. Most of the buildings were warehouses.

They turned left, and William realized he'd missed a street. He doubled back and paused in front of the dark, narrow alley. To his right a brick wall towered. Emma paused, staring fixedly at something. William stopped to look at an old one-story building. It was unappealing, its dark, broken windows gave him a sense that it had been abandoned some time ago. Moss grew unevenly all over the wall like a parasite, and a filthy board was propped up against it. William stepped closer. He lifted his right hand and used his sleeve to wipe the dirt from the board, revealing the Triskele symbol.

William entered the compound, Emma trailing behind him. He walked to the end of the wall, and realized the warehouse was huge. Then they crossed to the other side. Beside the loading bay was a steel door with tracks leading up to it. William wondered if it was time to call for backup. He heard a soft beep and a hissing noise. He turned to Emma, who stood in front of the open door.

"This is it," she whispered excitedly showing him the access card.

William hesitated for a moment before following her inside.

Beyond William's flashlight, there was only emptiness. The air inside the warehouse was stale and hot, and the ground was covered with dust, dirt, and tire tracks. Two clear sets foot and paw prints cleared a path through the filth. William examined the uprooted equipment leaning against the walls. In the dim light stood the white van.

New Jersey

Officer Jake successfully tracked Mario's mother. Mario had seen her two weeks ago. Tom and Joan drove to Constable Hook, New Jersey to question her, but after half an hour, it became clear that even his mother did not know his current whereabouts. The drug dealer had disappeared.

"There's no winning this case, is there?" Tom remarked, turning his hand on himself and pretending to shoot himself in the head.

"We'll find him," Joan said. Her mobile beeped. "It's William. He says he found the white van!"

Staten Island

William marched towards the vehicle and opened the back door; it was empty.

Emma sulked.

"What's important is that we found it," William told her. He climbed behind the wheel of the van, while Emma peeked through the passenger seat window. William took a few minutes to check the glove box, the floor, and the seats of the van, but found nothing. Disheartened, he jumped out and slammed the door shut.

Emma stood with her ear pressed against the wall. She moved away slowly. "There's something on the other side," she whispered.

William leaned close and heard a low humming. He angled the torch at the wall and walked forward. A pillar was partially hidden behind the wall. With his fingers, he felt the small gap between the black wall and the pillar. He spun around and rushed to the other end, kneeled, and saw a lever. He pushed it. A deafening thunder echoed throughout the warehouse, followed by a loud, dragging clamor. As the big door opened, William stood at Emma's side. The door halted with a powerful thud. Fear clutched at William, but he couldn't tear his eyes away from the dark void.

"What do you think is in there?" Emma asked.

William shook his head, swallowing hard. "I don't know. Let's look quickly and then leave."

Inside, it was chilly, and soft scents of wood permeated the air. Wooden boxes of all shapes and sizes filled the space. Trolley tracks marked the ground, their depth telling William that whatever they'd carried had been heavy. On the left wall was a large freezer. The compressor made a loud humming noise. William pulled the door open, icy mist collided with the warm air. Emma gasped. Three corpses laid in bags. Swallowing his fear, William reached out and unzipped one of the bags. Nigel Hawk's lifeless, decomposing face stared back at him. He closed the freezer, turning to look at Emma. Two weeks ago, he would have jumped with joy, but reflecting on the last few days he didn't feel like celebrating.

William walked over to the clusters of boxes, passing a sarcophagus and stopping to examine a medium-sized blue crate. He ran his fingers along the gold freehand markings that decorated it before prying it open. It was empty, but beautiful. Next, his eyes settled on two statues of women that had been positioned to face each other. Besides it was a large box. He opened it and his jaw dropped. It was full of pieces of gold, silver and raw diamonds.

"This place is full of ancient artifacts," Emma said squeakily, "and gems."

"Yeah. I think we—" William stopped himself mid-sentence and stepped toward a wooden door. He twisted the knob and pushed it open.

The next room was small. A thick layer of plastic protected the walls, and two large benches held innumerable beakers and containers. Any spare space was occupied by bulky weight machines. Small, transparent packages of white powder were placed all over the ground. William scowled. They'd seen enough. As he turned to leave, he noticed the quizzical look on Emma's face, her sights set on the wall behind him.

On the wall was a rusted panel. A green light blinked irregularly.

"What does that mean?" Emma asked.

"I don't want to know," William said. He reached for her arm, beginning to pull her away.

Suddenly, the light turned red. A loud screeching sound resonated, then a thunderous noise. Roars echoed in the small room. Pale shapes glided through the darkness, and two giant beasts moved towards them, jaws snapping.

"I really didn't have to open that door," William cursed. Just as the creatures jumped, William pulled the door shut. It vibrated with a heavy thud. Emma shook beside him, and a humming increased. He turned and saw the big door closing. "Emma, get out! Go!" he yelled. The hounds banged against the wooden door which shuddered and fought to break.

20

The Hounds Of Staten Island

Staten Island

Roumoult pushed the brakes, and his Audi skidded to a stop in front of the loading bay. It had taken him less than half an hour to reach Staten Island. The challenge was finding the address William had sent him. He stared up at the massive building and cross-checked the address on his GPS. William and Emma were nowhere in sight, and neither of them were answering their phones. Roumoult parked and was about to unbuckle his seatbelt when an uncomfortable sensation swept over him. His headlights flickered out, and there were no streetlights; it was pitch black. Roumoult was struck by the overwhelming feeling that something or someone was watching him. Reaching for the cup holder, he tilted the tray upwards and slid open the lid, grabbing his 9-millimeter gun.

Inside the warehouse, Roumoult found the van easily. He began to move toward it, then he heard a muffled cry. Roumoult stared at the wall. He'd recognize her voice anywhere.

"Emma!" Roumoult yelled, pressing his ear against the wall.

A suppressed scream was followed by a steady tapping noise. He stepped back and considered his options. Looking to the ground, he noticed the footprints. He followed them into the corner where he could just make out a small lever, caked in dust but with patches wiped clean by a fresh handprint. Roumoult stuck out a foot and kicked it.

A thud boomed. The wall moved, and Roumoult walked along with it, dragging his hand across its surface. He felt someone bump into him. Emma screamed.

He grabbed her. "Emma!"

A mixture of emotions filled her face—fear, relief, and confusion mingling. Her hands were filthy, and her hair was tangled.

"What happened?"

Another thud shook the ground.

"What's that?"

William came hurtling out of the darkness.

"William?"

"Roumoult!" William looked frantically behind him. "Run! Run! Get out!"

They ran down the dark hall and exited the warehouse. William quickly closed the door.

"What's going on?" Roumoult demanded. "What happened to you two?" Another heavy thump and a high-pitched roar made the hair on the back of his neck stand on end. "What the hell is that?"

"William," Emma choked.

Roumoult followed her gaze to a small steel panel with a flashing green light.

"Run!" William yelled again. They sprinted to Roumoult's car.

Roumoult threw himself behind the wheel. Emma buckled her seat belt in the passenger seat, and William climbed into the back. Roumoult twisted the key. With a groan, the car stuttered to life, its headlights cutting through the darkness.

"Roumoult! Go! Go now!" William cried.

"They'll kill us," Emma screamed. Her whole body shook with terror.

"What? Who?" Roumoult shouted back as he shifted the car into reverse and pressed his foot down on the accelerator.

"Hounds," William said. "Big bloody hounds!"

A flash of bright light pierced the night violently. "What the hell?" Roumoult said, shielding his eyes with his hands.

"Is that Joan?" William yelled.

"I don't think so," Roumoult replied. He slammed on the gas, and as he did, the green light on the panel turned red.

The hounds charged out of the warehouse and bounded toward the car.

"Oh, this is fantastic!" Roumoult roared. "William, how do you find these things?"

"This is not my fault!"

"Really?"

Roumoult did his best but driving backward was a challenge. He swung the steering wheel, trying to evade the parked cars. The beasts jumped over vehicles and lunged forward. The road ahead was straight and vacant. Now was his chance. "Hold on!" he yelled. He pushed the breaks hard. The tires screeched, and smoke gushed. Before losing momentum, Roumoult spun the wheel. The hounds smashed against the vehicle. The Audi twirled a hundred and eighty degrees and came to an abrupt stop. Roumoult pressed the throttle. The beasts got up, shook themselves off, and followed.

He reduced speed as he approached the roundabout. Suddenly, lights flashed startlingly bright. A four-wheel drive raced toward them.

Emma shrieked.

Roumoult steered the car. From the corner of his eye, he could catch a glimpse of a dark figure. "Get down!" he shouted.

A flood of bullets struck the Audi. Sparks flew off the roof. Roumoult winced and lost control. Frantically, he grabbed the steering wheel and spun it. Another crackle of gunfire. He ducked and heard a loud crash. The back windshield shattered, raining glass down into the backseat. "Who the hell are these guys?" Roumoult yelled.

"I don't know!" William shouted back.

"What did you do?"

"Hey. If you die, I die! Does that make you feel any better?"

"No!" Roumoult spat. "What was in that warehouse?"

"Treasure," Emma said. "They were guarding a treasure."

Roumoult glimpsed at her quickly.

"We have to do something!" William said.

"Call Joan?" Emma suggested.

"She's unreachable!"

Roumoult handed his gun to William. "Make every bullet count." He took another sharp turn.

"Surely, someone will call the police," Emma cried out.

"We might be dead by then," Roumoult replied.

The shooter appeared again.

"Watch out!" Roumoult shouted. He tried to put distance between the two cars. Bullets cut through the air and blew out the taillights. He noticed the gunman was reloading his ammo. He took his foot off the accelerator. "Now, William! Now!"

William aimed and pulled the trigger. The bullet struck the other car's bonnet. "Damn!" he said. He fired again and missed. "Oh, incoming!"

The gunman reappeared. Roumoult rammed the pedal to the floor, but it was too late. The bullets pierced through steel. Bits of the windshield's frame blew into the air. A stream of bullets narrowly missed Roumoult, tearing through the back of his seat. "Damn!" Roumoult said. He needed an edge. With the car still racing at eighty kilometers an hour, he turned to the GPS and studied the terrain. "That's it," he said. He made a sudden U-turn back toward the warehouse.

"What the hell are you doing?" William yelled.

"I have an idea."

With the assailants still on their tail, Roumoult drove past the warehouse and turned onto a narrow road leading toward the hills. The truck wasn't far behind.

"What are we doing?" William asked.

"Emma, on the floor," Roumoult ordered

"No!"

"Now, please. It's just a precaution."

"I wish you'd tell me what you're doing." She unbuckled her seat belt and slid down.

"William be ready," Roumoult warned as the Audi climbed up the hill.

"For what?"

He pushed the accelerator, took a sharp turn close to the rocks, and pressed the brakes. The protruding rock behind them would provide the perfect cover. He turned the headlights off; his left hand dangled over the gear stick. He turned the engine off and waited. Minutes passed slowly, no sound in the car but their breathing. Roumoult looked over at Emma. "It will be okay," he whispered.

They heard the roar of an engine. Roumoult grabbed and squeezed Emma's hand as a bright light streamed from behind them. The truck rushed ahead. They hadn't seen them. Roumoult swung back into action. He slammed his foot on the gas. "William now!"

William raised the gun, aimed, and fired two bullets at the truck's rear tire.

Boom! The tires blazed. The four-wheeler dangled, spinning out of control. Roumoult knocked his vehicle against it. Metal collided, sparks flew, and Roumoult kept pushing until the truck sped toward the edge of the cliff.

William took a shot at the passenger. The window shattered, and the vehicle skidded off the road, rolling twice and slamming against a tree. Roumoult hit the brakes.

"Yes!" William shouted.

Roumoult relaxed.

Emma's face showed a mix of puzzlement, excitement, and concern. "You, you..." she stuttered.

"Um..." Roumoult struggled for words.

The Audi fell silent. "You have got to be kidding me," Roumoult groaned.

Emma sat back in her seat.

Roumoult tried the ignition. Nothing. He paused at the sound of a low growl. He turned to Emma; she looked terrified. To their left, the growls grew louder.

"Roumoult, get us out of here," William cried.

Roumoult tried the ignition again, the car chugged to life.

Suddenly, a hound dove at the car, leaping right through the cracked glass.

Staten Island

Joan looked at her mobile. "I think it's on the other side," she said, pointing to the drawbridge.

Tom couldn't believe it. William had sent them the address, but they couldn't find it. He was trying to get in touch with Roumoult or William, but neither of them were picking up.

"Where are they?"

"Let me check the GPS in the car," said Joan.

Tom held his head in frustration. A loud crashing noise sounded a little way off. He surveyed the hill across the river.

Staten Island

Emma screams echoed in Roumoult's ears. William flailed, trying to kick the hound out. Its fangs tightened around William's right foot. "Help!" he shouted.

Before Roumoult could think, the second hound pounded the window. The car spun out of control. He frantically twisted the wheel. He glanced behind him. Gone.

"Gun," he demanded. "Where's the gun?"

"It fell off," William yelled.

"Take the bloody shoe off!" Roumoult roared. He could see something ahead.

Roumoult urged the car forward, driving closer to the mountain where a huge rock bulged out. "Hold on!" he shouted.

At that moment, Emma reached down to her foot and removed her shoe. She to hit the hound over the head "Get off him!"

The car jolted, throwing Emma off balance. The beast howled as it collided with the mountain. It lost grip on William's ankle and slid from the window. Roumoult noticed the blood that streaked the rocks. He glanced at William, who was staring at his bloodstained socks. "Are you okay?" he asked.

"Yeah, I think so," William breathed.

"It's okay now. We're going downhill. If we follow the same road we came down, we'll—" The Audi lurched. "No, no." He slammed his fist against the steering wheel.

"What is it?" Emma asked.

"It's one of the tires."

The car slowed, and something hit the driver's side window, cracking the glass. Roumoult couldn't believe it. The second wounded hound was chasing them.

"What are these things?" Emma called out in horror.

Roumoult scanned the road. Their chances of getting out of this alive were bleak. Sweating and panting, he drove. A sign caught his attention: *Drawbridge*.

"I found the gun," William said.

In the rear mirror, Roumoult could see smoke pouring out of the tires, but with the hound on their tail, he didn't dare reduce his speed.

Staten Island

Tom stood in front of an old and rusted panel. He wondered if it worked. Joan was still struggling with the maps, and no one was picking up their phones. Then he heard it again—the roar of an engine. He squinted and made out headlights. He stepped forward, accidentally bumping into the panel. A thud resonated. The clamps below the bridge disconnected, and the two parts started moving upwards.

Staten Island

"Is it just me, or is the drawbridge moving?" William asked.

"Oh, no!" Emma cried.

It was becoming increasingly difficult for Roumoult to maintain speed. The hound would not give up. Suddenly, the beast jumped and smashed against the cracked windshield. It shattered completely, sending the car spinning. It skidded a full circle before screeching to a halt. Roumoult gripped the wheel, sat back in his seat, and froze. The creature stood on the bonnet. Blood trickled from its head, and saliva dripped from its mouth. It flashed its fangs.

Bang!

Roumoult jumped, covering his ears.

"Damn!" William snapped as his bullet missed the hound. The bridge groaned. "Roumoult, drive," he ordered.

Roumoult didn't need to be told twice. Shaking his head, ignoring the ringing noise in his ears, he drove.

Tilted to one side, the Audi dragged itself towards the bridge. Rubber tore off the blown tire, and steel rubbed against the road, leaving a trail of sparks. The beast followed at an alarming pace.

"William, watch out," Roumoult yelled.

The hound roared and plunged forward, sinking its teeth into the back seat.

"Ah!" William shouted.

Roumoult pinned the accelerator to the floor, and they drove up the bridge at full speed.

Staten Island

Tom was thunderstruck. It was Roumoult. "Joan!" he shouted as the bridge raised higher and higher. "Oh, Lord!"

Headlights appeared at the top. The engine roared as the car jumped over the small gap and skidded down. "Oh God, what have I done!"

The bridge was almost vertical. The Audi skidded sideways before correcting itself. It struck the road. Puff! Puff! The airbags released, crushing the passengers. The vehicle stood vertical for a second, and then it landed on the roof with a bang.

Tom scrambled to help but stopped dead in his tracks. An enormous hound stared unblinkingly at him. The beast lowered onto all four limbs and growled. Viciously, it lunged towards him. Tom drew his gun and fired. But it was too late. It rammed into him.

21

Treasure

June 23, 2015

Staten Island

Adrenaline flooded Roumoult's system. His eyes opened. His heartbeat loudly. He shoved the airbag away from his face. "Is everyone okay?"

He heard groans.

"Emma! William!"

No answer.

Trying to breathe normally, Roumoult unbuckled his seatbelt and crawled out of the window frame. "Oh, not again," he muttered. He stood up but immediately grabbed the car door for support, worried that he'd collapse. He leaned into the vehicle and found Emma pinned to her seat. "Emma!" he said, helping her out. "Are you okay?"

She shivered in his arms.

"It's okay, it's okay. We're okay."

"Yeah, don't mind me," William huffed, crawling out.

"Where is it?" Emma asked surveying their surroundings.

"I don't—" Roumoult's voice was drowned by a loud cry. He turned and recognized the beast's newest victims. "Tom! Joan!"

"Help! Tom!" Joan cried.

Roumoult ran as fast as he could, almost tripping over the sidewalk.

"Oh, God no!"

Using every ounce of strength, he had left, he pushed the heavy hound away. Tom's torn shirt was drenched in blood. The hound's sharp claws had dug into the skin on his neck and shoulder. Roumoult shook him roughly.

Suddenly, Tom coughed. His eyes sprung open, and he cried out, holding his chest.

"Oh, Tom!" Joan cried.

"Are you okay?" asked Roumoult.

Tom tried to sit up, but Emma stopped him. "Stay. I need a med kit."

"There should be one in the car," Roumoult answered getting to his feet. He rummaged through the glovebox until he found a first aid kit. Then he returned to help Emma treat Tom's wounds.

"Tom. Are you all right?" Roumoult asked again.

Tom put his hand to his chest as if checking for a heartbeat. "I-I don't know. It came out of nowhere. It could have killed me."

Roumoult rested a gentle hand on his shoulder.

The ambulance, a tow truck, and four police cruisers arrived at the same time. William was on the phone arranging for someone to pick up the rental car. Roumoult wished he had never come to this damn place. He looked at his car. In the moonlight, the Audi sat upside down. Smoke poured from the hood, and countless deep dents, bullet holes, and scratches marked the doors. All the windows had been smashed out of their frames. For the first time, Roumoult checked his watch. It was one a.m.

Staten Island

Roumoult sent his car for repairs before joining the others at the warehouse. He was frustrated, but he wanted to have a look inside; he hadn't gone through the chase for nothing. The place was swarming with cops. The CSU unit was busy checking the van. The heavy door opened with a loud thud, and over a dozen beams of light entered the gloomy hall. William directed the police officers toward the freezer, while Roumoult walked with Tom toward a large crate. Tom popped it open, and Roumoult's jaw fell. It was full to the brim of what had to be hundreds of glittering coins.

"Oh my God," Tom said.

Roumoult picked up a coin and turned it over. It looked like gold, heavier than most modern coins, oval shaped and with the word *Nero* engraved on it.

"Detective!" someone called.

Roumoult threw the coin back into the crate and followed Tom. They stopped in front of a half-opened stone box.

"You've got to see this," said one of the police officers.

Four officers carefully lifted the lid. Roumoult covered his nostrils, but he couldn't look away. A skull with a half-broken jaw and hollow eyes stared back at him, strands of worn cloth unraveling from around it. Roumoult looked closer. A cramped child-sized figure sat inside the box, dressed in an aging cloth wrap.

"It's a mummy," said Roumoult.

Tom turned to Roumoult. "This explains why they wanted you dead. This place is loaded with antiquities. Stuff here must be worth millions."

"Yeah. Protected by deadly hounds."

"You guys were lucky. These dogs were Rottweiler, one of the most dangerous breeds. They were probably trained to hunt down anyone entering the premises. They must've caught your scent, followed and attacked."

Roumoult sulked and noted Tom's torn shirt and the bandages on his neck. "Are you okay?"

Tom shook his head.

Cranston House

Roumoult was thankful to Tom, who despite his injuries, volunteered to drop Emma, William, and him at home. Fatigue dominated every part of Roumoult's body. He walked toward the main door. It flung open.

"Where have you been?" Fred demanded. "I've been trying to call you."

"My phone battery died."

"Where's the car?" Fred asked.

Roumoult ruffled his hair with his hand and said nothing.

NYPD Precinct

Tom had to go to the hospital to take care of his injuries. He had company. William needed to consult the doctor about the bite on his foot. After returning home Tom couldn't sleep, so when the Captain called, it was almost a relief. He wanted Tom to come to the Precinct immediately. The media was fast, and the headlines everywhere read: *NYPD Discovers Hidden Treasure*. The National Museum of History wanted the artifacts. Since Dr. Payne was involved in the case, he was acting as a liaison between the cops and the Museum.

Tom entered the Captain's office and found Dr. Payne pacing the floor.

"Good morning Detective," said the Captain in a calm tone.

"Good morning, Sir," Tom replied, noticing a coin in an evidence bag on the desk.

"Take a seat, gentlemen."

Tom did as he was told and waited for the Captain to begin speaking.

"Dr. Payne, it's evidence," the Captain explained. "The CSU needs to examine for prints…"

"Absolutely not! You will destroy them!" Dr. Payne argued. "These are incredibly delicate and rare items. They belong in the Museum and should be handled by experts. You can't—"

"It's evidence in an active investigation," the Captain repeated firmly.

"Perhaps I can change your mind. Let me show you something," Dr. Payne said. "This coin," he picked it up and held it in front of them, "is called the Aureus. One of the most precious ancient Roman coins. I presume it was minted in the fourth century and weighs about forty grams. Note the blur of the letters and the engraved face, the wear is similar. This hand-minted coin was made by melting gold and pouring it into a mold. Then it was placed in a hinge die set, which produced a uniform engraving on both sides." He flipped the coin. "See? These tiny waves were probably made during the minting process."

"Your point?" Tom asked.

"The point," the Captain responded before Dr. Payne could, "is that this is an authentic Roman coin, and we have several others downstairs."

"And they are worth millions."

"But the one I saw was different. It had the word *Nero* on it," said Tom.

"That's another famous ancient Roman coin imprinted with the Emperor Nero's face. It's very rare, and a collector's delight," said Dr. Payne.

"What about the mummy?" Tom asked.

Dr. Payne opened a file. "From the pictures, I can tell that they moved the mummy from its original location and placed it in this stone box, which they probably thought was the best way to preserve it. They were wrong! And this mummy is not Egyptian."

"What?" Tom raised his eyebrows.

"It's from South America, specifically from Peru. Have you ever heard of the Chinchorro?" Dr. Payne asked.

"Nope."

"The Chinchorro lived over two thousand years before the Egyptians on coastal areas of Atacama

Desert, now known as Peru. They mummified their dead. They cleaned their bodies, removed their organs, packed them with clay, and stitched them back up again. Note the black paint above the skull and on the limbs. As a part of the ritual, they painted the corpses black. With time, the paint has withered away. Egyptians did not paint mummies. The strands, the cloth, is a hoax."

Tom sat back. "But why?"

"It's rare, unique and these smugglers knew that. They probably disguised it so that it could pass as Egyptian mummy probably until they found a buyer. Any collector would pay a handsome price for it. Now we have it and the situation could become political as once the South American people learn of its existence, they will want it back. We need to act fast."

All Tom wanted was to catch the murderer. "What do you propose?"

NYPD Precinct

After a thorough discussion, they agreed to release the artifacts to a secure room at the Museum. Half a dozen cops drove alongside the truck to ensure the treasure's security. Dr. Payne and the CSU unit were to work together.

Tom wondered where Joan was. He is looking forward to going home and catching up on some sleep. But there were other pressing matters.

The lift halted, and the door to the basement opened. He walked through the long dim corridor to step into the small room. Wagner, Hawk and Garrison bodies laid silently, as if frozen in time. He stood by William and waited. Racheal stood by her father with a subtle smile. Mrs. Garrison remained indifferent. Ms. Garrison stood a bit away from her brother's body.

Racheal stepped forward, "Is it over? Can I take him home now?"

William answered before Tom, "Yes. We have got everything we need from other sources."

"And the murderer?" asked Ms. Garrison.

"We are working on it." Tom replied.

Racheal and William left.

"What about me?"

"You can return to your normal life."

"How?"

Tom knew her pain too well. "Well, you begin with talking with people." he replied and handed her his card. "Call me anytime."

She smiled.

Tom returned to his office, feeling much better. Joan was not there.

Officer Jake appeared at the door. "Sir, we have Mark Weldon and his lawyer in the interrogation room."

The Weldon's had been almost impossible to question, but with APTOS now under formal investigation, there'd been good reason to lure them in. Tom entered the questioning room carrying the case file.

"Am I under arrest?" asked Mark Weldon.

Tom didn't answer, calmly taking his seat. Mark's lawyer was a bald man with a calm demeanor.

"Mr. Weldon, did you know these men?" Tom laid out the pictures of Wagner, Nigel, Garrison, and Alex.

"Is my client under arrest?" asked the lawyer.

"We just want some answers. Do you recognize any of them?"

Mark pointed towards Alex's photo. "Only this one. I saw him on TV. Fred shot him."

Tom collected the photos and put them aside. "What can you tell us about Dr. Wheeler?"

"He was an exemplary employee,"

"Do you visit all your exemplary employees at home?"

Mark's face turned to stone. "What the hell are you talking about?"

"You met Dr. Wheeler twice the week before he died. Why?"

"That's none of your business."

"He was building chemical bombs in a secret lab under your company. So, it becomes my business."

"I'll tell you the same thing I told the reporters," said Mark coolly. "We didn't know."

"Are you certain? Your actions tell a different story. We know that you visited APTOS in the middle of the night. Why?"

Mark sat back.

"If you didn't doubt him," Tom pressed, "why visit him at home?"

Mark twisted his jaw and his cold eyes locked on Tom's.

Tom leaned closer. "You had doubts, didn't you?"

Mark didn't reply.

"Oh yes, you had doubts. Didn't you?"

"Are you done?" asked the lawyer.

Tom ignored him. "Tell me, why did you visit Dr. Wheeler?"

"This is ridiculous." Mark stood up abruptly and began to button his coat. "Detective, I suggest you stay away from me and my family, otherwise..."

"Otherwise what exactly?" asked Tom, looking at him intently.

The door swung open, and Joan walked in. She handed Tom a folder.

"Mr. Weldon, I suggest you sit back down," she said.

Mark eyed her. "You can't tell me—"

"The ship of the dead," Joan interrupted. "What do you know about it?"

Mark looked as if all the blood had drained out of his body.

"Maria Weldon and Kathlyn Weldon were on that ship. Killed. Brutally murdered..." Joan said.

"H-how do you know?"

"Sit down," Joan said again.

"It's about revenge, isn't it?" said Tom.

Mark collapsed into the chair looking as if he'd lost everything. Tom glanced at Joan as Mark picked up the photos of his family.

"Mr. Weldon, you are searching for the man who murdered your family," said Joan. "You hired Dr. Wheeler to manufacture that gas to get back at the gang responsible for the massacre on the Nefret."

"What are you talking about?" Mark said. His voice was losing strength.

"You killed Wagner, Garrison, and Hawk, pawns of the man who orchestrated the attack on the ship," said Tom.

Again, Mark got to his feet. "What? No. No. It's not true! I had nothing to do with any of this!"

"Mark, I suggest we talk in private," Mark's lawyer said.

"Are you telling me that a madman chopped your family to pieces, and you didn't even think of revenge?" Tom yelled, getting up to meet Mark's eye. They stood no more than a few inches apart.

"Mark..." the lawyer repeated.

"Stay away from my family," Mark said heatedly. He stormed out of the room, leaving silence in his wake.

"Good work partner," Tom told Joan proudly.

"Thanks. I finally got hold of Raker West, the journalist who wrote that article. Guess what? He had the complete passenger list of the Nefret."

Tom grinned. "Nice timing!" he said, looking at the door. "He knows something. Let's find Walter Weldon."

Within an hour, Joan had traced Mark's uncle. But it wasn't going to be as simple as expected. Getting behind the wheel of his car, Tom asked, "Are you sure?" He was getting sick of running around the city.

"Yes," Joan replied.

Tom grunted and shifted the car into first gear.

"I spoke with Walter's secretary. At first, she said we could see him after the next meeting. Then she called and said Walter had suddenly changed his plans and was leaving the country."

"Where's he headed?"

"She didn't know. He's taking a private jet from Teterboro Airport, New Jersey."

"Why the rush?" Tom asked.

Joan smirked. "She didn't know that either."

Teterboro Airport, New Jersey

Tom pushed the throttle and turned on the siren. It helped them cut through the traffic, but as soon as they reached Lincoln Tunnel, he had to reduce his speed. Cursing under his breath, he swung the wheel around, driving down the opposite lane until the on-coming traffic became too much and he had to return to the road. The Tunnel was a piece of work and Tom didn't like it. It was too long, too narrow, and it made him claustrophobic. He usually tried to avoid it, but this was the most direct route to Union City.

It made sense now. The Weldon's had the power and the motive; one of them could be the white king. Tom parked and jumped out of the car. He rushed up the stairs; the glass doors slid open. He ran towards the gates showing his badge to the security guards who were trying to stop him. He emerged on the other side. Several aircrafts waited out on the runway. A white jet with blue strips stood elegantly at the far end of the airfield. Its engines were running, and a man was walking in its direction.

"Hey, where are going?" called out a flight attendant.

"NYPD!" Tom called back.

"No wait! The plane is going to take off soon."

Tom ignored him, running toward the aircraft. "Mr. Weldon!" he shouted. Tom slowed his pace and came to a stop. Walter Weldon was nothing like he had expected. He reminded him of the laughing Buddha. He was a short, stout man with soft blue eyes, a broad forehead, and very little hair. Wrinkles creased his face, and his thin lips curled into a disarming smile.

"We need to talk to you," Joan said breathlessly.

"Ah, you must be the cops. This isn't a great time. I have to go."

"Mr. Weldon, what do you know about the ship of the dead?" Tom demanded.

Weldon's face hardened.

"We know your sister and niece were on the Nefret," Tom said.

"There's nothing to tell."

"Are you sure?"

"Detective, I warn you."

"We think the four murders linked to APTOS Pharmaceuticals are a result of what happened on that ship."

"That was Wheeler," said Walter. "Just him."

"No, there's someone else," Tom insisted. "Someone powerful who is pulling the strings."

Walter shook his head. "Look, I don't know. This is over your paycheck Detective."

Tom's blood boiled.

"I am leaving," said Walter. "We'll have words later."

"You can't leave the city," said Joan.

Walter turned to look at her. "Do you have a warrant?"

Tom cursed.

Walter smiled. "You have nothing on me except that Wheeler manufactured the toxin, and my family was killed on the ship. For your information, Wheeler was nuts. He was solely responsible for what happened. And over fifty people died on that ship. It could have been any one of them." Walter's demeanor hardened. "I will return in ten hours. Call me then, I'll try to clarify things. But Detective, do not involve my family in this." He turned and disappeared into the jet. An attendant disconnected the staircase, moving it away. Tom and Joan walked to a safe distance to watch the plane speed down the runway.

"Wow," said Joan.

"I know. The Nefret brings out the worst in everyone," said Tom.

"Do you think he'll return?" Joan asked.

"Well, family is important to him, and Mark is family. I have a feeling he will."

With nowhere else to go, they stood and watched the jet take off and gain altitude.

"What's our next move?" asked Joan.

"I have a sinking feeling that he found the—" Tom was cut off by a loud noise. An explosion boomed like thunder, and a lightning flash blinded them. Fire burned brightly then turned into a cloud of black smoke. Debris of the plane rained down to the ground. Tom's brain desperately tried to make sense of it. Weldon was dead. The white king had won again.

Cranston House

Roumoult sat in the large chair with his feet on the table. He sipped his drink and watched the breaking news. Walter Weldon was dead. His photo flashed on the screen as the journalist listed his life accomplishments. Another life lost. Roumoult bowed his head and stared at the glass in his hand.

"It's a dark day, and our hearts go out to the Weldon family," said the reporter.

Roumoult rolled his eyes. "You don't give a damn!" It was just another story for them, but not for him, not for his father, his friends, and especially not for Mark. They were living the story. They were living the nightmare. Roumoult recalled the night his father told him his mother was gone. He remembered the feeling of hollowness, wretchedness, and pain, he still felt it.

NYPD Precinct

Tom entered the vacant men's room. He'd failed again. Tears flowed.

"Ah!" he yelled, kicking a toilet door. He sunk to the floor and sat with his head buried in his knees. It was on him. It wouldn't affect Roumoult, William, or Joan. But if he didn't get this murderer, he'd lose his job and his reputation. This case would kill his career. If he failed again, and someone died, he didn't think he could live with that. He got to his feet and washed his face with cold water.

When Tom emerged from the bathroom, he found Joan waiting for him in the office. He thought she'd left.

"We're running out of time," he told her.

"I know," Joan replied. "I don't understand."

"He was not the white king. We were wrong. That leaves Mark."

"Let's dig out Walter's projects over the last two years. Let's talk about other leads. Did we find out who blew up our tearoom and killed Alex?"

"We have his picture," said Tom, "but he's not in the system or on DNV database. There is a chance he wore a disguise. Tim Larson's drug dealer, Mario. Did we find him?"

Joan shook her head.

"The cigar boxes?"

"Untraceable."

"Fine," Tom said. "Let's focus on Walter."

22

Wolf In Sheep's Fold

June 24, 2015

Cranston Law Firm

T he night guard looked surprised to see Roumoult at this hour. The Firm was silent, and the Detective Agency was closed. Roumoult opened the door to the lab and was unsurprised to find Jack still working.

"Boss?"

"Hello Jack. Are you done? I need to use your computer."

"I am leaving," Jack said getting up. "Your username and password should work."

Roumoult placed the three files on the desk and began to work. He sensed Jack hovering around him. "Goodnight Jack," he said pointedly.

"Boss, what are you doing?"

"Looking for a wolf in a sheep's fold." He opened the file and started from the beginning, the day the three bodies arrived at the Morgue. He realized he still wasn't alone.

Jack pulled a chair beside him. "So," he said, "how do we look for this wolf?"

NYPD Interrogation Room

Sunlight blazed as another humid day began. Tom traced Walter's activities over the last two years, and one thing stood out: his visit to Egypt earlier this year. Only specific members of the team had joined the expedition, and the National Museum of History had played no role at all. Since Walter was gone, Tom contacted the next person on the list: Dr. Marian Watson.

"Thank you for seeing us Dr. Watson," said Tom.

"Anything I can do. Please be honest with me. Was it an accident or murder?"

Tom glanced at Joan. "Someone sabotaged the plane and rigged the tank to blow after takeoff."

Tears welled in Marian's eyes.

"We're sorry," Tom said gently.

"He was a good man," said Marian. "Why?"

"We think he got involved in something he shouldn't have," Joan answered. "Tell us about your visit to Egypt this year?"

Marian sat back. "Of course! The Nefret."

"The ship of the dead," Tom stated.

"Yes"

"Did you find it?" Tom asked.

"Yes, we did," said Marian.

Tom and Joan looked at each other. "Tell us everything,"

"In 1975, Walter's sister and her daughter were touring Egypt when they were brutally killed. Its broke Walter. The locals were petrified, because they thought a green demon had possessed everyone on the ship, leading to the massacre. An article said it was a heist by a gang, but no one gave it any merit. No one wanted to board the ship or retrieve the remains. They wanted to burn it; they thought it would get rid of the demon. Walter traveled to Egypt and worked with the Embassy and the police to release the remains of his family and the other passengers, but he remained tight-lipped about the ship's location. Walter returned with his family's remains, adopted Mark, and went on with his life."

"What changed?" Tom asked.

"At first, Walter dismissed the article about the heist on the Nefret," said Marian. "Then, two years ago, he announced he wanted to find it. I don't know why. We nicknamed it 'The Walters Project'. Honestly, I wasn't interested. It wasn't an artifact; it was a grave. And I sensed that Walter knew more than he was telling us."

"Like what?" Joan said.

"A few days before we found the ship, we sat together for a drink. And out of the blue, he told me that a vicious, red-eyed monster had chopped his sister and his ten-year-old niece into pieces."

Tom straightened up. "Wait a minute, how would he know that?"

"Exactly! But he did."

"Did you ask him about it?" said Joan.

"Yes. He refused to tell me anything more."

"Okay," said Tom. "What did you find on the ship?"

Marian's face turned white. "A massacre. Stepping onto that ship was like walking through a time warp. You could smell rotting flesh. You could hear the cries in the desert's silence. Dried blood coated the deck and..." Her voice shook and trailed off. "It was a slaughterhouse. The journalist was right. It was a heist, because we discovered jewelry, artifacts, cash, and other valuables in two bags. We informed the FBI, and they took samples and began an investigation." She paused. "The police lied when they said they removed all the bodies. We found two on the lower deck, hidden in a closet. They'd tried to save themselves and died of starvation. And the corpse in the Captain's chair with a big hole in its head." Marian looked Tom in the eye. "The expression on that thing was haunting."

A chill made its way down Tom's spine.

"What did the FBI find?" Joan enquired.

"I don't know, ask them,"

"Did you find anything else?" Tom urged.

"Oh, yes! We found the pearls."

"What's special about them?" Joan asked.

"They're one of a kind, iconic to the Weldon family, passed down through generations. They're worth up to three million dollars."

"Wow," Tom reacted, "That explains why they targeted the Nefret."

"But Walter didn't go for them?" Joan asked.

"No, he wanted to know what happened to his family."

"Where are the pearls now?" Joan said.

"They pressured Walter to display them at the Gala. After that, they'll pass onto Mark Weldon,"

"What Gala?" said Tom.

"It's an exhibition," Marian explained. "We worked on three sites for over a decade and identified, gathered, and cataloged hundreds of artifacts. It's a celebration of our accomplishments. It's too bad Walter's not here. And I feel worse, because I'll lose the entire collection."

"Why?"

"Walter made a pact with the governments and the Museum of National History. We could dig them out, study them, and display them at the exhibition. The Gala marks the end of this project. After that, we have to return them to their respective countries."

"How many artifacts did you collect?" Tom asked.

"Around three hundred."

Tom raised his eyebrows and eyed Joan, who did the same.

"Detectives, you do not put on an exhibition for a few artifacts. This is Walter's work. Our team's decade of commitment to human history. I know its cliché, but Walter and the board members wanted to celebrate its end."

"How much are they worth?" Tom asked. "The artifacts?"

Marian's face went blank. "Well, the pots and cutlery aren't worth much. You can find them anywhere. But the sculptures, the mummies, the knives, golden plates, they're priceless." She looked between Tom and Joan. "It's history. You can't put a price on it!"

Cranston Law Firm

Roumoult rubbed his eyes. He was ignoring client calls and had asked Alice to take care of everything. Jack slept peacefully with his head on the desk. The last two weeks had been unforgettable. He thought about the clues they'd collected. William's files on Hawk, Wagner, and Garrison. The print outs of the payments made to them by Alex. Information about blue lily, Dr. Wheeler, and everything about the Nefret. He flipped through the photos of the unidentified man, material on Tim Larson's dealer, and artifacts they'd uncovered at Wagner's warehouse. A picture began to form in his head. For several moments, he sat motionless, thinking. Suddenly, he got up and dashed out.

NYPD Precinct

If Tom was right, Walter was after the black king because he was responsible for the massacre on the Nefret. It got him killed. Tom informed the Captain of the FBI investigation, and the Captain assured him he would look into it. Tom and Joan had just started to eat lunch when Roumoult and William arrived. Tom noticed that Roumoult's hair was messy, and he hadn't shaved or changed his clothes. "You look like hell," he said.

"Thank you," replied Roumoult. "Nice to see you too."

Tom chuckled. "Lunch?"

"I'm not hungry,"

"What's on your mind?"

"Since the beginning, I've been asking one question," Roumoult said. "Why did the black king need Hawk, Garrison, and Wagner? The black king is ruthless, powerful, and a blackmailer. Garrison needed money and probably killed his would-be brother-in-law. Hawk and Wagner had money. Wagner had a soul and felt guilty. He was probably pressured to work with black king. Hawk was greedy, narcissistic, and disliked by everyone. But we missed one minor detail about Hawk."

"What?"

"He had diplomatic immunity."

"So?" William asked.

"So," said Roumoult, "the black king might have influenced Hawk to use his diplomatic immunity to smuggle the artifacts into the country."

Tom dropped his sandwich. "How did we miss this?"

"We didn't look at it that way," Joan responded.

"And he lied about his trips," Roumoult said.

"How do you know?" Tom asked.

"Two weeks before his death, Hawk traveled to London for business."

"Yeah, we knew that," Joan replied.

"Posing as his secretary, I called his hotel in London to enquire about his meeting," said Roumoult.

William hung his head. "There was no meeting, was there?"

"There was one meeting and nothing else scheduled. So, what did he do for five days? I called Heathrow Airport, and they confirmed that Hawk flew to the Middle East for two days and then returned to London."

"Son of a bitch," Tom muttered.

"If you retrace Hawk's steps, you'll find that he traveled to many places, including South America, and he used his immunity to smuggle artifacts."

Tom shook his head. "Okay. The black king needed Hawk for smuggling. What about Wagner?"

"To hide artifacts," Joan answered.

"The warehouse," William added.

"He might have blackmailed Wagner," Roumoult said. "He might have caved in to protect his daughter. Wagner didn't like helping the black king and felt mortified. When the white king began hunting him, he knew his time was up. He couldn't involve his daughter, so he left the clue for Emma to find."

"This is making sense. Hawk for smuggling the artifacts, Wagner for hiding and storing them. Why Garrison?" William asked.

"That's the best part," said Roumoult. "I spoke to Garrison's boss. He told me that Garrison was a good worker and a hot-headed loner. And he volunteered."

"Volunteered? That's bullshit," Tom said, thinking of Ms. Garrison's experience.

"Let me finish," Roumoult replied. "The next question I asked is where did he volunteer? I looked at the list. Sure, he did projects involving houses, apartments, and retirement homes. But most of the projects were in art galleries, exhibitions, and museums. The last project he worked on was the Egyptian Gala & Exhibition at the Weldon's Exhibition Hall in Flushing."

Tom's jaw dropped.

"Garrison was the black king's eyes and ears," Joan said. "That's the mission. That's what he's after! Walter's collection."

"And the white king knows it," Roumoult said. "And he will come after the black king and kill him. We should warn—"

"No!" shouted the trio.

"They've always been one step ahead of us. This time, we have them! Not a word, Roumoult," Tom said.

Roumoult folded his arms. "You don't get it, do you? You want to use the artifacts as bait, but I wouldn't risk it. Hundreds of people will be at the Gala. After everything that's happened, I don't think the white king, or the black king will spare anyone. It could be another massacre. Let me ask you, how much blood are you willing to spill, and can you live with it?"

Tom swallowed hard.

"Because I can't!"

NYPD Precinct

Roumoult waited with the detectives as the Captain spoke with the Commissioner. They had to stop the Gala. He knew it wouldn't please anyone, but that didn't matter. The Captain banged the handset on the receiver.

"Sir?" said Roumoult.

"They're not listening!"

"What?"

"According to them, they receive threats every day. And we don't have enough evidence that the white king is planning carnage."

"But he'll kill everyone!" Roumoult exclaimed.

"It's all speculation, we have no hard evidence. We can ask the bomb squad to search the building and put cops everywhere. But that's it. Like it or not. This party is going ahead."

"Like hell it is," Roumoult said and stormed out.

Queens

Tom wanted to join the bomb squad in the search, but Officer Jake called him and said they found Larson's dealer, Mario. Tom parked the car in front of a one-story house. The unpainted stone building appeared to have been built in the nineteenth century. The officer was waiting near the gate.

As soon as he entered the house, Tom smelled something burning. "I thought you got Dr. Larson's dealer."

"I did,"

Tom followed him to a door under the staircase. They took small steps and passed through another door. Tom gulped as he walked in the modest, dimly lit room with its pale green walls. It smelled like someone had burned pork with the doors closed. His throat went dry. A charred body of a man sat on a chair in the middle of the room. His feet were in a wooden bucket and surrounded by wires linked to a battery. Tom wasn't sure if he wanted to move closer. He walked around and saw that the victim was bound to the chair with rope.

"After torturing him, he burned him alive and left," said Officer Jake. "The smoke reached the top of the stairs and triggered the alarms. The firemen found him and called us. I'm sorry we didn't get him earlier."

A cloud of gloom loomed over Tom as he stepped out of the house. No one deserved to die like that.

"This is getting out of hand," said Tom. "It's time we put surveillance on everyone, including Mark Weldon."

Officer Jake nodded. "You know what this means, right? Mario worked for the black king. Now the white king knows the new identity of the black king."

"And we don't know what any of them look like," Tom muttered.

Cranston House

Roumoult hit the brakes and parked in front of the main door where Fred stood leaning against his car. He had been struggling to reach his father for the last hour. It looked like he'd gotten his messages.

"Hey Dad."

"Hey, where have you been?" Fred said. He looked down at Roumoult's clothes. "Did you sleep?"

"Dad, do you know anyone at the National Museum of History?"

"Yes, the board members and a few archeologists. Why?"

They entered the house and Roumoult informed his father of a possible genocide.

"Oh my God! And the Captain can't do anything?"

"He can search the premises and he can put cops everywhere, but he can't stop the Gala. Dad, you always boast about how much power you have in this city. It's time to prove it."

Fred arched his eyebrows. "Okay, no pressure."

Roumoult rushed up the stairs.

"Are you going to the Gala?" Fred asked.

Roumoult halted and faced him. "Dad, did you forget? I hate parties." He entered his room.

Fred followed reaching into his pocket for his phone. It was time to start making calls.

Roumoult entered the bathroom, brushed his teeth, and shaved. He could hear his father talking on the phone. Under the water, his body relaxed. He dried himself and walked to his closet.

Fred paced the floor. He didn't look happy. He finished his call and crashed on the bed.

"Let me guess,"

"I made over a dozen calls," Fred sighed. "The Museum has no control over the Gala. The Weldon board of directors orchestrated it. I know two of the board members, but they don't want to ruin Walter's life celebration. They'd rather impress the trustees, the Mayor, and the Commissioner than take action."

"I have to do something," said Roumoult.

"What?" asked Fred.

Roumoult didn't respond.

Fred sat up and studied his face. "What?"

"What if there was a fire?"

"No!"

"Mass murder versus a small fire. I think the building can take it. What's the worst they could do to me?"

"Roumoult!" Fred warned.

"They could sue me..." Roumoult said thoughtfully. "Unless..."

"Unless what?"

"He did come back from the dead." he muttered. "Dad, you are a genius!"

"I am?"

"Stay here, I've got an idea." Roumoult said and left without another word.

NYPD Precinct

Tom couldn't believe it when the Captain told him that the FBI had shared Ortiz Stalin, the black king's, information with the NYPD. The case made more sense now. He flipped through the file and discussed it with Joan. "Born in New York, he's a well-known gang member, but he disappeared from the police radar in 1974. Ortiz took over the gang after killing his boss, Vincent. His operations always remained in the dark. No one has met him except his trusted comrades. He targeted Egypt and other Middle Eastern territories, and he raided boats for artifacts. Van Gerkins worked for him and burgled several ships. Everything was running smoothly until the Nefret. Something happened. Van turned into a monster and attacked and killed the passengers on the Nefret and his own men."

"The PCP?"

"Or another hallucinogen. Whatever it was, he lost it."

"The FBI found his corpse in the Captain's chair. After Van's death, the looting stopped in Egypt but continued in other countries. For several years, Ortiz eluded the FBI, until Walter stepped in."

"How did he help?" Joan asked.

"The locals didn't trust the law enforcement and wouldn't talk them. But Walter was different. He was a humanitarian, his team was there for over a decade, and he'd earned their trust. Walter wanted to get back at Ortiz for murdering his family, so he acted as a middleman. He gathered information and tipped off the police. He uncovered Ortiz's location in Egypt. The FBI acted fast, and in the exchange of gunfire, two of Ortiz's men died and he fled."

"It fits," said Joan. "He returned to America, probably with Hawk, and changed his identity. Then they lost track of him."

"Until Mr. Meddler, Dr. Sterling, dragged us all into this," Tom said.

Cranston Law Firm

Roumoult was back in Jack's lab, speaking on the phone with Raker West, the journalist and the best source on the Nefret.

"Yes, are you sure?" he said eagerly into the mouthpiece. "They got everyone they could find... How many?" he asked, grabbing a notepad.

"Forty-one on the ship, whatever they could recover," said Raker in his thick hoarse voice.

"Of course." Roumoult felt Jack watching him.

"Five were found in the river,"

"People?"

"Well, parts that belonged to people."

"Fine, that covers the passengers and the crew. What about the unidentified bodies?"

"You mean the gang?"

"Yeah."

"Nine,"

"Nine? Counting the one in the Captain's chair?"

"Yes."

"So, they recovered fifty-four people. But according to the passenger list there were fifty-five people on that ship."

"What?" Jack asked. He was quickly shushed by Roumoult.

"Well, I don't think anyone survived,"

"But the numbers don't tally,"

"Look, Mr. Cranston, it was challenging for the police to put them together. Even to find them in the first place! These are very spiritual people. They hated doing it. It's possible that there was a body that wasn't uncovered, but if anybody was missing, the family would have contacted the authorities."

"Maybe."

"So, when do I get that exclusive interview with you?"

"My secretary will call you. Thanks for your help, Mr. West." Roumoult hung up and turned to look at the figures. He studied the passenger manifest. Someone was missing. Everyone thought all the passengers on the Nefret were dead. What if they were wrong?

Cranston Law Firm

Angelus touched his wound as he walked toward the Firm. He'd seen everyone except Roumoult. As usual the Firm was busy, and he found Alice at her desk. "Where's Roumoult?"

"I don't know. He's completely distracted. I had to cancel all his appointments," Alice huffed.

Angelus tried calling him again. He didn't answer the phone.

"Where's the boss?" Jack asked joining them.

"Somewhere," Alice muttered.

"Angelus, I think boss is in danger," said Jack.

"What do you mean?"

"His curiosity is going to get him killed! He's determined to solve this mystery at any cost."

"Uh-huh," Angelus grunted. "What happened?"

"The ship of the dead. He talked to some journalist, Raker West. Something about the bodies not adding up."

Angelus arched his eyebrows. He withdrew his phone and dialed Tom's number. "Good morning."

"Good morning. Make it quick, I'm busy."

"You have a tail on Roumoult, right?"

"Yeah."

"Good. I'm sending Joe as a backup."

"Why?"

"It's a shot in the dark, but Roumoult thinks someone survived the ship of the dead. We need to keep an eye on him."

New Jersey

Joe was glad to be back. Sitting on the sidelines had been eating him alive. For the last two hours, he'd been tailing Roumoult. It was time to call Angelus.

"What have you got?" asked Angelus.

"Here it goes. First, boss went to a cemetery. I'll be honest, that's creepy, but I'm glad it's not the middle of the night and he is not carrying a shovel. He spent half an hour chatting with the warden, then he went and stood over a grave. I shadowed him to New Jersey. Now we're in the parking lot of a retirement home."

"Okay. Keep a very close eye on him. Understood?"

"Understood."

NYPD Precinct

Tom examined the blueprints of Weldon's Exhibition Hall. The one-story building had a large hall space and two small exhibition rooms on the first floor. On the ground floor, there was a big lobby, a security office, and two art galleries. The basement below the building was mainly used for storage, with six big rooms secured by automated steel doors. Monitoring hundreds of people was challenging. Tom wiped the sweat from his brow. The event managers were stubborn, and it had been difficult to chalk out a tight security detail.

The phone rang, and Joan answered. "What?" she said.

Tom looked at her.

"How could you let that happen?" she spluttered. There was a pause. "Well, just find him!"

Tom gulped.

"Mark Weldon has disappeared."

"You're kidding."

"He left the house this morning, got to work, then left his office about an hour ago. Our men followed him. He drove to 7th Avenue, then turned onto Eighth Avenue. They tracked him until Columbus Circle, but then they lost him. He just disappeared!"

New Jersey Specialty Aged Care

As he walked toward the exit, Roumoult's hands were shaking. He knew everything. He had to tell Tom. He unlocked his phone and dialed his number with trembling fingers. As he left the building, a warm burst of air greeted him. He shielded his eyes from the bright sun. Tom didn't answer. He tried again. No response. Roumoult headed for his Mercedes, which had replaced his Audi. For the first time, he took notice of his surroundings. A well-kept green lawn and an eight-foot wall surrounded the facility. A broad driveway led from the parking area to the gates. The building itself was a massive eight-story complex. There were a few other cars and a catering truck in the parking area.

Tom answered the phone. "What's up, Cranston? We're busy."

"I know, but this is important."

"Okay."

"I know the identity of the white king."

"Really? How?"

"Man, this guy is smart. Thanks for giving me the number of the journalist. I spoke to Raker West. There were fifty-five passengers on the Nefret. At first, they thought they'd found everyone, or whatever was left of them. But they were missing the remains of four people. After a week, they declared them lost."

"Until Walter rediscovered the Nefret,"

"Yes. Walter's team discovered three skeletons. Two in the closet and one on the Captain's chair. So that leaves one. I know this sounds crazy, but what if someone survived the massacre?"

"The white king?" Tom asked.

"Exactly. They found remains of all the adults on the ship which leaves the children. There were six children including Ms. Weldon, on the passenger list. But they never found the body of a six-year-old boy named Zachary Madison. The manifest shows two Madison's were on that ship: Zachary and his mother, Valerie."

"Okay," Tom said slowly, taking the information in.

"Valerie died of gunshot wounds on the ship. They recovered her body. But Zachary's was never found. I tracked the remains of Valerie Madison. Her husband's mother, Mrs. Olivia Madison, buried her here in New York."

"Her husband is dead?"

"Yes, he died in a car accident in 1972. I visited Valerie's grave and guess what I found."

Tom remained silent.

"Flowers... Take a guess which ones?"

"Blue lilies," Tom breathed out.

"Yep. I had a chat with the gardener, a retired chap who spends the better part of his day taking care of the plants. He confirmed that a man in his late thirties, well-dressed, about my height with dark black hair, visits the grave every week or so."

"A name would be good,"

"Let me finish. I spoke to Mrs. Olivia Madison. She believes that her grandson is dead. After burying her only family, she was severely depressed. She took a fall down the stairs and sustained a brain injury and was in a coma for a year. She woke up but never fully recovered. A few friends came around, but over time, most of them stopped visiting."

"But someone showed up?"

"Yes, Mr. Hilton comes to visit, and he sees to her every need. Everyone thinks he's just a nice young man."

"But you don't think so,"

"No, because his first name is Zachary, and he looks like the man who visits Valerie Madison's grave."

"He changed his name."

"His last name, yes." Roumoult thought he heard something and paused for a moment. "I went through the list of people under Walter's banner," he continued. "There is a Hilton on that list."

"He was with Walter when they found the Nefret!"

"Go get him. You owe—" Roumoult broke off. A sharp pain shot through his neck.

"Hello... Hello," Tom's voice echoed through the dropped phone.

Roumoult felt the earth spin.

"Roumoult?" Tom called.

Roumoult couldn't speak. His eyes rolled, and his body went numb. His muscles failed him, and he lost his balance, sinking to the ground.

Joe saw Roumoult fall and jumped out of the car. A man advanced toward the Mercedes. Joe stopped. Before he could reach for his weapon, the man lifted his hand and aimed. Gunshots cracked into the air.

He threw himself to the ground and armed himself. Screams echoed. He looked around, but the man was gone. An engine roared, and the Mercedes raced for the gates. Joe got to his feet and ran after the car. It was too late.

Joe came to an abrupt stop. "Damn!" He raced to the SUV, where Jake waited.

"Who the hell was that?" Joe asked.

"I don't know. He has Cranston," Jake said. He pressed his foot down on the accelerator.

The SUV darted out of the gates and followed the kidnapper. The Mercedes swung left, almost running over a pedestrian. Jake twirled the wheel, and Joe grabbed the dashboard.

"Can you get a clear shot?" Jake asked.

"No, he's too fast," Joe replied. He cursed his decision not to tag along with the boss. They couldn't let him get away. "Faster! Faster!"

The Mercedes turned right and then left. Jake pinned the accelerator to the floor, and the SUV shot ahead. Suddenly, the Mercedes made a sharp right, and Jake followed at full speed. Out of nowhere, a large truck careened across the road and hurtled straight for them. Jake lost control. The SUV jolted and jumped onto the footpath before crashing into a fence.

Joe gasped. He looked at Jake, who shook his head. The Mercedes vanished at the next turn. "He's getting away!" Joe said.

Jake threw the car into reverse. The SUV jolted; he changed gears, pushing his foot down flat on the gas.

"Left, he took a left," Joe yelled, pointing his index finger.

"Okay, okay!" He turned left and eased his foot, causing the SUV to slow. The street was empty, and the Mercedes had vanished.

Brooklyn

Tom and Joan drove to Zachary Hilton's house. Tom felt like the world was coming to an end. Zachary had kidnapped Roumoult and telling Angelus about it had been one of the hardest things he'd ever had to do. Time was of the essence; he couldn't afford to let anyone else die. They had to find Zachary.

As Tom drove down Metropolitan Avenue, East Williamsburg, a sinking feeling engulfed him. He knew the white king wasn't stupid enough to hang around his house, but he had to check it out.

Brooklyn grew each year. New people were arriving, and buildings were developing fast. It was a quiet afternoon, except for a couple of teens hanging out on the street. A few cars passed by as Tom parked near the red and white row house.

Tom and Joan knocked and waited. A short old woman shuffled to the door. Her gray hair dangled over her face, and her blue eyes looked enormous behind her thick glasses.

"Mrs. Jenkins?" Joan asked.

"Yes."

"Is Zachary Hilton home?"

"I don't know," she croaked. "Why are you disturbing me?"

The detectives showed her their badges. The woman leaned forward, closer and closer, peering at Tom's badge until her nose was no more than an inch away from it. Tom rolled his eyes.

"You're cops?" said the woman.

"Zachary didn't turn up at work," said Tom. "Do you know where he is?"

"No."

"Okay. Can you show us his apartment?"

Her shoulders slumped. "I stay on the ground floor. I mind my business." She gestured upstairs. "That's Zachary's apartment. You want to talk to him, go knock there. Don't disturb me again."

"Yes ma'am," muttered Tom, heading for the stairs.

No one answered the door. Tom glanced downstairs. They were on their own.

"What are you doing?" Joan asked uneasily.

"We don't have time for a warrant," he muttered, searching his pockets.

"But..."

He held his right index finger to his lips. Taking out a bunch of skeleton keys, he said, "With any luck, we'll be out of here in minutes."

Navy blue carpet covered the floor of the living room in the two-bedroom apartment, and to Tom's left was a small kitchen with well-arranged appliances. To his right, two recliner chairs sat in front of the TV. He hurried into one of the rooms. Zachary's bedroom was small rectangular and neat. Unremarkable. Tom headed for the second door. It was completely dark. He searched for the light switch and flicked it on before slowly stepping forward, Joan following close behind him. Tom felt a knot grow in his stomach as he noticed the plastic drapes dangling from the roof. The place was devoid of any noises or smells. He reached for his gun and used it to push the plastic drapes aside. Under the light sat an overstuffed chair, a large table, a computer, a printer, two cabinets, and a number of files.

Joan marched ahead.

Tom observed coins kept in a transparent container and a big magnifying glass beside them. The pictures on the wall caught his attention. His heart skipped a beat when he recognized his, Joan's, Roumoult's, and William's photos on the wall. Then he saw photographs of Wagner, Hawk, Garrison, and Alex.

"He's been watching us." he whispered.

23

Haunted

June 24, 2015

Weldon Exhibition Hall

C rowds of people entered the Exhibition Hall. Women dazzled in beautiful costumes and men stood proudly beside them. The media was out in full force. A chopper flew over the building, and reporters were busy interviewing celebrities and iconic families. Several historians, archeologists, artists, and writers joined the crowd.

Tom and Joan entered the majestic building. Tom couldn't help but feel out of place. He wore a sweat-stained white shirt with filthy-looking pants. He touched his face and hair, trying to remember the last time he'd looked at himself in a mirror. The Captain dressed in a handsome tuxedo, stood at the end of the stairs. Tom and Joan rushed towards him.

"We haven't seen Zachary Hilton or Ortiz Statin," the Captain said shaking his head. "I don't think they'll come."

"Oh, they will," Tom replied. He dropped his voice. "What about the bomb?"

"The squad checked three times. They didn't find it."

"Did they check the ventilation system?" Joan asked.

"Yes. Nothing."

Tom looked around. Arches, paintings, and the extravagant ceiling lights gave the lobby a heavenly appearance. More people poured in, and soon the room was full of buzz and excitement. The body scanner beeped continuously as one by one guests entered the building. A conveyor belt carried their belongings through a scanner. As an extra precaution, guards conducted body searches. Tom looked over his shoulder and surveyed the huge room. A feeling of uneasiness coursed through his body.

Officer Jake sprinted toward him. "Detective, I might know where Cranston is."

William, Jack, Joe, and Angelus joined them. "We already searched the Museum and opened every box we could," said Officer Jake. "Then I went through the list of the artifacts under Zachary's name. He's handled several artifacts over the last six weeks, including four custom-made stone boxes from China, which were sent over here late this afternoon."

"Why send them here?" Tom asked.

"Because it's part of the deal," Angelus replied. "After the exhibition, they'll send the boxes back to China."

"Are they on display?" Tom asked.

"Not these, they're in storage. We need to find them."

"Do you have a photo of the boxes?" Angelus asked.

"Yes." Jake showed them a picture. "They are large and creamed-colored with a blue freehand design."

"Where were they stored?" asked Tom.

"Basement."

"You guys find Roumoult. We'll track down Zachary and Ortiz."

Roumoult felt lost. Every time he tried to wake up, his eyes weighed shut once more. Through his eyelids, he made out two flashes of light. Strange voices jumbled together. Feeling stiffness in his neck and body, Roumoult tried to stretch, but he couldn't move his hands. Slowly, he peeled his eyes open and cast a glance over his shoulder. Silver duct tape bound his wrists. He tensed and tried to wriggle his feet. His ankles were strapped together. Frustration hit him hard when he noticed the tape over his mouth. He looked up, realizing that he was crouched inside a big box with no memory of having been put there.

It was a struggle, but Roumoult tried to recall. He'd been at the aged care center, he'd spoken to Tom, and then...? Legs aching, he tried to shift his feet and hit something. A ringing noise startled him. In the dim light, he noticed a black blanket. It took effort and patience to maneuver in the box. He reached for the blanket and pulled it.

He sat back. It looked like a small Christmas tree, upside down and decorated with balls filled with green gas. It was connected to a bunch of brown wires that escaped the box through a small hole. Roumoult moved back to his original position. Ignoring his pounding chest, he counted over twenty glass balls. Sweat dripped down his face as he sat across from a narcotic killer gas, powerless and speechless.

Weldon Exhibition Hall

With time running out, Tom was losing patience. The Egyptian collection was in the biggest on the first floor. Arched doors formed a magnificent entrance. Most of the artifacts stood along the walls, and a few items sat on white tables in the middle of the room. The hall was well-lit, and excellent food and wine was being served. Music saturated the space. People moved around slowly, admiring the artifacts. A few danced in a far corner, and several people mingled in groups. He left to scout the other two smaller galleries on the same floor. He soon returned to the main hall and observed.

An hour passed without an incident. Joan moved around with the crowd. Tom stood beside an owl sculpture. His face was stern as he watched the crowd intently. In his ugly clothes, he could almost have passed as a part of the exhibition.

Roumoult yanked and tugged until his hands came free, bleeding. He stripped the duct tape from his mouth. He gasped for fresh air and rested his head against the side of the box. With every passing moment, it was becoming more difficult to breathe. Resting his hands on the lid of the box, he tried to push it up. It was too heavy. He sunk into the corner, panting, and peered out of the two-inch square holes. He saw a white wall.

"Hello?" he called out. "Anyone!" His voice echoed and then died out. He was on his own. He felt the surface of the lid with his fingers; it wasn't wood. It was stone. Gathering his strength, he reached for the lid and began to push sideways. His fingers slid over the rough surface. He paused, and he tried again. He had to get out.

"Bloody ancient thing..." he grunted. The stone shifted with a grinding noise. Roumoult's arm started aching, and his head spun. He gathered all of his strength and continued to push. After several attempts, a small beam of light entered the box.

Museum Basement

Joe panted as he pushed open the door. Angelus and Jack followed behind him. Officer Jake and William were looking next door. They searched the vast room, tapping and knocking on boxes.

"He's not here!" Jack said.

Joe pointed toward a big door. The guard swiped his card, and it opened. Joe turned the lights on and stared at hundreds of boxes. A loud thud echoed through the hall. They stopped. His attention was drawn to a large steel door at the end of the room. The security guard turned the latch and pushed the door. Together, they entered the well-lit hall, which was full of ancient stone boxes. Two of them were open.

Joe saw the pieces of silver duct tape and an ancient-looking sword on the floor.

"Who's that?" demanded the security guard.

Joe followed his gaze and noticed a pair of legs dangling from the ventilation shaft.

"Roumoult?" he called.

Roumoult jumped down from the shaft.

"Boss!" Joe said happily. "Where the hell have you been?"

"In the box!" Roumoult huffed.

Jack stepped forward. "Don't ever do that again."

Officer Jake leaned over and peered into the box. "Oh, God. What the hell is that?"

"That's the bomb," Roumoult replied. "I've disconnected the wires. Did we get him? Did we get Zachary?"

"We don't know," Angelus replied. "We were looking for you!"

First Floor of the Museum

A modest-looking gentleman kept looking over his shoulder. He didn't socialize or look anyone in the eye. Tom thought it was odd. He took a risk. Swiftly crossing the hall, he casually came to stand beside the man, and pretended to admire the set of long, beautiful knives in a glass showcase.

Tom kept his voice low. "Hello, Mr. Ortiz Statin."

The man gasped and stumbled back. "I think you're mistaken!"

"I think not. No one forgets their real name," Tom replied, signaling for backup.

"My name is Franklin Oxford," the man insisted.

"Say what you like. I know who you are."

The cops approached, and Tom ignored the two men standing behind them.

First Floor of the Museum

The group rushed toward the stairs, "Joe and William check with security. See if they found them." Roumoult ordered. "We'll find Tom."

They entered the hall and spotted the detective. Tom was talking to a short, stocky man.

"Roumoult," Angelus whispered, ushering him toward a man in a white suit, who was leaning on a cane. His hair was curly, he wore thick glasses, and his face was covered in wrinkles. His eyes scanned the room suspiciously.

Ignoring the stares of guests, Roumoult crossed the hall. He wasn't wearing a tuxedo. Hell, he hadn't even had time to wash his face. "It's over Zachary," he said plainly.

The man jolted. A set of cold steel-gray eyes fixated on him.

"It's done. They have him. He's not going anywhere. It's over."

A flicker of momentary defeat spread across Zachary's face as he removed his wig and mask. "Do you think you can beat me?" he said in an emotionless tone.

"Angelus, I think—" Roumoult began, but his voice trailed off at the sight of Zachary smiling.

"You can never beat me," he said. The lights in the hall glowed red. The fire alarms went off. A loud hissing noise spread through the air. Roumoult looked up. His eyes widened in horror as green gas gushed through the vents. Screams resonated throughout the hall as panic spread.

First Floor of the Museum

Using the panic as a distraction, one of the Ortiz's guards punched a cop and drew his gun. He aimed steadily at Tom, who ducked just in time. The bullet hit a glass display, smashing it to pieces. Tom withdrew his handgun, but he couldn't get a clear shot. The crowd rushed toward the exit, elbowing each other out of the way. Another thunderous noise echoed through the hall. Tom spun. A huge iron door was moving downward. He saw Ortiz and his two bodyguards racing toward the other exit. His first impulse was to follow them, but he couldn't let himself lose sight of his priorities.

"We have to get everyone out of here!" Joan shouted.

Tom nodded.

Ground Floor of the Museum

William heard an unmistakable beeping noise. Stepping out of the men's room, he found himself in the middle of chaos. The terrified crowd hurried downstairs, the halls overflowing with screams. He looked up the stairs toward the first floor. The doors were closing, and green gas clouded the air. Horror struck him. Everyone he cared about was up there.

William tried to shove his way through the mob, but they threw him to the floor. Two women fell on him. He yelped as he felt a sharp pain rip through his leg. Flipping onto his stomach, he crawled as fast as he could until he reached a wall where there was just enough room to stand. Machine guns boomed. The glass beside William smashed into pieces. He yelled and ducked.

First Floor of the Museum

Roumoult heard the sounds of machine guns. Grief washed over him—all those people. And he thought he'd successfully disabled the bomb. He saw Ortiz trying to open the small exit, and Zachary heading straight for him. One of the two guards tried to tackle Zachary, but he punched him in the face, then drew a knife and thrusted it violently into his chest. Roumoult staggered back, knees weak. Though he couldn't hear the screams, he watched Zachary's victim go into rigors and drop dead on the floor. A strong arm grabbed him.

"Let's go," Angelus said.

"But…"

"No. We have to leave. Let them kill each other!"

"Was that a machine gun?" Roumoult asked. He hoped he was wrong.

"Yep. Ortiz had a backup plan."

Museum Security Office, Ground Floor

Joe stood in the office, shock and adrenaline coursing through his veins. On every screen, he saw people running for their lives. Officer Jake had joined the cops in their attempts to tackle the assailants. He wanted to check on his team, but the exit door was closing. The only way he could help was to make sure it stayed open.

"What the hell?" The head of security ran his hands over his bald head.

"What's happening? You told me you could keep that door open. We have to get them out!"

"Someone's tampered with the controls. I'm locked out!"

"What?" Joe shouted. His felt a lump in his throat. "Can we open the doors manually?"

"No, no. It's all computerized."

"We have to get those people out. How do we fix this?"

"We need a computer guy."

A bulb lit up in Joe's head. "Keep trying. I'll be back."

Ground Floor of the Museum

"Get up! Move," William said pushing a man off him. The old man trembled, making him feel bad. "Stay down. Okay?" The man sat helplessly in a corner.

The door had almost closed. William looked around at the carnage, and his heart skipped a beat. Two women were slumped on the floor, blood pooling around them. "Oh, no, please, no." He crawled toward them.

Several shots echoed. The Captain and a group of cops fired madly at the assailants. Lying flat on his belly, William checked the women for pulses. They were alive but unconscious. Maybe that was a good thing. Careful to stay out of sight, William dragged the injured women away from the gunfire.

First Floor of the Museum

Outside the hall, Tom, Joan, and Jack were helping people get out through the closing door. "Jack take cover," Tom shouted.

Jack opened his mouth to protest.

"I'll get Roumoult out," Tom yelled.

Jack hesitated, peering over the railing.

Tom knew there was nowhere safe. "Just lie low!" he told him.

As the door closed, Tom and Joan did their best. Tom was breathless, his hands and back screaming in pain, but he didn't stop. He had to get them out, or Zachary would win. He couldn't let him win. Not this time. "Hurry up!" he roared.

First Floor of the Museum

Inside, Roumoult and Angelus were trying their best, but it was becoming increasingly difficult. Roumoult was on his knees, pushing people toward Tom, who grabbed their arms and pulled them towards safety. Roumoult glanced at Angelus. The stab wound was slowing him down, putting strain on his breathing. The gas was flooding the hall; they couldn't outrun it. Suddenly, an idea popped into his head. He signaled for a cop to take over. Without asking, he snatched Angelus' mobile phone from his back pocket.

Ground Floor of the Museum

Like everyone else, Joe was terrified, but he had to get to Jack. They didn't have time to drill or break the steel door. Dodging bullets was becoming tougher. Joe waved his hands and called out, but Jack remained curled on the floor in a corner. He was scared to death. Joe ran up the stairs, threw an arm around Jack's shoulders.

"Jack! You okay?" Joe asked. He couldn't believe it. Jack was on the phone. "What are you doing?"

"Talking to the boss."

"We need you in the security office,"

Putting the phone away, Jack glanced nervously at the door. "Okay, boss told me to do one more thing." He stood up and rushed downstairs.

"Jack, be careful!" Joe yelled, running after him.

First Floor of the Museum

Roumoult picked up a chair and threw it at the window. It bounced and fell. Desperately, he looked around. He saw a small stone statue. He grabbed and threw it. The window cracked, but it didn't break. A cop fired two bullets; the crack became bigger, but the glass didn't cave.

"Great!" Roumoult rested his hands on his knees, trying to catch his breath. The door was closed. The green cloud was descending. He looked around for Zachary and Ortiz. They'd disappeared. Roumoult coughed as he felt the air in the hall thinning. He hoped Jack understood his instructions.

Museum Security Office, Ground Floor

"What?" asked the security guard.

"You control the ventilation system, right?" Jack asked.

"Naturally. So?"

"Reverse the exhaust fans. Instead of sucking the air in, send it out."

The guard turned to the console.

"Jack, look at this," said Joe, pointing at another computer. "Zachary has control over the automatic doors. He has locked out the guard, can you help?"

Ground Floor of the Museum

"Good, keep firing! Take them down," shouted the Captain.

Six gangsters with machine guns lurked behind parked vehicles. They were heavily armed, and the cops only had handguns. Four police officer were down, two severely injured. William was on his stomach, his hands held to his head. He glanced up and saw Tom still standing near the door. His friends were trapped in there. The gas would kill them, turn them into madmen. But there was nothing he could do.

First Floor of the Museum

A group of twenty people huddled close to each other, shaking. Roumoult hated himself. He wished he could do more. His attempts to break the glass had failed. He surveyed the scene; his heart sank when he saw Ortiz's guards' lifeless bodies. A big part of him wanted to find Ortiz and even save Zachary. Roumoult was pulled out of his thoughts when the hissing ceased. He looked up and saw a ventilation shaft about ten feet from the ground. He heard a dragging noise, and then the gas began moving towards the ventilation shaft. Roumoult smiled wryly.

Museum Security Office, Ground Floor

"Yes, it's working!" said the guard.

"Great work!" said Joe. Then he shifted his attention to Jack. "Well, what do you think?"

"This is professional work. They've designed the program to hijack all systems one by one. I'm trying to access the doors, but I'll need to break the code. We don't have time for that, and I don't have my algorithms."

"What's our next best option?"

"Guess the password," Jack said, typing into the little box.

"Can you do that?"

Jack tried several times. "This is taking too much time!"

"Hold on, who would have chosen the password? The person who developed the program or the user?"

Jack froze. "Either."

"Let's assume it's the user. What password would the white king use?"

Jack grinned.

"Oh, no, no!" shouted the guard.

"What now?" Joe demanded.

"The program took over the environmental system. I'm losing control of everything. He'll kill everyone in that hall!"

First Floor of the Museum

Joan and Tom were standing outside, helpless.

"Damn!" Tom said, kicking the door. "Roumoult... How many?"

"Around twenty,"

Tom covered his face with his hands.

"We should help the Captain," Joan said.

"Look, they're in there," said Tom. "Roumoult is in there!"

Joan was about to argue with her partner when they heard sirens approaching.

First Floor of the Museum

Inside, Roumoult was in serious trouble. The duct had reverted and was spitting out green gas again. The monstrous cloud was descending on the room. Roumoult covered his nostrils, trying not to breathe it in. A tremor ran through the wall behind him, and he heard a loud thump, followed by a scream. He spun, and his eyes filled with delight. The door was slowly opening.

Museum Security Office, Ground Floor

"Bloody blue lily!" Jack exclaimed. "That's the password!"

Joe jumped, hardly able to contain his joy. "How did you know?"

"I remembered it because William was droning on about it being five hundred years old," Jack replied as they watched the door open.

"Doesn't this thing go any faster?"

Jack glared at him. "I can't control the speed."

Suddenly, the lights flickered out.

"Now what?" Joe asked.

Red lights sputtered to life, casting an eerie glow. They turned to the security guard.

"The program took over the system. Everything is offline."

First Floor of the Museum

The door halted; the hall turned crimson. Everyone screamed in terror and confusion. Roumoult eyed the gap. It might have opened just enough.

"Everyone, move! Go, crawl out! Move, move!"

A woman crouched down and crawled through the gap between the iron door and the ground. Tom pulled her free from the other side. Roumoult assisted an older man as others slid under the door. Soon, everyone was out. Roumoult looked for Zachary. A strong arm hooked onto his.

"We're leaving," Angelus ordered.

First Floor of the Museum

Ortiz hid under the dinner table. His plan had failed. Someone had sabotaged the small exit door. As soon as he realized, he wanted to leave with the other guests, but the place was swarming with cops, and a madman was killing his bodyguards. So, he hid. Ortiz still felt the killers grip on his neck. He'd almost been strangled, and narrowly escape because of one of his bodyguards.

The green smoke began to choke him. Ortiz crawled out from beneath the table and sat up coughing. He rubbed his eyes to stop them from burning. "Hello! Anyone?"

Staggering on to his feet, he stood up straight. The hall was empty and silent. He saw his men, stabbed in the heart with the very knives he wanted to steal. He felt like he was falling apart; he had eluded everyone in his life. How had he finally been caught? He marched toward the exit.

"Where do you think you are going?" said a deep, hoarse voice.

Sensation left Ortiz's body. Trembling with fear, he turned and faced his nemesis. He watched in pure disbelief as the man sucked in the green gas.

"Who are you?" Ortiz shouted, ignoring the burning in his throat. "Who are you? What do you want from me?"

"I am Zachary Madison."

The name meant nothing to him. "What do you want? Money, power? I can give you anything!"

Ortiz began to cough vigorously. His chest felt like it was on fire.

"I've had a dream since I was eleven," said Zachary.

A beam of hope appeared on Ortiz's face.

"I dreamed I would kill you. The same way you murdered my mother and destroyed my life," Zachary spat.

"You're the hunter. The wolf on the phone!"

Zachary smiled wickedly. "I will say, I have enjoyed it. Killing your men one by one. I used Walter as a shield and did everything in his name. You killed him for no reason at all. Tut, tut. That was bad of you. He was a good man."

"That's on you!" Ortiz shouted, "Walter died because of you. You got him involved. It wasn't my fault."

"You are a cancer. And I want you erased. I tortured and killed your men...gradually. I loved it. They died in fear, fear of their own demons, fear of me. It was a pleasure to watch them suffer the consequences of their actions."

"Please, please," Ortiz choked. "I'm begging you. Let me go."

"Yes. Beg. Beg, get down on your knees! But I won't spare you. I am the devil, and you made me!"

"B-but I've never met you," Ortiz shrieked. He tripped over and landed on his back.

"Remember... 1975, Egypt... The ship of the dead."

Ortiz's face fell.

"The cursed ship, the doomed ship. You hired Van Gerkins to loot the Nefret? What were you after? The pearls? Walter's pearls?"

Ortiz gulped.

"On your orders, Van Gerkins attacked and looted the ship. Those scoundrels dragged me and my mother to the deck. Everyone was there. They ransacked the ship and were about to leave when we heard a loud cry. A green cloud emerged. Through the green mist an evil man appeared. First, he slaughtered his own men. Then he turned towards us. I can still hear the screams. After Gerkins slaughtered my mother and the other passengers with a machine gun, I was left alive. Alive surrounded by the bodies of innocent people. I was buried under my mother. I can never forget her lifeless eyes, her pale white face, her arms around me. She died protecting me." Zachary paused. "Do you know what it feels like when a six-year-old boy watches his mother die? To watch his mother slaughtered to death," Zachary pressed on. "No, you don't. When the firing stopped, I tried to revive my mom. But she didn't move; she was gone. Everyone around me was lost. Innocent souls wiped out. I wept in silence, fighting to stay quiet. Then he started chopping the bodies up, as if slaying them wasn't enough! The ax drew nearer. I could hear him. Then he found me. I couldn't move. He looked like a demon with bright red eyes. A green cloud hung over his head." He paused, "Till this day I do not know why he spared me. He hit me in the head and threw me into the river. I wished, I still wish, he had killed me that day." Zachary stepped forward, drawing a long knife. "But that's not the end of my story. When I woke up, I was a prisoner to a native Egyptian tribe. I soon discovered they were smugglers, looters. Just like you! Just my luck. They hit me, burned me, tortured me, and assaulted me. I was their slave, and I almost died. Eventually, local police found them and killed all of them, but I survived, and they threw me in jail. Thanks to you, that's where I spent ten years of my life."

Ortiz watched a glimmer of sadness cross Zachary's face before it hardened once more.

"After a decade, I escaped with the help of a few inmates. I wanted to go to the American Embassy, but I was afraid of Egyptian police. I joined a local excavation team, made some friends, and hitched my way out of Egypt. When I finally came home, there was no home. My mom was dead. My father was gone, and my grandmother did not recognize me." He looked down at Ortiz. "Do you know how it feels to be haunted by your past every day? How it feels to wake up in the middle of the night screaming, feeling the heat from the iron rod? Having visions of people being murdered?"

Ortiz took a step back. "Look, whatever happened, it just happened, okay?"

"It has haunted me all my life. I fought it. Tried to be a good man. But then I stopped running, and I decided to haunt you."

Fear ran through Ortiz. He shrieked in terror as Zachary transformed into an enormous figure with bright red eyes. Ortiz screamed in agony, feeling his hands blister and burn. Fire erupted around him.

The huge figure raged towards him, brandishing a long sword.

First Floor of the Museum

Inside, the gallery smelled of blood and gunpowder. The gas still flooded it. Tom raised his right hand and pointed. Like ghosts, the SWAT team vanished into the green mist.

Tom felt uneasy, listening to the sound of his own breath rattling inside the mask. They couldn't flush the gas just yet. He glanced at Joan; she was at his side, ready and alert as they walked ahead.

"Joan be careful," Tom said.

"I..." she replied, but her voice died out.

Tom immediately looked over his shoulder. Joan was staring at something straight ahead. Tom followed her gaze. He lowered his gun.

Zachary looked up at them; his eyes were red, swollen, and protruding. His skin was pasty, and he looked like a zombie. Ortiz lay dead on the floor. Half of his face was lacerated, and blood flowed down his neck, soaking his shirt. Zachary stood motionless, his eyes wide, staring sightlessly, lost in an abyss. Blood dripped steadily from the knife he held in his right hand.

"Zachary, you are under arrest," Tom said.

He didn't move.

"Put your hands in the air!"

Zachary's face transformed, his human features restoring. He looked down and studied his hands. "It's done." He looked toward the sky, smiling. "It's done," he repeated.

"Put the knife down and come with us," Tom said, raising his weapon.

Zachary moved his head mechanically. "This is more fun than I thought. No wonder Wheeler enjoyed it." He looked past Tom and beamed. "Mother, you are here!"

Tom spun around. There was no one there.

"I'm sorry it took so long, Mom, but I did it. I avenged you. Now you can rest in peace, and so can I."

"Zachary, it's time you come with us," Tom said softly, careful not to make any sudden movements.

Again, Zachary's expression changed. His eyes locked on Tom's.

"You are under arrest," He remembered Alex and Wheeler. Could Zachary still be saved?

Zachary spread his hands and began walking toward them. "You can't do anything to me."

Tom gripped the gun tighter.

"I see hope in your eyes," Zachary stated, pausing for a moment, as if reading his mind. "You want all the answers, don't you? Detective, I have been watching you trying to save people. Save Alex. Save Wheeler. Save Ortiz. Now you want to save me."

Tom felt his hand tremble.

"You think you can reform me, bring me back," Zachary said, moving forward.

Tom hesitated. He'd killed Ortiz, he'd enacted his revenge, why go on? Why not give himself up?

Suddenly, Zachary lunged forward. Tom stumbled back. Joan kicked Zachary. He tumbled. With his heart pounding, Tom watched Zachary climb back to his feet. He still hesitated to raise his gun. Joan stepped between them. Zachary charged at her. "Zach—" Tom started.

Joan fired. The bullet struck Zachary in the head. He fell with a sickening thud.

"Joan!" Tom yelled.

Joan turned to him with her mouth slightly open. Shock marked every line of her face.

Tom shut his eyes in frustration. He stepped closer, bent, and checked Zachary's pulse. His pale, ghostly face remained frozen. The white king was dead; his reign had ended.

24

Epilogue

July 1, 2015

Cranston House

U nder the pavilion in the backyard, Roumoult sat with his feet on the table. He glanced at the car keys and smiled. Charles turned on the sprinklers to water the grass. Roumoult took a long breath in and relaxed in the overstuffed chair. After the incident at the exhibition, he'd decided he'd had enough and taken a vacation. For the last week, he'd been relaxing at home, not bothering about work. The wounds on his hands were healing, but like everyone else who was exposed to PCP, he remained under medical supervision.

Roumoult wanted to be alone, but that seemed impossible. Alice sat on a chair playing a game on her phone. Angelus was reading a newspaper.

"We need to talk," Alice said.

"I am on vacation," Roumoult replied.

"You should check your emails. Did you see the Audi's bill? Why didn't you just buy a new car?"

"Alice, stay away from the Audi," Roumoult growled.

"And the Museum wants to sue you for breaking artifacts."

"And I thought we deserved an award for stopping a massacre," Roumoult retorted.

"Unfortunately, the bureaucrats don't see it that way," Alice continued. "They're also going after the NYPD. I think we need a debriefing."

"Okay. Arrange it. You know what, we should sue the companies who make stupid computers."

Jack came up behind them and took a seat beside Alice. "For the last time," he said, "computers and mobile phones are not stupid."

"Why are you here?" Roumoult demanded.

"Why are you unreachable?"

Roumoult bowed his head.

"Paul called," Jack said. "Fred recommended us to him. He said he wants me to build a prototype computer for a ship."

"We don't work with ships," Alice pointed out.

Before Jack could answer, they heard footsteps approaching.

"Ah, isn't this a welcoming sight," said a familiar voice.

"Don't you have work to do?" Roumoult asked William as he took a seat.

William ignored him. "How's Patrick Burns?"

Alice and Roumoult exchanged glances.

"A happy man," said Alice. "As it was him who brought this to light, Mark was very generous and has rehired him to run APTOS. So, he got his compensation and more."

"Good for him," William said.

"You didn't answer my question," Roumoult said, looking at William. "Why aren't you at work?"

William eyed Jack and Alice.

"He's been trying to kick everybody out," Alice replied smiling.

"I came to check on you, then I'm having lunch with Joan."

"I see," Roumoult replied. He shook up his sleeve and showed him the time on his watch. "It's lunchtime. Where's Joan?"

Fred approached the group. "Ah, so glad to see all of you together."

Soon the detectives joined them. Fred offered them drinks and snacks.

"So is the NYPD happy?" Fred asked.

"The Captain's glad it's over," said Tom. "We found the killers and the damage—"

"Is done," Alice finished in a low tone.

Jack and Roumoult looked over at her, but she turned her head away.

"It could have been worse," Angelus said.

"You don't seem happy," said Fred.

Tom's eyes lowered. "It's a paradox. I feel bad for him."

The men gave no response, but the women glared at him angrily.

"I dug up Zachary's story and read his diary. It's unfortunate what happened to him. Van killed his mother, and he saw it all," Tom continued. "The only living witness to a mass murder. Then a group of smugglers captured and tortured him. When the smugglers were killed, he was sent to an Egyptian jail. I can't even imagine what he went through. He escaped and worked as a laborer at an excavation site. It took time, but eventually he got out of Egypt and found his way back to America." Tom paused and looked down at his coffee cup. "But he had nothing left except a drive for revenge. He kept his cool for years, got his degree in archeology, had friends and girlfriends. He even went to therapy. But the dreams, the visions... His past tormented him. The memories were so intense that he even tried to erase them. He tried hypnosis. He took drugs to control his emotions. When that didn't work, he underwent experimental brain surgery."

"Let me guess, it didn't help," Fred offered.

"No," Tom affirmed. "He gave in, and his thirst for revenge grew. He was already a renowned archeologist, and he knew Ortiz's weakness. It was a slow process. He had no money, no power. Then, two years ago, he met his red herring, Walter Weldon. He found that Walter was eager to find whoever had murdered his family and bring them to justice. He earned his trust, used his money and power to get all the information. And then one by one, he hunted them down. Although he used him, he admired Walter like a father figure."

"But he killed him," Fred said.

"No. Ortiz killed Walter, not Zachary," Joan replied.

"I can't help but wonder, was he beyond help?" Tom said.

Roumoult gave him a cold stare. "Tom, that's your perspective. In Zachary's view, everyone in that Exhibition Hall had to die, regardless of whether they'd killed his mother or destroyed his life. He crossed the line, just like Wheeler and Alex. You wanted to reform him; do you think he wanted to be reformed?"

"I just wish things ended differently."

Silence spread over the pavilion.

"About the werewolf," Tom muttered.

"Wagner hallucinated." William said.

"But why?"

"He hit his head." Joan replied.

"No, he saw the animal before the accident."

"What did you find?" Roumoult asked.

"I couldn't stop thinking. Was it an accident or attempted murder?"

"Explain."

"Wagner definitely hallucinated, but PCP was not detected in his blood. Why? There was only one explanation."

"Someone switched them." Roumoult concluded.

"Exactly. I asked the CSI Unit to check Wagner's car. They found traces of PCP in the air conditioner's vent. Someone had mixed it with the refrigerant. Wagner had three cars and that car had returned from service two days before his accident."

"Wonderful," remarked Angelus.

"Hey, speaking of Zachary, any thoughts on how he got the boss into an ancient box?" Jack joked breaking the tension.

"Let's keep that a mystery," Roumoult answered.

"No, let's speculate," William said.

"There's no need to speculate," said Joan. "After misleading Jake and Joe, he drove to the Museum.

Zachary had those boxes for six months. He could have transferred Roumoult and the bomb into them at any time throughout the day. Then the box was transferred to the Exhibition Hall."

"I don't get it," said Roumoult. "I disconnected the bomb."

"You disconnected one," Tom explained. "Zachary had planted six cylinders way before anyone of us got to the scene."

"But the squad cleared the building," Roumoult insisted.

"They did. Unfortunately, they didn't check the ventilation tubes. Someone had to crawl inside the tube and install the gas cylinders."

"But why kidnap boss?" Jack asked.

"Perfect distraction. You all would focus on finding him," Tom explained. "And Roumoult knew his identity."

"What about Ortiz?" Fred asked.

"He was a smuggler, a mass murderer, a thief, and a blackmailer. His bodyguards were the same men who attacked you guys at the warehouse," Joan said.

"About Mark," Tom added excitedly. "Apparently, he was doing an internal investigation of his own. He secretly visited APTOS to check the inventory of the boxes. Next, he spoke to Wheeler and discovered that he wasn't acting alone, but Wheeler was loyal to Zachary. From what Mark gathered, he owed the guy. Mark got as far as getting Zachary's name. Then Walter died, and he got distracted. Zachary grew suspicious of him and lowered him into a trap, hit him on the head, and disappeared. Later,

Mark woke up in an alley near Central Park and took a cab to the hospital."

"What about the doctors?" Fred asked Tom.

"Dr. Larson will suffer the consequences of his actions. The Dean of St. George Hospital recognizes the difficulty of his circumstances. He won't lose his job, provided he becomes sober in the next few months. Dr. Meyers is continuing her residency in the ER."

Silence fell once more.

"It has been an interesting case," William said, breaking it.

"You started it," Roumoult said.

"Just imagine if they'd never stolen those bodies." William speculated.

"You would have discovered the PCP, and we'd still have had a case," Tom said. "I have to say, I never expected hounds."

Everyone laughed.

"Yeah. I wonder what's next?" Jack thought out loud.

"Stop right there," Fred warned.

Roumoult laughed.

"Are you ready for lunch?" Joan asked William.

"Yeah," William replied, but he was looking at Roumoult. He got to his feet and stood with his hands on his waist. "You okay?"

"Just leave me in peace."

"Fine. By the way, Mom said hi."

Their eyes met, and Roumoult gave him a warm smile.

Next, Alice hugged Roumoult, said goodbyes to the others, and walked herself out.

Roumoult and Angelus glared at Jack.

"What?" he asked warily.

"Jack, do this one thing for me," said Angelus. "Stop playing around. Alice could have any man she wanted, but for some stupid reason she likes you."

Jack gulped nervously, throwing a glance at Fred. "We went out for lunch."

"You can do better," Angelus said.

"You're right!" Jack stood up and gave a quick goodbye before running after Alice.

Fred sniggered. "I didn't know you two liked to play cupid. First William, now Jack."

Both men scrunched up their faces in revulsion.

"Jack needed the push," Roumoult said. "William didn't need a cupid, he needed direction. I had to turn him away from that crazy woman and push him towards Joan."

"So, you are cupid."

Roumoult narrowed his eyes at his father. "Dad, you and I both know, I'm no angel."

Fred and Angelus laughed.

Cranston House

That evening, Roumoult called Emma. They went on a walk through the busy streets.

"I heard you took a vacation," she said.

"I had to. It was too much."

"I know he took you..."

"Yeah, let's not talk about that."

"I had breakfast with Joan," Emma said. "It was fun. It's good to have friends."

"You have friends and admirers," Roumoult replied.

Her eyes showed surprise, but then her face fell. "Did you hear about Tim?"

"Yes. If I were you, I wouldn't be so hard on him. He had no choice. They threatened his family."

"Really? But they're saying—"

"It's gossip," Roumoult interrupted. "He's a good man, and he cares about you."

"Joan says the same."

He put his arm around her waist. "Why did you walk out of my office that day?"

"I-I didn't know what I was supposed to do. I've made so many mistakes. And I thought you were still angry with me." She wrapped her arms around him. The noise died out.

"How about a drive?" Roumoult asked.

"You fixed the Audi?"

"Of course."

Tilting her head, a hint of mischief glinting in her eye, Emma said, "Where did you learn to drive like that?"

Lower Manhattan

"Hey John," said Tom cheerfully. "Good to see you!"

They sat in a local bar to watch football and drink beers. Tom noticed that his ex-partner looked ageless, fresh, and had put on some weight. He realized how much he'd missed him.

"I heard you had a crazy case," said John.

Tom nodded. "It took me back to the academy."

John arched his eyebrows. "But I heard many people died."

"Unfortunately, yes."

"How do you like your new partner?" John asked after a moment of thick silence.

"She's good," Tom replied absentmindedly, then he added, "not as good as you."

John eyed him. "Uh-huh. So, what's new at the precinct?"

"Well, we got a new tearoom, because Zachary blew up the old one." Tom laughed. "The Captain's gained a few pounds. Detective Quin is still dating both Kelly and Mandy."

"Still? And they don't know!"

Tom chuckled. "No. No. Joan is dating William, and Alice likes Jack."

John put his drink on the table.

"Fred is dating Evelyn," Tom continued.

"Wow," John said, reaching for another sip of his drink.

"And, if I'm not mistaken, Roumoult is in love. He just doesn't know it yet."

John swallowed hard. "That's impossible!"

"It's true. Ask anyone."

"Cranston? Seriously? Man, this is nuts! I feel like I'm in a parallel universe or something. Fred and William, I get it. I thought Cranston was cold and calculating. Solving mysteries and getting into trouble was his top priority. Next, you'll tell me that Angelus is having a baby."

Tom raised his eyebrows. "No, things aren't that bad."

John's shoulders slumped. "Or you got hitched."

Tom pressed his lips together.

"It's not fair! I left, and all the fun stuff started happening."

"Her name is Jenny. Man, she is beautiful."

John smiled proudly. "Good on you. So, you are happy Cranston was around for this one. He took over the case, didn't he?"

Tom tried not to let his prejudice guide him. "I have to admit, I couldn't have done it without the Cranston team."

John nodded.

"And if you ever repeat those words, I will have to kill you."

John busted into laughter.

Tom rubbed his hands together. "So. You want all the juicy details of the case?"

John's eyebrows shot up. "Damn the case! Tell me, how did everything change?"

About the Author

H.G Ahedi holds a PhD in biomedical sciences and is a fictional writer. Haunted is her second book. She spends a lot of time writing and when she is bored of her desk; she wants to hop on a plane and travel the world. As that is not always possible, she explores local Sydney beaches, parks, and enjoys a nice cup of coffee.

Loved Haunted? Please leave a review! Thank you very much in advance.

Want to know what happens next? Join the world of Cranston and his friends. Subscribe to the club by visiting
harbeerahedi.wordpress.com/author/hahedi/

Other books by H.G. Ahedi

Printed in Great Britain
by Amazon

49412818R00203